matter. It was only much later, when they retrieved their luggage from the rack, that they took note of a case that wasn't theirs. Small, a little battered, of thick, tan leather that had been inexpertly repaired at the corner and reinforced with a panel darker than the rest.

'That young man,' the husband said, 'must have left his suitcase behind. Silly young fool.'

The woman frowned and fingered the label, tied to the handle with coarse string. 'Joseph Levy,' she said. 'We should tell the guard. What can the boy have been playing at?'

Her husband shrugged, already dismissing the incident as no more than a curiosity. On leaving the train, they duly reported the bag to the guard and thought no more about it.

Idly, Joseph peered at their reading matter. The man was absorbed in the business pages of Friday's *Financial Times* – two days out of date, Joseph thought, so either he was desperate for news or he only fancied himself knowledgeable. The wife, if that's what she was, very properly, if drably clad in a slim-fitting tweed skirt and camel coat, read Evelyn Waugh, which Joseph considered very unsuitable reading matter for a respectable woman, especially in a public place. The front cover of the girl's magazine, *Woman's Way*, featured a young flapper in a red cloche hat. To his eyes, it looked racy and he wondered if Rebecca ever read such things. Not if her father had anything to do with it, that was for certain, but Becky was proving to be surprisingly independently minded. And anyway, what Becky and her family – or his family – thought really didn't matter now.

Solutions were lacking if they were to please their families and still grasp at a little happiness for themselves, and it had become obvious that Joseph must take action. Joseph had previously had no objection at all to marrying Becky. Far from it, in fact. He was content to be partnered with a young woman he'd known from childhood and who genuinely liked him as much as he liked her. But sometimes, he thought, life knocks you and your plans for six and makes no apology for it.

A few stops later, when the train pulled into Bardney station, the girl with red hair prepared to alight.

Joseph was puzzled, confused. He waited for her to be visible on the station platform, craned forward, resisting the temptation to open the window and lean out, saw the gay red hair beneath the dark-blue hat, his gaze hungry for the brightness of the flash of green dress beneath the coat.

Suddenly, Joseph was on his feet, grabbing his hat and then hurrying past the couple and out into the corridor without so much as a word.

The man looked up. 'I say, he was in a frightful hurry. Do you think he forgot he was getting off here?'

His wife looked up and then out of the window. 'Some kind of argument going on,' she said. 'That young woman who just got off and a young fellow in a flat cap.'

The train pulled out and they both returned to their reading

PROLOGUE

3 February 1929

It wasn't that she was exceptionally beautiful, more that she was striking. Colourful. And on such a drab February day as this one, colour and vibrancy were more than welcome. He had been looking out for her, and she had got on the train one stop after him. He couldn't recall the name of the village; this train stopped everywhere. Slow and tedious and not particularly warm. She had glanced into the compartment he occupied – he and a couple he assumed were married. Sitting opposite one another, the husband with his nose buried in a newspaper and she with her eyes fixed on a book, they had said little to one another since the journey began, so it was hard to judge the exact status of their relationship. But the presence of the older woman meant that she felt at liberty to enter the compartment and sit down in the corner furthest away from him. A quick glance was all she had shot in his direction, also taking in the couple and their bags on the luggage rack, but it had been enough for him to admire her eyes, a browny grey, like smoky quartz, and her hair, beneath the dark-blue hat, a vibrant, almost ruby red. Her dress, peeking out from her dark coat, was an equally extravagant and almost emerald green.

Startling, he thought. Exotic, and the thought made him smile.

She was not obviously beautiful, not like Becky. Becky was pale, a real English rose – for all that her parents were anything but – with dark hair and hazel eyes. Small and fragile, like a bird; he knew that she was gorgeous and that everyone said he was a lucky young man . . . so why was he so drawn to this more robust and curving beauty sitting across the carriage from him? She did not look his way, after the brief nod of greeting that took in everyone in the carriage, and soon also had her attention taken by a magazine.

This first world edition published 2019
in Great Britain and the USA by
SEVERN HOUSE PUBLISHERS LTD of
Eardley House, 4 Uxbridge Street, London W8 7SY.
Trade paperback edition first published
in Great Britain and the USA 2020 by
SEVERN HOUSE PUBLISHERS LTD.

British Library Cataloguing in Publication Data
A CIP catalogue record for this title is available from the British Library.

ISBN-13: 978-0-7278-8888-4 (cased)
ISBN-13: 978-1-78029-609-8 (trade paper)
ISBN-13: 978-1-4483-0226-0 (e-book)

All Severn House titles are printed on acid-free paper.

Severn House Publishers support the Forest Stewardship Council™ [FSC™],
the leading international forest certification organisation. All our titles that
are printed on FSC certified paper carry the FSC logo.

MIX
Paper from
responsible sources
FSC
www.fsc.org   FSC® C013056

Typeset by Palimpsest Book Production Ltd.,
Falkirk, Stirlingshire, Scotland.
Printed and bound in Great Britain by
TJ International, Padstow, Cornwall.

THE CLOCKMAKER

Jane A. Adams

THE CLOCKMAKER

ONE

The constable had come into the Central Office of Scotland Yard and told Henry that he had a visitor waiting downstairs in reception.

'A gentleman, sir. His name is Abraham Levy and he says that you know him. He requests a few minutes of your time.'

It took Henry a moment or so to remember who Abraham Levy was and then a moment more to wonder why on earth he had come all the way to the headquarters of the Metropolitan Police at Scotland Yard, instead of taking his problems to the local division. Henry tidied the files on his desk and then went down to see what the clockmaker wanted.

Abraham Levy had cropped up in an earlier investigation, but only as the landlord of someone whose unfortunate death Henry had investigated. Detective Chief Inspector Henry Johnstone recalled that he had spoken to Abraham Levy only on a couple of occasions but that he had liked the man.

Abraham had seen him coming down the stairs and unfolded himself from the hard wooden bench set near the door, an uncomfortable seat and draughty spot that Henry always assumed was established to dissuade anyone from staying too long. Abraham held out his hand; Henry shook it and then sat down beside Abraham.

'I can try to find some office space so that we can talk or we can chat here. The constable said this would only take a few moments.'

If Abraham was put out by this slightly dismissive attitude, he did not show it. Instead, he set his hat on his lap and folded his hands neatly behind it and looked at Henry carefully. 'When we met, it struck me that you are a just and careful man,' Abraham said. 'Some policemen I have known, they go through the motions only. They look as though they are doing something and they collect their pay and they go home and nothing has been done, but I do not think you are that kind of man. I come to you because so far I have only met *that* kind of policeman and I need someone different. Someone who will not just pretend to be concerned and go away thinking, "Oh, this is just a Jew boy I'm dealing with, so what concern is this of mine?"'

Henry considered for a moment and then he said, 'I think you might begin at the beginning.' He stood. 'There is a café just around the corner; perhaps this might be better discussed over a pot of tea.'

He glanced up, catching sight of a familiar figure coming down the stairs: his sergeant, Mickey Hitchens, who looked curiously in their direction and then clearly recognized Abraham.

'Mr Levy,' he said. 'And what brings you here?'

'A problem I cannot deal with on my own.'

Mickey frowned. The streets where Abraham Levy lived had been ruled by one Josiah Bailey and his family for quite some time, but had recently undergone a change of owner-ship – although the new ruler, Clem Atkins, had simply taken over both Bailey's lieutenants and his criminal schemes. It was Mickey's first thought that this was the source of the trouble.

'No,' Abraham reassured him. 'Mr Atkins continues the work of Mr Bailey, you might say. Little has changed and the protection money we pay as businessmen has not gone up dramatically since the change of management. No, this is a personal matter. A missing person. I fear perhaps a *dead* missing person, and as no one else will help me, I have come to you.'

They walked to the Lyons' Corner House that was set on the intersection of the Strand and Craven Street, and Henry ordered tea for them all. At two in the afternoon, they were between the crowds of lunchtime rush and the partakers of afternoon tea, and they found a table in a corner with a fair degree of privacy.

'So, tell me,' Henry said. 'Who has gone missing, and why do you feel that no one has been of assistance to you?'

Abraham arranged his cup carefully on his saucer, positioning the spoon so that it protruded at the opposite side to the cup handle. He looked suddenly awkward. He had long, slender hands, Henry noted, with well-clipped nails. Hands that were used to being occupied now found themselves ill at ease.

'On the third of this month my nephew caught a train,' Abraham began. 'His name is Joseph and he had been to visit his young lady – his intended. They are both young – Joseph is only nineteen years old and his fiancée is a year younger than that – and they are to be married in the autumn.'

'It is very young to be married,' Mickey observed.

'In our community, not so young. We think it's better that our children are safely married and have someone to care for and to care for them. Young ones often spend time living with their in-laws until they are ready to set up home for themselves. Anyway, Joseph and Rebecca are to be married – or were. Then Joseph caught the train to come home and he did not arrive.'

Mickey took out his notebook and set it on the table. 'The train from where?'

'He was travelling from Lincoln to London. He caught the train in Lincoln; Rebecca's family saw him off there, so they know he got on the train. But he did not arrive.'

'That's a long journey,' Henry observed. 'He could have got off at any station in between. From what I remember, there are a great many going up towards Lincoln. Where would he have changed trains to come back to London?'

'At Peterborough. Lincoln is on the loop from the main line that leaves Peterborough and, yes, there are a great many small stations on that line. Once in Peterborough, he could get the train back to King's Cross – an easy journey, if a little long, but one he has made more than a dozen times.

'His family contacted the police and were told that he was an adult and that adults go missing all the time and there should be no cause for concern; he would probably turn up. His family contacted the girl's family, in Lincoln, and were told that he and Rebecca had argued before he left and had parted on bad terms. When the police heard this, they decided

that the boy was not so keen on the marriage, after all, and
had chosen to go off on his own somewhere.'

'It's certainly possible,' Mickey said. 'As I said before, they
are both very young, and young minds can be changed – young
people can be impulsive.'

'All of that is true,' Abraham agreed. 'But that was on
Sunday February the third and this is now Wednesday the
twentieth. There has been no news since. He has not
contacted his family or his fiancée or his friends. I know
Joseph; he is not a boy who would put worry into the hearts
of those he loves. If he had decided he did not want to
marry, everyone would have understood. No one is being
forced into this. But I do believe that he and Rebecca love
one another.'

'How long have they known each other?' Henry asked.

'Since childhood. Our families grew up within a few
houses of one another. Then Rebecca's family moved when
she was twelve years old, but Joseph used to go up and stay
there, and it was always understood that one day they would
marry. But if either one of them had said no, we prefer
to choose for ourselves, that would have been accepted,
believe me.'

'But it would have caused awkwardness, at the very least,
I would suppose?' Mickey suggested.

Abraham shrugged. 'Awkwardness for a little time, perhaps,
but it would have been accepted and people would have got
over their upset. No one wishes our young people to marry
and be unhappy. But we believed them to be happy.'

'What was the quarrel about?'

Abraham hesitated, clearly uncomfortable with discussing
his family business. 'The argument was loud,' he said. 'The
family overheard, of course. It seems that Rebecca wished to
wait until at least next spring before they married. She said it
was because her sister and brother-in-law would be coming
to visit then and she wanted them to be at the wedding. Joseph
was content to wait, but he did not believe her reasons and
he challenged them. He asked if she really wanted to marry
him, and she became angry, saying of course she did, but that
she wished to wait just a little longer. Rebecca's mother tells

me that Joseph tried to be understanding and calm, and he suggested to her that she just had the usual reservations and that this was understandable. He said that he would be willing to wait, but Rebecca just became even more angry until Joseph said that he didn't believe this was her reason at all, and that maybe she had another man.'

'And is that likely?'

'Not that anyone knows about, but young girls . . .' He shrugged again. 'Young men, too – their heads can be turned by the attention of someone who seems more exciting. So I don't know. It's possible. But she's a good girl and I don't believe she would deliberately hurt either Joseph or her family.'

'And no one at all has had word from him? Friends might have heard and not told anyone?'

'None of Joseph's friends are so heartless. They have seen how we've all suffered, how worried we've been. His friends are also people he has known since childhood, who have known his family since childhood. We are a close-knit community, Inspector.'

'Which might make him even more fearful of your disapprobation,' Henry suggested. 'Did he have any money with him?'

'Not enough to have lasted all this time. He had enough for his journey, and emergency money, should he have to stay overnight somewhere, but little enough else.'

'And have the police investigated?'

'Investigated! Is that what you call it? They confirmed that he got on the train at Lincoln – there are witnesses aplenty for that – but as no one knows where he got off, all they could do – all they *said* they could do – was send a message down the line to ask at the stations. Our family have printed pictures and have these positioned at any stations that we have been able to reach, and Rebecca's family have done the same. Police refuse to believe this is anything more than a young man who has chosen to go off by himself for a time. They seem to have spoken to no one; they seem to have found no evidence of Joseph's existence after he left Lincoln.'

Mickey and Henry exchanged a glance. It seemed to them

that all that could be done probably had been done. This was a big distance to search, and if there were no clues as to where the young man had left the train, then there would be no clues as to where he might have ended up.

'And have there been any communications, any witnesses who have seen the posters and might've seen him?'

Abraham shook his head. 'There have been a few individuals who have contacted our families to ask if there is a reward and who have obviously been giving us false information. Rambling stories that don't make any sense. We've ensured that one of the menfolk has spoken to each one of these, but it soon became clear that they are all deceivers. It does not help that we are Jews.'

Henry opened his mouth to object to that last sentence and then closed it again, thinking that Abraham was probably right. He witnessed anti-Semitism all the time in his work, most of it casual and unthinking, rather than deliberately targeted, but nonetheless . . .

'Who is handling the case now?'

'Local constables in Lincoln and here. The railway police have been involved, of course.' He reached into his pocket and took out a list of names. 'These are the men we've had dealings with,' he said. 'No one has been helpful.'

'And I'm not sure we can be of any more use,' Mickey said frankly. 'He could have gone missing anywhere along that route. He could have made a deliberate decision to go away for a time, found himself some casual work and lodgings, and not want to be found.'

'And if that was the case, then we would leave him alone. But we would still need to know. You understand that?'

'Mr Levy – Abraham – we are murder detectives. This is not directly within our purview.'

Abraham regarded them solemnly. 'Joseph would not just *go*,' he insisted. 'Inspector, Sergeant Hitchens, believe me when I say that it is only a matter of time before this becomes your business. I believe that Joseph is dead. Had Joseph still been alive, he would have contacted his family; he would not have left them to suffer the way they have. He's a good boy . . . Or he *was* a good boy. I am fearful – no, I am *certain* – that something bad has happened to him and that he is no longer alive.'

There was silence at the little table. Mickey picked up his cup, drained it and set it down gently. 'It would do no harm to call in the files,' he said. 'I can take a look on my own time, but for now, Abraham, that is all we can do. You understand that?'

The clockmaker nodded. 'When his body is found, which surely it must be sometime, you will need me to make introductions. As I've said, we are a close community and a closed one too in many ways; you will need someone from the inside of the community to open doors. You understand that?'

'Let's hope it doesn't come to that, eh?' Mickey said.

Abraham nodded, then retrieved his hat and took his leave.

'We both know he's right,' Henry said as the café door closed behind him.

'More than likely, but we also know there's not a lot we can do until a body turns up, and it's a long way from Lincoln to London; the boy could have got off anywhere – or been thrown off.' Mickey frowned.

'True,' Henry admitted. 'Perhaps he was having second thoughts about the wedding after the argument and has simply taken off somewhere. That would be an alternative.'

'Better to be heartbroken than a murder victim,' Mickey agreed. 'I'll call in the files from the various constabularies and the railway police, see what we can find out. I doubt there will be much.'

'And there is an outside chance that the boy may yet turn up,' Henry said, but he did not sound at all hopeful.

'He *is* just a boy,' Mickey said quietly. 'Though it's not long since boys of that age were deemed fit to be fodder for the machine guns and mortars.'

'And that was wrong,' Henry said flatly. 'And still is. No, you are right. If we don't look into it, no one else will. We'll give it an hour or two of our time – see if there is anything to be followed up. But, frankly, Mickey, I doubt there will be anything. Abraham will be as much in the dark after we have examined the files as he is now. And even if we do find something, unless the local constabulary ask for our help, we can still do nothing, and they will not ask unless the worst happens and a body is found.'

Mickey shrugged. 'Cross that bridge,' he said.

TWO

C ynthia was packing. Her maid had directed Henry to the dressing room and, after kissing his sister, he dropped, with a deep sigh, into the green nursing chair beside the narrow stained-glass window.

'Sudden trip?' he asked.

'Decided this morning, at breakfast,' Cynthia confirmed. 'I am taking my husband away for a week or so. It's for his own good; he is becoming very morose.'

'And the reason for that?'

'The reason for that, Henry, is that he knows he has recently made some bad decisions and is being pressured into making more. My thinking is that if I take him away for a while, he'll have time to rehearse his polite refusal without the fear of getting it wrong and consequently losing face.'

'Hatry's mob?' Henry guessed.

'"Mob" is the right word for them,' Cynthia replied with some asperity. 'For all their titles and position, that's exactly what they are.'

'And how over-extended is Albert?'

'So far, within the bounds of what we can afford to lose without too many long-term regrets. To be truthful, Henry, I'm hoping this whole business is starting to sting. He can be a fool, that husband of mine, though there's no one else I'd say that to.'

Just before Christmas, Albert had been offered a 'sure-fire for certain' business opportunity by one Clarence Charles Hatry, who invited Albert to invest in his company, General Securities Limited, adding the bait that one of his main backers was Henry Paulet, Marquis of Winchester, a man Albert wanted to cultivate. Cynthia, doubtful that any deal was 'sure-fire' *or* 'for certain', had looked into the previous business dealings of this Hatry, and what she found had frightened her enough to warn Albert off. A multiple bankrupt who left in

his wake penury and wrecked lives, but who always seemed
to come out well himself.

Albert had abided by Cynthia's advice back then, but it
seemed he was now under further pressure.

'So, where are you taking him?'

'As far away as I can. We catch the plane from Croydon
airport tomorrow morning and will be in France by afternoon.
I have arranged for a car to take us to Lyon.'

'Lyon?'

'First place I could think of. I told Albert I'd always wanted
to see it. Malina was good enough to make the arrangements
and do the bookings. That girl is a real treasure.'

Henry smiled. Malina Cooper had joined his sister's house-
hold, ostensibly as her secretary, also just before Christmas.
Initially, Cynthia had been simply asked to give the young
woman shelter for a few days, her life being threatened, but
events had taken over. Malina had become a valued member
of the staff – and rather more than that.

'And Albert agreed to this sudden arrangement?'

'Albert was looking for an escape route. All I did was open
the door.'

'It's *that* bad?'

'He can see it getting that way. Henry, I know the work
you do is useful and that you bring some truly evil people to
justice, but frankly I believe the biggest criminals are those
way beyond your reach.'

'Well, unless they commit murder, there's not a great deal
I can do,' Henry admitted. 'Cyn, how worried are you?'

'Henry, you dimwit! I'm packing, aren't I? We're leaving
in the morning. What does that tell you? Once that lot have
their claws stuck in, who knows what will happen. They'd
drain him dry if they could, and then spit out his corpse and
grind it into the dirt without a second look.'

'But you've taken steps . . .' Just before Christmas, Cynthia
had persuaded her husband to sign over a portion of his estate
to her sole control.

'Oh, if it all falls over, we won't starve! I have control of
sufficient money and of his property portfolio, and I have all
of that tied up with so much red tape that Hatry and his ilk

could have me floating in the Thames and still not be able to touch it. Nor Albert, for that matter. It's all in trust for the children, should I die, and portioned out carefully so they can't get all spendthrift when they turn twenty-five. But it's what it's going to do to Albert if all of this goes the way I suspect it will. He's already suffering abuse for listening to a mere woman; if he shows himself, publicly, to be an even bigger fool when he *doesn't* listen to his bloody wife, well . . . Henry, I don't know what will happen to him.'

She turned from her packing and flopped down into the chair beside his. 'Strange and unfashionable as it might sound in this cynical age, I do happen to be fond of my husband. He's a good man at heart, and I don't want to see him in despair, derided by those who really should know better.'

It occurred to Henry that Cynthia was doing her own packing and that her maid, Gwenda, had skittered away once she'd informed her mistress that her brother had arrived. Things must really be out of kilter. 'Are you taking Malina with you?'

'No, just Gwennie.'

Henry reflected that in most other households Gwennie would have been renamed Dorcas or Smith or some such.

'It's just going to be me and Albert. We're going to drive where we like, stay where we want and talk or not, depending on what's necessary. I need to save my husband from himself, Henry. I'm damned if I'm going to let the likes of Hatry and the rest prey on him.'

Henry, knowing just how fiercely protective his sister could be, rated her chances better than those of her opposition.

'I will miss you,' he said.

'I know,' she smiled. 'And I will write, daily. And you'll come and see Melissa and Georgie?'

'Of course I will. Does Cyril know of your plans?' Cyril, the older boy, was away at school.

'He does, and he has a clear understanding of why.'

'Is that wise? He's only a child.'

'He's almost thirteen, bright as a button and with a sense of responsibility that would shame most adults. Henry, Cyril almost caught me in a lie at Christmas. He knew there was something on my mind. Albert and I, we sat him down and explained what we had agreed to do. And, no, Henry, I'm not sure if that was wise or foolish – only that it had to be done. I'm not a believer in lying to children; they only imagine the worst and then suffer for it.'

'I've rarely see you this upset,' Henry said gently.

She clasped his hand and smiled. 'And I'll get over it. Now, how was your day? Tell me about crimes that are obviously so and that have simple solutions.'

Henry, thinking of the likes of Abraham the clockmaker and his nephew, wondered if crimes were ever simple.

THREE

It was Monday, five days after they had spoken to Abraham, by the time the files had all been sent through to the central office. Mickey and Henry brought sandwiches to their desks and took their lunchtime to read, dividing the task between them.

The material itself was scant. They had statements from the family Joseph had been visiting in Lincoln, who had definitely witnessed him getting on to the train. They had statements from local constables at various stations that he must have passed through if he had taken his expected route. There were interviews with station masters and their staff from a number of different locations, but no one remembered a young man of his description. There were also pictures of the young man and a handful of fliers that the family must have given to the police to distribute to the public, but they remained in the folders, unused. It was evident that the local constabulary had gone through the motions, but there was little for them to go on, and little action they could take beyond questioning those who might have seen Joseph at one of the stations en route.

'He should have travelled from Lincoln to Peterborough and then picked up the London train from there,' Mickey said. 'So it is logical to think that he left the train somewhere between.'

'There is one possible sighting,' Henry said. 'At the station called Bardney, a married couple who regularly travel on that train suspect that they had seen the young man. They reported that he had left the train but had not taken his suitcase with him.'

He handed the brief statement to Mickey, who read it through. 'So, Mr and Mrs Parker think the young man who got off at Bardney station was our Joseph Levy. It was certainly his luggage, judging by the luggage label. Do we know what happened to the suitcase?'

'If they reported it, then it's probably in a left luggage store somewhere, waiting to be claimed. We have to hope it's in Peterborough, or that it's made its way to King's Cross or somewhere just as easy to access. Looking at the route, it seems there are a great many more stops on this line than I suspected.'

A timetable and a rail map had been tucked into the folder containing the Lincoln statements. Henry laid it on the desk between them. 'So, this Bardney is only a few stops out of Lincoln. Is it possible he only made it this far?'

'And why get off the train there? Why leave your suitcase behind? The Parkers seem not to have voiced an opinion on this and no one seems to have asked them anything useful.'

'If the Parkers simply reported a lost bag, it might not have occurred to anyone to ask them anything more. For all we know, they might be wrong about him getting off at Bardney. It could have been the station before, or the one after.'

'He could have chosen worse,' Henry said. 'The train he caught is on something called the Lincoln Loop, or Witham Loop – apparently, it follows the course of the river. At Bardney, this splits off: one line goes on to Peterborough and the other goes to Louth. He could have picked up another train at Louth and we'd have no idea of his journey from there.'

'Nice little town, Louth,' Mickey said. 'Even if it is in the middle of nowhere.' The previous year, a double murder had taken them to the market town. 'And why leave his suitcase?'

'So, for the moment we set that possibility aside and we focus on Bardney. Constable George Young is our man on the spot there. I suggest we contact the constable and ask him to spread his search a little wider. Beyond that, there is little we can do unless or until our man turns up as a corpse.'

'Which is more than likely,' Mickey agreed morosely. He took out his pocket watch. Worn smooth with use and the polish of hands and pockets, it was a much-loved timepiece. He opened the case and studied the white enamel face. 'Well, we've given this the time we allocated. If one of us telephones the constable later this afternoon, then we'll have done our duty by both of the Levys for the time being. Frankly, I'm hoping the young man just got cold feet and decided to make

a run for it, and that sooner or later he'll feel sheepish enough
to make contact with his family.'

Henry nodded. He gathered up the folders and consigned
them to a desk drawer. 'And now,' he said, 'to more pressing
business and Mr Clement Atkins.'

Clem Atkins had taken over the territory and dealings of his
erstwhile employer, Josiah Bailey, in what, under the circumstances, had been a relatively bloodless coup, the major victim
being Josiah Bailey himself. The Baileys had controlled the
turf around Commercial Road for two generations, a little
island of streets crushed between the holdings of other criminal
gangs, but they had held their own and rumour was that Clem
Atkins intended to expand his territory. A body had been fished
out of the Tobacco Dock two days before, an associate of Mr
Atkins, and now the rumour said Clem was looking for whoever
had knifed his lieutenant and dumped the body, not even
weighting it down, but making sure that it would easily be
found. It was not lost on anyone that the warehouses in the
Tobacco Dock had housed the boxing club that had been
the centre of Josiah Bailey's empire and, as yet, no one was
quite sure what to make of that.

Was it someone who had a grudge against the late Bailey?
Or someone warning Clem Atkins that this was as far as he
went, the docks being a dividing line between himself and
two other gangs.

The post-mortem report had just come in, as had witness
interviews taken by local constables, and although this was
not their case, Mickey and Henry Johnstone had a particular
interest in the goings-on within Clem Atkins' territory and
liked to keep themselves apprised of developments. Clem
Atkins had staged his coup late the previous year, deposing
Bailey himself at a time when Henry and Mickey had been
investigating the untimely demise of two of Bailey's men.
Atkins had been implicated, but they had not been able to
prove anything. Nor had they been able to prove that Atkins
had arranged for Bailey, once his boss, to be removed by
violence – even though everyone knew he must have been
behind it.

'Toby Ince, aka Tom Timmins or Rex Paul. That last one sounds a bit pretentious,' Mickey laughed. 'Had history with the race gangs a few years back, but since then he's been an odd-job man, mostly for Bailey and now, presumably, Atkins. Was known to put the frighteners on anyone new to the area who might not believe in paying their dues; had the usual convictions for illegal betting and other petty crimes.'

'A single stab wound to the back that pierced a kidney, and then he was thrown in the water,' Henry said. 'Word is that Clem Atkins wants to know who did the deed, but he doesn't seem to be making too many waves. Atkins isn't like Bailey; he's better at the long game. He'll wait until he's certain of his target and then he'll strike. Bailey would have been piling up the bodies by now.'

Mickey closed the file. 'Well, I suppose we can be thankful for small mercies, but there's trouble brewing from that direction, you mark my words.'

'I don't doubt it,' Henry agreed. 'But the one thing you could say of Bailey is that you knew where you stood. I still don't know how to figure Clem Atkins.'

Mickey paid a visit to Abraham Levy that evening, taking a detour on his homeward route. Mickey liked to walk; it soothed his mind and gave him some thinking time. He was in no hurry, anyway, to return to an empty house. His wife, Belle, was away on tour with the theatre company. He wished she would give up her travels and stay at home . . . but if she did that, then she would not be Belle.

He knocked on Abraham's door – his home rather than the clockmaker's shop next to it – and wondered if Abraham had replaced his lodgers yet. One had left because his family had need of him; the other had been murdered at the tail end of the previous year, which was how Mickey and Henry had become acquainted with the clockmaker. He was aware of the twitching curtains. A stranger and one who obviously did not belong was sure to attract attention, and Mickey was reminded also that he was in Clem Atkins' territory. He wondered if he'd been wise to come to visit Abraham. Perhaps he should have simply sent a message. He was loath to bring more trouble to the man's door. From what Mickey recalled, this side of the street was mostly Jewish, the opposite houses occupied by Irish and Poles. It was an odd quirk of these little streets that you could practically stick a pin in the map and be able to tell who might live there in terms of ethnicity and religion. There were Irish streets and Jewish streets – or half streets – and pockets of Armenians, Poles, Irish . . . When William Booth had carried out his famous survey of East End poverty, sending out his surveyors in the company of constables local to the area, he had been surprised by this pattern of identity. Mickey recalled, from his early days on the beat, a local officer telling him that there was no problem between communities as long as you didn't try to mix direct neighbours. A Polish family living next to a Jewish family, living alongside the Irish was a recipe for a storm. But if they kept to their own street or their own side of the street, he had said, then everyone got along famously.

People were odd, Mickey thought. Very odd.

Abraham opened the door and his eyes lit up at the sight of Sergeant Hitchens. 'You have news? Come along inside. You will take tea?'

'Tea would be welcome,' Mickey said as he stepped over the threshold and into the small front room. 'But I've not much to tell you, I'm afraid. We called in all the information that could be had, and the boss and I went through it today. From what I can see, everyone did as thorough a job as they could.'

He watched as Abraham absorbed that and the light in his eyes faded. 'I'm sure you've done what you can,' he said. 'You would like to sit in here?'

Mickey glanced around the front parlour. As with most such rooms, it was clean and neat and obviously rarely used, kept for high days and holidays and special guests. In this particular context, Mickey really didn't want to be a special guest. 'In my opinion, kitchens and back rooms are the place to be,' he said.

Abraham smiled. 'My feeling also,' he said. 'Come through and be at ease.'

They drank strong tea as Mickey talked through what little they had discovered in their review of Joseph's disappearance.

Much was already familiar to Abraham, but he became animated when Mickey told him about the suitcase left on the train and also that his nephew may well have broken his journey at Bardney.

'That is progress!' Abraham declared. 'Information we did not have. We can go to Bardney – I don't mean you, Sergeant Hitchens; I am aware that this is beyond your purview. But we – his family – we can begin there. And the suitcase? You know where that might be?'

Mickey shook his head. 'We know it's been handed in. It was reported to the guard on the train, so I expect it will have been taken to Peterborough. We will telephone in the morning and let you know if it's fetched up there. It's possible, of course, that it came all the way to King's Cross and we will ask there first, although I don't see that finding his suitcase will tell us much about the whereabouts of your nephew.'

Abraham shrugged. 'It is something,' he said. 'It is more than we knew yesterday. We must be grateful for small mercies, Sergeant Hitchens.'

There was a photograph on the mantelpiece of a very young baby, cradled by a very pretty girl, and Abraham noticed Mickey's gaze. 'My wife and child,' he said.

'What happened to them?' Their absence was almost a physical presence in the house.

'Dead, just a few weeks after that picture was taken. Influenza, after the war.'

'I'm sorry,' Mickey told him. 'You never wanted to marry again?'

'You mean, it's unusual for a Jew of my age to be a bachelor,' Abraham laughed. 'And it is, I suppose. But I love my wife. I would have to love her less to love another more, and since I can't do that, I don't consider it fair to ask any woman to take her place. It would be wrong.'

Mickey nodded thoughtfully. 'Makes sense,' he said. 'When you have loved that powerfully, anything else would be second best. I have a wife,' he added, 'who came to me later in my life than I suppose is usual, but I'm grateful to whatever powers I don't believe in that she did.'

'That you *don't* believe in?' Abraham was clearly amused.

'It can be hard to believe in an almighty and omnipotent God when you do a job like mine,' Mickey said. 'Though for some of my colleagues, of course, the job sends them the other way, right into the arms of one church or another.'

'Do you go to church?'

'My wife likes to sing. I go when she's home.'

'When she's home?'

Mickey shrugged but did not elaborate. 'And you, do you go to synagogue?'

'I go as often as I feel needful. More lately, I suppose. However much we turn our backs, it's human for misery to want company, don't you think?'

Mickey had to agree with that.

Abraham was silent for a moment or two and then he said, 'You have to understand, it's more than just fearing that he's dead. It's knowing that if he is, he's also unburied, unmourned . . .' He hesitated, as though not sure how his guest would judge his next words. 'According to our beliefs, until his body is in the earth, properly buried according to our customs and our ways, then his soul is in turmoil. He is lost, in pain, apart from the community that nurtured him and that will always love him and to which he belongs.'

'Do you believe that?' Mickey asked gently. 'As a man who goes to synagogue only as often as he feels necessary?'

'It's not about that.' For the first time, Abraham sounded almost impatient. 'It's not about worship; in my head, it's not even about the Almighty, as you call him – it's about belonging. Sergeant Hitchens, however much we try to pull up our roots, our roots are always anchored. Cut them off and the remnants are still in the soil. We are always, in some measure, what we are born to, for good or ill, and in times of joy or sorrow it's only natural that those roots pull us back. So yes, as things stand now, I do believe that. My brother and his wife have cried themselves dry. They need to know that their son is safe. Maybe not alive, but safe. Do you understand?'

Mickey nodded. 'We'll do what we can,' he said, 'but I won't make promises I might not be able to keep; you must understand that.'

'I do and I'm grateful.'

Mickey retrieved his hat and made ready to go. 'If we track down the suitcase, can you come and look it over? Just in case there's anything significant?'

'Of course. I'll do anything you need me to do.'

'Do your brother and his wife and the rest of the family know you've come to us?'

Abraham smiled broadly. 'Of course, and I've told them that, as good and honest men – even though you are *goyim* – you will not rest until you have answers for them.'

FOUR

On the Friday of that same week, there was an incident in Clem Atkins' territory. A youth, thought to be about eighteen or nineteen, had found himself in the wrong place at the wrong time and been badly beaten. It was said that he was from the Elephant and Castle mob and should not have been in Atkins' territory. The local constables had reported back and Mickey, finding himself curious, took a wander down on his way home. The young man had been taken to hospital with slash wounds on his face and arms, concussion and broken ribs. None of the wounds were life-threatening, but Mickey was told that he would bear the scars for the rest of his life.

Mickey was worried that this was the start of something more. If the victim was a member of a gang, and in particular a member of the Elephants, then they would take revenge sooner or later. Mickey had seen such clashes before and had no wish for them to be repeated – and certainly no wish for them to be repeated a matter of a mile or so from where he himself lived.

There was a larger police presence than the streets normally attracted. Constables were still out doing door-to-door, although as Mickey watched, he was amused to find that nothing had changed. The constable knocked on the door. The door opened, words were exchanged, the door closed. The constable went away. It was a given that no one would have seen anything, know anything or say anything – not unless Clem Atkins wanted it to be seen, known or spoken about. The injured was not one of theirs, so why should they care?

Mickey paused to speak to the officers and get further details. In the street where the incident had taken place, the blood was still on the ground, soaking between the cobblestones.

'Witnesses say he was being chased by some of the kids round here,' the constable said. 'But of course we've no names for the kids involved. They caught up with him just here, and two men came out from that alleyway – one with a stick from the looks of him, one with a razor. Not a bare blade; the wounds aren't deep enough for that.'

Mickey nodded, understanding, and asked which hospital he had been taken to. He had no doubt that he or Henry would be talking to the boy at some point, for all the good it would do them. The boy would be as tight-lipped as the locals were.

Mickey rounded the next corner and headed towards the King's Head, the pub that Clem Atkins had chosen as his headquarters. He had refurbished the building and now lived above the bar, a hostelry frequented by his own people rather than the general public. He seemed unsurprised to see Mickey and had a pint ready and waiting for him.

'Sergeant Hitchens, make yourself at home.'

Mickey settled himself in a tub chair and took a long draught. 'You keep a good pint here; I'll say that much for you.'

'You hear that, boys? The copper reckons we keep a good pint.'

'So what happened here, then?'

'A brawl, someone got hurt, you lot came, they took him off to hospital. End of story.'

'As yet he seems to be a young man without a name.'

'Well, he's not from round here, so you can't expect anyone who *is* from round here to know who he is,' Clem said reasonably.

Mickey acknowledged that and took another drink.

'I hear you've been paying our clockmaker a visit. About that nephew of his, was it?'

'Mr Levy asked us to look into it. Of course, unless the boy turns up dead, there is little we can do, but we took it upon ourselves to review the evidence.'

'Murder detectives wasting their time on a simple missing person. Or is it likely to become a missing corpse?'

Mickey shrugged his shoulders. 'From all accounts, he is not a young man who would go missing willingly. His family is concerned.'

'Young 'uns do things their families don't expect,' Atkins said with a wise nod. 'Likely there's a woman involved.'

'Better that than a murder involved.'

Mickey glanced around the bar. The floor was scuffed but well swept and the wood on the bar top polished and gleaming, along with the brass. The walls were clean, and Mickey could smell fresh paint. It was a far cry from the underground boxing den where Josiah Bailey had held court. This place had windows – windows through which Clem Atkins could observe the crossroads of his world. It was an interesting change of tactics, Mickey thought, and interesting also that whereas Josiah Bailey's headquarters had been on the periphery of his territory, this old pub was slap bang in the centre. The space was dotted with cast iron, marble-topped tables and bentwood chairs, with the addition of a few more comfortable tub chairs like the ones in which he and Atkins were seated. Groups of men sat around drinking, playing cards – and Mickey had no doubt they had been playing for money before he came in – studying the betting form or just engaging in idle chat. But there was an atmosphere in the room of barely contained aggression. Anyone mistaking this bar for a common or garden hostelry would only have to stick their heads through the door to have their minds changed.

'Not that it's my concern, of course,' Atkins said in a tone that belied his words, 'but you hear rumours about the Kikes, don't you?'

Mickey ignored the epithet. 'Rumours?' he asked. He didn't bother to hide his interest; Clem Atkins was not a man who appreciated the playing of such games.

Atkins set his glass down on the table and beckoned Mickey closer. 'Family used to live round here,' he said. 'The brother's family and that of the girl this Joseph was supposed to marry.'

'Apparently so,' Mickey told him.

'Know why they left, do you?'

'Get away from the likes of you, I should imagine.'

Clem Atkins laughed. 'More than likely,' he agreed. 'Wanted that veneer of respectability, didn't they? You know, that veneer folk reckon they get by leaving their past behind.'

Mickey sighed but knew he had to ask, 'And what past was that, Clem?'

Atkins brushed imaginary dust from the sleeves of his jacket.

'The girl's family made out they'd not got two shillings to rub together, didn't they? But then they go and buy that big old place up north, set up a bit of a boarding house – only for their own kind, mind you. And only for their own kind that happen to be travelling in from certain places.' He raised an eyebrow at Mickey, inviting him to enquire further.

'Well, go on, enlighten me,' Mickey told him. 'I can see you're burning to.'

'Me? I don't burn for nothing, Sergeant Hitchens; I leave all that to lesser men. But I will tell you anyway.' He leaned closer, whisky-soaked breath in Mickey's nostrils. '*Diamonds*,' he said. 'Come in from Antwerp. Or so the rumour goes. Not that I give a lot of credence to rumours, you understand.' He turned from Mickey and tapped the table, indicating that his glass needed a refill.

Mickey knew he had been dismissed, but he took his time moving. Leaning back against his chair, he said, 'Rumour also has it that the lad beaten half to death today has connections to the Elephants. You might want to consider that.' He paused. 'Ah, but, of course, you don't pay attention to rumours, do you?'

'There's rumours and there's rumours,' Clem told him. 'I'm sure you know that to be true, Sergeant Hitchens. And speaking of rumours, I suppose you've heard what is said about Abraham Levy?'

Apparently, Mickey thought, he'd not been dismissed after all. He waited.

'An agitator,' Clem Atkins said. 'A communist, so it's said. Stands on his soapbox of a Sunday and exhorts the working classes to rise up against their masters. Tells them they should be the ones benefitting, not the sweatshop owners and the slum landlords.'

'Not an uncommon message in these parts,' Mickey observed.

'Ain't that the truth! I hear he almost got himself arrested, month or so back, standing on his box outside the labour exchange and delivering his commie message to the queue. And you know that ain't legal – not outside the labour exchange. Your lot just moved him on – some young officer, new to the beat, who didn't fancy taking on the crowd, I imagine.'

'You seem to know a lot about this clockmaker,' Mickey observed. 'Seem to spend a good deal of effort keeping him under observation.'

Clem Atkins drained his glass and tapped it on the counter again. Magically, it was refilled and Clem drained it again. 'He causes me no worries,' he said. 'I just like to keep my finger on the pulse, if you get my meaning.'

Atkins stood and nodded to two men who'd been drinking at a side table. They too drained their glasses and came across to join their boss. 'Well, it's been good yarning with you, Sergeant, but I'm sure we've both got work to do, so I'll wish you a good evening.'

Mickey watched him go and then wandered back out into the street, thinking how much had changed since Atkins had reopened this pub and taken over this little patch of a dozen or so streets from the previous incumbent. Josiah Bailey had not been in agreement with the change and had now been dead for almost three months, although on the face of things, Mickey reflected, not much had actually changed at all. The reopening of the King's Head was the only surface difference. Even that had little impact on the local community; as far as Mickey could make out, it was reserved for Clem Atkins and his cronies. Bailey's preferred headquarters, the boxing gym, was below ground, easily defended, invisible to most, and although Mickey knew that Clem Atkins still frequented the place, it seemed that the new boss preferred to be a degree or so more visible than his predecessor. That perhaps was the biggest shift; it spoke, Mickey thought, of Clem Atkins' personality compared with Josiah Bailey's. The impression he got was that Atkins was just feeling his way at the moment, not yet as tightly ensconced as he would like to be.

On reflection, Mickey had not been surprised by what Clem Atkins had said about Abraham Levy. There were a good many Jewish communists active in Whitechapel, Limehouse and even Golders Green, although the more orthodox community did not encourage such overt activity, and Abraham seemed to be a man who cared for the welfare of others. It might mean that he had a police record, though, Mickey thought; if so, he and Henry needed to be aware. It was likely that this business with the missing nephew had some quite different foundation, but if the uncle was an agitator, had the boy followed in his footsteps and been led into trouble because of that?

Unlikely, Mickey thought, especially considering he'd gone missing from a Lincoln train and not in the capital. What was more interesting was Clem Atkins' reference to the diamond trade. It could all be so much gossip, of course; it was common-place, whenever the Jews were mentioned, that someone would also mention wealth and alongside that would be a reference to either money lenders or diamond traders. Those who did had most likely never witnessed the hand-to-mouth poverty endured by the East End Jews – alongside the East End Irish, Poles, Russians, Armenians and everyone else – but the idea still seemed prevalent and immovable, whatever the evidence to the contrary. But prejudice against the Jews was embedded even at government level, and it had been the influx of Yiddish-speaking Ashkenazi Jews, visible and in larger numbers than previously, that had impelled the government towards legisla-tion and the Aliens Act of 1905 had come into force. Now all incoming aliens had to be registered with the police, and it had become convenient since the rise of Bolshevism in Russia to claim that you were from this now Soviet country, as the government had decided Russian émigrés could not be deported back to their homeland.

Mickey had encountered his fair share of non-Russian speakers who claimed Russia as their mother country, but so many arrived without papers and it was difficult to prove anything one way or another. And he could never find it in his heart to blame those fleeing poverty for trying to make the best of a bad job, although he knew this was a minority opinion within the Metropolitan Police.

He had reached the streets close to his home now and stopped off at Pritchard's corner shop for bread and bacon. Young Eddy, taken in by the Pritchard family a few months before, served him, weighing out the bacon and counting his change with care. He looked clean and well fed, Mickey noted with satisfaction. One small story with a happy ending out of all of those that had none.

'So, how's school, young fella?'

Eddy grimaced. 'Hard work,' he admitted. Education had not been a regular feature of Eddy's previous life. 'But Mr Pritchard says I have to just keep at it, and he helps me with my numbers and my reading.'

'Good lad,' Mickey approved. Malc Pritchard's wife had died some years before and he had raised his clutch of sons largely single-handed, a feat that had raised more than a few eyebrows, lone men not generally reckoned to be suitable parents. But he'd done a good job of it, as far as Mickey could see, and they'd taken on this young 'un and given him a home when most would have turned the boy away.

'Bacon for tea, is it?' Malc himself appeared from the room behind the shop, wiping his hands on a cloth. 'You get on and get yourself fed. Food's on the table,' he told Eddy.

'I've some eggs at home. I thought bacon, eggs and a bit of fried bread would set me up just right. And a large pot of tea. How's the boy doing? He looks well.'

'Still having the nightmares, but only once or twice a week, so that's a big improvement. He wets the bed once in a while, but we just wash the sheets and don't make a fuss about it. I put a rubber sheet over the mattress, so it's no matter. What that boy's gone through, there's no surprise he's still fretting. He'll be fine, given a year or so.'

'Good to hear. Poor little scrap.'

'I hear you had some fun over the way this afternoon? Clem Atkins' lot?'

'Beat a boy – one of the Elephant gang, so the rumour mill says, strayed too far.'

'Strayed a long way too far,' Malc observed, and Mickey nodded thoughtfully in response.

'You're right there,' he said. 'Truth is, Malc, I'd not thought about that. It would take more effort than a simple walk up the wrong road.'

'Elephants testing the lay of the land, maybe? See what this new man will and won't take?'

'Could be. Atkins is no Josiah Bailey. Bailey could be relied upon to strike before provoked and figure out after who'd done the provoking. Clem Atkins is a different sort. More like a snake, lying in the grass. Quiet like, not drawing attention, but you step too close and he'll strike before you even know he's there.'

Malc nodded. The shop doorbell rang, announcing another customer, and Mickey took his leave. Malc's comment had struck a chord; it resonated uncomfortably but he could not, as yet, quite make out the notes. All the way home he'd been aware of an unease in his mind, something that went beyond the simple wrongness of the fight, the injuries and his conversation with Clem Atkins in the bar, and Malc had put his finger on it. The Elephant boy could not have just wandered into Atkins' territory; he'd have to cross two, maybe three, other gangs' territory to get there and, yes, he could have managed that by the simple expedient of taking a bus, but why bother? What was he doing there? As Malc said, it could have been to test strength and purpose, but Mickey would have expected the Elephants to turn up in bigger numbers if that had been the case.

Mickey put his key in the door and swung it wide. The house felt empty and cold without Belle. Knowing it was selfish, that he'd known what her life was like when he'd asked her to be his wife and that she would not surrender her hard-won independence, he still wished she'd just choose to settle down and stay full-time. He went through to the middle room of his terraced home and put a match to the fire he'd laid before leaving that morning and then dropped his shopping off in the kitchen before filling the kettle.

Food and a very big pot of tea were definitely required, Mickey thought, and a conversation with the young man who'd been so badly beaten, should he be in a fit state to have one, the following morning.

FIVE

As it turned out, the suitcase belonging to Joseph Levy had made its way back to London. Having arrived at Peterborough and been identified as a piece of abandoned luggage, it had been examined for an owner's address and, this being on the label, dispatched to London and lodged in the lost luggage store at King's Cross.

Henry had sent word to Abraham, and the two of them now regarded the battered and much mended piece of luggage laid out on a desk behind the ticket office. The sound of the trains, departing passengers, hiss of steam and swift footsteps, muffled by the walls and the conversation between those selling tickets and those requesting them, drifted through.

'This was his grandfather's case,' Abraham said. 'Our father travelled with it all the way from Odessa on the Black Sea. You see this repair?' He pointed to the strip of leather that had been carefully stitched to reinforce a corner. 'He borrowed a needle and thread from a woman in Paris, and cut a piece from an old boot that even he could no longer repair.' He smiled. 'Stories. Who knows which are true or have some truth in them and which are just stories? Does it matter anymore? In the end, it is the stories that remain.'

'There is no key?' Henry asked.

'No, just the latches and then the straps with buckles, to keep them closed. I don't recall anyone ever having the key.'

Henry unfastened the buckles and then released the catches. He stepped back. Abraham lifted the lid and slowly removed the contents. Two shirts, a spare pair of trousers, some underclothes and a purse containing a ten-shilling note and some coins.

'He kept this money in case of emergencies,' Abraham said, 'but the silly child didn't even keep that with him when he left the train. He would have had little more than pocket change on him.'

'He left the train in a hurry,' Henry said. 'Probably intending to get back on before it left the station.'

'So why did he not?'

Henry took the remaining item from the suitcase. A small leather frame that held two photographs. One, formal and redolent of an old-fashioned studio, depicted an older couple, and the other, casual and candid, a young man and a girl.

Abraham pointed. 'His father and mother, and this is Joseph and his intended. Handsome, are they not?'

'A good-looking couple,' Henry agreed, although it seemed to him that the girl was somewhat distracted. The young man, half smiling, looked straight at the photographer. The photograph was informal and small, probably taken by a friend or relative and on a camera similar to the one he and Mickey used for photographing crime scenes. Something like a Vest Pocket Kodak camera that had become so popular during the war. The couple seemed to be sitting on a park bench, water and trees behind. The girl looked past the photographer. She too was smiling but, to Henry's eyes, she seemed to be looking at something or someone behind whoever held the camera.

'Are they happy?' he asked.

Abraham sighed. 'As far as I know. To be honest, I know little about the young woman. She was a child when she left London, and I knew her family only as one more family in our community. I remember being surprised when they moved to a place that had no community, as far as I know. The closest place of worship is in the port of Grimsby. Joseph knew her from childhood; the families judge it to be a good match.' He shrugged and Henry got the impression that he was expounding this as much for his own benefit as for Henry's.

'A good match does not always make for happiness,' Henry observed, pursuing the subject even though he had asked the same questions before. Perhaps the answers would be different now that Abraham had had more time to think about them. 'Perhaps your nephew had met another girl or the girl had met another young man . . .'

'And as I said before, if they had, there would have been

no blame. Inspector, my brother's family is not so deeply orthodox that such a course would matter. If either chose to marry out, now that might cause some family arguments, as you might imagine, but as far as I know, neither had spoken against the marriage and neither seemed unhappy. My brother and his wife viewed Rebecca as another daughter.'

'And *her* family?'

'Any family would have been glad to welcome Joseph as a son.'

Henry turned his attention back to the photographs. The frame was old, red leather, a little scuffed and somewhat dated with its pattern of interlaced gilding. He gently removed both photographs, checking for anything concealed behind, but was disappointed, and there was nothing written on the reverse of the photographs either. He returned the photographs to the frame and the frame to the suitcase.

'What business is your brother in?'

'He runs a general store just off Commercial Road and has three jewellery shops. He has done well for himself. His wife brought money and connections into the marriage, and Ben worked hard to build the businesses. I will give you the address. No, I will make introductions.'

Abraham's sudden eagerness bothered Henry. He held up a steadying hand. 'If it becomes necessary, then I will meet with them. The boy may yet turn up.'

'Inspector, you and I both know that isn't going to happen.'

'Unless or until a body is found or there's firm evidence of foul play, I can't investigate. You are aware of that.'

'And so what are you doing now? If this is not investigating—'

Henry cut him off. 'And the girl's family?'

'They run a boarding house and also have shops selling mid-priced jewellery, watches, that sort of thing.'

That tied in with what Clem Atkins had told Mickey. 'And trade diamonds? Or so I'm told.'

For a second or two the clockmaker stared in disbelief and then he laughed aloud. 'And you see our family dripping with riches, do you? With all the gold we could buy, all the houses and the clocks . . . Inspector, where did you hear such nonsense? My brother has done well, as have the Goldmanns, the family of Joseph's fiancée, but believe me, they have grappled for every penny and worked their way to where they are now across the generations. There has been no easy way and certainly no diamonds unless they are little stones in engagement rings.'

Henry closed the suitcase and handed it to Abraham. The clockmaker took it reluctantly, as though by receiving the bag he was accepting that Henry had no further interest.

'Our grandfather,' he said, 'was a cutter. He was born in Antwerp, went to Odessa to marry and took his trade with him. Some of the family are still in the trade, I believe, but not our branch of the tree. We fled here, along with, what, a hundred thousand like us? What did we bring with us, Inspector? My mother arrived with the clothes she stood up in and a few coins sewn into the hem of her coat. My father arrived with even less, but he had a skill and a trade, and he found work with an old man about to retire and who had no son to pass his business on to. I now live next door to that business instead of above the shop, as my parents did, and I rent out those rooms above, as you well know. We raised enough between us to set my brother on the path with his first shop, and then, as I say, he married well. Perhaps our distant kin in Antwerp or Odessa have had better luck with their skills, but, Inspector, I know nothing of them and they know nothing of me. All I have is what my parents made with their hands, their hearts and their determination.'

'And you have no apprentice and no heirs,' Henry observed. He realized at once, from the expression on Abraham's face, that he had said something wrong, that might be taken as uncaring or cold, even though he had merely meant it as an observation of fact. He felt the lack of Mickey Hitchens. Mickey who could pour oil on any manner of troubled waters.

'I meant no offence,' he said and hoped that would do.

'I've taken enough of your time, Inspector.' Abraham extended his hand and Henry shook it. 'I thank you for expending energy on this when others would not.'

Henry watched him as he walked away. Of course,

Abraham was right, Henry thought. The boy was lying dead somewhere; now it was only a question of whether or not he'd turn up so that his body could be ritually laid in the earth before the earth took it upon itself to absorb his flesh and cover his bones.

SIX

Mickey Hitchens had taken himself off to St Thomas's Hospital before he went to Scotland Yard in the morning and was shown through to the long ward where the injured boy lay in the end bed. He was a mass of bandages and only the one blue eye looked out at Mickey with cautious curiosity.

'I'm told that it hurts for you to talk,' Mickey said, 'so I'll keep it simple and you can shake your head or raise a hand if that suits you better.'

The lips moved to form words anyway. Mickey could see the end of the gash at the side of the mouth, partly covered by dressing. 'Nothing to say.'

'Well, I'm going to ask you some questions anyway,' Mickey told him, settling himself in the uncomfortable visitor's chair.

The boy turned his head away. A shock of black hair emerged from the dressings and lay on the pillow. Dark, curly and quite long. And he was young, too. No doubt had been popular with the girls and was now wondering what life had in store for him.

'You've not given the doctors a name, and my constable said you had nothing on you, apart from a knife and a few coins and a pocket handkerchief, so how do you expect us to get you back to your family if you aren't going to tell us who you are?'

He thought he saw a tear creep out from the corner of the single blue eye. 'Blinded the other one, did they? A razor blade will do that – split it wide open. But the rest of you will heal; you know that. You left an eye behind, but the rest of you will want to go home, and your family will want you back.'

The boy in the bed shook his head, and Mickey could see he really was trying very hard to hold back the tears. This was just a kid, Mickey thought. He had been told that the boy was in his late teens, but Mickey now doubted that. 'How old are you? Fifteen, sixteen? I'm betting not even that. Your mother will still be missing her baby boy.'

'I ain't no baby.'

'To our mothers, we are always babies,' Mickey said. 'So I hear you got chased down, attacked by another group of kids, then two men came out and beat seven shades out of you, cut you to ribbons. That's about the size of it?'

No answer.

'Rumour is the Elephant mob sent you. Or was going to beard Clem Atkins in his den your idea? After all, there are all kinds of stupid.'

Still no answer, but Mickey didn't really expect one.

He paused at the nurses' station to talk to the matron and ask what the prognosis was. As he suspected, although the boy had been badly beaten, there seemed to have been no intent to kill.

'His face is like someone planned to play hopscotch on it,' Mickey was told. 'And, of course, he put up his hands and arms in defence. As for the rest, he's lost an eye, he has some broken ribs and his body is black with bruising, but he will live and, after a fashion, he will recover. And the wounds were straight and easily stitched, so I suppose that is a small mercy.'

Mickey left thoughtful and somewhat depressed. One more young casualty. He hoped that the constables would be able to track down the boy's family. Word of the incident would have spread by now. Someone would come and claim him, and even though the boy seemed upset at the idea, Mickey knew that what he really wanted was the comfort of his own people. He'd tried to be a man well before his time and this is where it got him. Another life ruined.

SEVEN

Constable George Young wasn't keen on being told how to do his job, nor was he keen on having his judgement questioned. He had, as far as he was concerned, already done his bit, first tracking down the couple who'd told the station master about the suitcase that had been left on the train and then having a telephone conversation with said couple, who had told him about the young man leaving the train so precipitously. In pursuit of a young woman with red hair and wearing a green frock, so his informant had said, and it was George Young's experience that young men in pursuit of young women did not act wisely.

Questioning of the station staff satisfied him that no one had been left standing on the station platform when the train had departed and no one had come running up, complaining that the train had gone. It was Constable Young's belief that the young couple – if couple they had become – had either most likely adjourned to the local pub or found themselves some place or other where they could be private. It was also most likely, he thought, that when the young man had had his bit of fun, he'd have caught the next train out and the young woman, likewise, would have gone on her way.

However, whatever he might think about the situation – or the morals of young people today – a degree of sensitivity, brought on by recalling how precipitous he might have been when younger, had discouraged George Young from broadcasting this interpretation of events. He had no wish to bring the reputation of either into disrepute.

But George Young was also a man who knew his duty, and if a Scotland Yard inspector requested that he have another check, make sure the young man was not still on Constable Young's patch and that no harm had come to him while he was there, then Constable Young saw it as his reluctant duty to go and investigate.

Eventually.

The request had actually been made a week ago. Constable Young had made a few enquiries at the local hostelries and questioned a few locals who lived near the station in case they might have noticed anything untoward, but he'd told himself that he didn't have the resources for a full-scale wild goose chase.

He'd pretty much put the matter out of his mind, confident that there was nothing to be done. Until this morning. This morning everything had changed and Constable Young's lot was certainly not happy as he anticipated the phone call he was about to make to the Scotland Yard inspector.

They had deposited the body in the disused dairy at a local farm, that being the only available space cool enough and with a door solid enough to keep the curious at bay. Constable Young had decided not to cover the high windows, which were barred but unglazed, hoping that the through draft might diminish the stench, the body in question now being 'well rotten', as Jed Fox, the farmer's boy who'd come across it, had said.

'So, you were rabbiting.' Constable Young had already heard the tale but he wasn't eager to make the telephone call and thought he'd do well to check the facts again.

'Like I said. I'd got two brace and I'd promised to take a brace over to old Jenny Webster. Poor old lass could do with a couple for the pot. So I cross the field where the water turns back on itself, away from the railway track. Water's been high, as you well know, but it's dropped a bit this last day or two. Sally was running on ahead, sniffing, like she does, and all of a sudden, like I told you, she picked up a scent and she took off, wouldn't come back when I called her or nothin'.'

Sally, hearing her name, lifted her head and regarded the constable with solemn brown eyes. She was part spaniel, part something larger and longer-legged, but she always had her nose to the ground when Constable Young saw her.

'And Sally led you to the body.'

'Started barking, didn't she? Sally don't ever bark. She knows better when she's out with me. Barking's for night-time, when strangers might come near and not be about proper

business. So I run up and there she is, standing by the water
and there's the body, half in and half out of the water, and at
first I think it's someone half drowned, trying to lift theirselves
out, but then I see it's a dead 'un. And he stank, didn't he?
Stank to high heaven.'

He did indeed, Constable Young thought. Stank as much
as any corpse would that had been sitting in or close to water
for three or more weeks and was now also coated in mud from
water that had been stagnant for most of that. He did indeed
stink to high heaven and then some.

Jed had run to the farm and brought his boss and foreman
back with him. They'd taken a tarpaulin and tumbled the
body into it, dragged and carried it back across the fields
and roused the constable. He'd taken charge and comman-
deered the disused dairy and taken statements, and now he
had to telephone the inspector.

Knowing he could put things off no longer, Constable Young
dismissed young Jed, telling him he'd have to make himself
available when the inspector arrived. Then he called the
exchange and made the trunk call to Scotland Yard, knowing
that the story would be round the district by now and news
of his phone call would be following the tale within minutes.

He was relieved to discover that Chief Inspector Henry
Johnstone was out and that Sergeant Hitchens, who took his
call, was a little less austere.

'I take it,' Mickey Hitchens asked, 'that you are formally
requesting the help of a murder detective?'

'Well, I suppose I am,' Constable Young confirmed. 'So,
when can I be expecting him to arrive?'

Mickey glanced at the board that listed those on call.
Protheroe was first up, but Mickey doubted he would mind if
he and Henry took the shout, as they were already informally
involved. 'You can expect us on the morning train,' he said.
'We'll need to see where the body was found and interview
those who found it. And, Constable, it's a shame it had to be
moved, but there's no help for that now. Just make sure it's
not further disturbed until we get there.'

Constable Young assured him that no one was likely to want
to disturb it further and, anyway, he had the only key. He

ended the call feeling slightly relieved that he'd not had to speak with the grumpy one.

Mickey replaced the receiver and stared thoughtfully at the phone. They'd have to tell Abraham, he thought; tell him that his worst fears had been realized and that it was now up to Mickey and Henry to find out the how and the why.

EIGHT

'I have to come with you tomorrow,' Abraham insisted. 'He's been alone too long. Someone has to watch over the body until burial. Someone has to prepare him for the grave . . .'

Henry held up his hand and Abraham fell silent. 'I can't take you,' he said. 'This is a murder investigation and you have to let us do our job. If his next of kin are in London, then we will arrange for the body to be brought here and the post-mortem carried out by one of the pathologists on our list, probably at Barts or St Mary's . . I can't promise where, but close by. Abraham, that's the best I can offer.'

'But someone must be with him.'

'And once he's brought back, we'll do what we can to accommodate that,' Henry promised. 'We should notify his next of kin.'

'I can do that.'

'It should be made official,' Henry objected. He caught Mickey's look and relented. 'Very well. You can inform your brother and the fiancée, but I'll need to speak with everyone concerned upon our return.'

'But they have done nothing—'

'No one is being accused,' Henry snapped. He sighed.

'What the inspector means is that we have to speak to the family in all cases like this – see if they can shed any light. People often think they know nothing, but a small fact, something out of place, can often as not lead to us finding out the rest of it.'

Abraham leaned back in his chair and rubbed his face wearily with his palms. 'I do understand,' he said. 'I will do whatever is needful.' He shook his head sadly. 'Nothing prepares you for death, not even the expectation of it. I still dared to hope that he was safe.' He looked once again at Henry. 'You are certain it is him?'

'Unless someone else wore his coat, went missing at the same time, fetched up dead in the same place he was last seen.'

'Then I should come and identify him.'

Henry and Mickey exchanged a glance, and Mickey said gently, 'It may well be that a final identification is made by dental records. Perhaps you could find out the name of his dentist for us?'

Abraham stared hard at Mickey Hitchens, allowing the implications of his words to sink in. 'He is so badly—'

'It's been three weeks or more, Abraham. He's been out in the open and some time in the water.'

'I see,' Abraham said. 'No, of course, I should have thought of this. Of course, I should have anticipated . . .'

Mickey got to his feet and clasped the man by the shoulder. 'We must be going,' he said. 'We've an early start and you'll be wanting to contact your brother and such like.'

'I was harsh,' Henry acknowledged as they closed the front door and stood for a moment on the step.

'That you were.'

They walked on in companionable silence for a while. 'Well,' Mickey said, 'I'm off that way and home. You're welcome to come and have a bite to eat.'

'Thank you, but I promised I'd call in and see Melissa this evening and then I must pack my bag ready for the morning. You are all prepared?'

'As if we were first on the board,' Mickey said, referring to the time they'd have to be ready if they had been first on call. He had no doubt that Henry was similarly fixed but guessed that the inspector needed to go through the motions of packing and sorting to get his brain in order. Whatever had disturbed his equilibrium needed dealing with in Henry's own way, and Mickey had no doubt that his boss would reveal all in good time. 'Give my love to young Melissa,' he said. 'Tell her it's been a while since I had one of her wonderful letters.'

Henry made his slow way to Cynthia's house. He chose to walk rather than taking bus or taxi, knowing that he needed to get what Cynthia called his grumps under control before he saw his niece. He wished Cynthia was back; he'd had a letter from her that morning, announcing her intention to take her husband travelling for a little longer, and Henry realized that he missed her terribly. Cynthia was his foundation, the one constant in his life, a steadying influence that not even Mickey could match, and he had to admit that Cynthia's letter was one part of what had upset him that day. The second had been a brief encounter with Clem Atkins when Henry had gone to view the spot where the boy had been attacked.

He'd had the news that morning that the family had come looking for him; news of the assault had travelled and the family had already been out looking for the boy and checking hospitals. They had finally made their way to St Thomas's.

While Sergeant Young had been on the phone to Mickey, Henry had been talking to the boy's parents and trying to persuade them that the action they viewed as their right was indeed unwise and that he would have no hesitation in pursuing them should they venture into Clem Atkins' territory looking for revenge.

He and the matron had eventually calmed the scene, but he had no doubt that they would get just as riled up again later when the bandages came off and they took the boy home. The seeds of conflict had been sown and they would reap the harvest, whatever he said.

He had therefore gone to view the scene himself, and although he knew that Mickey had already spoken to Clem Atkins, he felt he should add his presence. The least he could do was to make Atkins fully aware that he was being watched – from all sides.

Henry disliked the man far more than he had ever disliked Josiah Bailey – senior or the son of the same name – and he could not quite explain to himself why this bothered him so much. After all, he wasn't exactly meant to like the criminal classes with which he had to deal, day in, day out. Bailey had been a mean, vicious and unpredictable individual, given to violence and bouts of rage. Atkins – although Henry had no doubt he was equally vicious – exercised a tight and uncanny control over his own moods. He was intelligent, Henry allowed, in an animal sort of way. And every bit as dangerous as Bailey.

The difference was Bailey had been impulsive, given to mistakes – making an exhibition of those who crossed him. Atkins, Henry sensed, was craftier, more skilled at hiding his play, and he filled Henry with revulsion in a way that Bailey, even in his excesses, never had.

But now it was more than that, he reminded himself. During the conversation, Clem Atkins had compared the two of them, himself and Henry, and it had played on Henry's mind for the rest of the day, adding to his restlessness and pointless irritation at the fact that Cynthia would be staying away longer than he'd hoped.

'Two sides of the same coin, we are. I'll make a bet with you that we had the same childhood – the same bastard fathers, the same weak mothers. I could have been standing where you are and you could be standing in my place, Inspector Johnstone.'

'No,' Henry said softly as he stood at his sister's door. 'No, we are not.'

Henry had Cynthia to guide him, to protect him, to ensure he became the man she trusted he would become, and that made all the difference.

Melissa and Nanny were eating supper by the fire in the nursery. Henry joined them, sinking down into one of the comfortable old leather armchairs that had been in Albert's study before they became too tired and worn. Melissa had claimed them then and Nanny had crocheted afghans for them both.

'You look as though you've had a long day,' Nanny told him. 'I'll get cook to send up some sandwiches and tea for you.'

Henry thanked her, leaned back in the chair and closed his eyes.

'Are you tired, Uncle Henry?'

'I suppose I am. And I have to catch a train tomorrow, up to Lincolnshire.'

'So, someone is dead, I suppose.'

Henry opened his eyes and regarded his niece thoughtfully. 'Do you think that's the only reason I go anywhere?'

She thought about it. 'Usually,' she said. 'I mean you're not like Mummy. You don't exactly like to go on holiday, do you?'

Henry laughed. 'No, I probably don't. Maybe I should. I had a letter from your mother this morning.'

'So did I. She and Daddy are staying away a bit longer. I thought they might do.'

'Oh? And why is that?'

Melissa pushed back a strand of auburn hair from a freckled face and for a moment she looked so much like Cynthia that Henry felt his heart cramp. He could not have borne it if Melissa had to suffer as her mother had done.

'Because she needs to keep Daddy away until the men who want him to sign up to some rotten deal have left for New York, and I did as Mummy asked and forwarded the clippings on to her about the two men she's trying to avoid. They haven't gone yet. The newspaper said that one of them was staying on to do some car racing, so Mummy has to keep Daddy away from them a bit longer.'

Henry laughed. 'Oh, my goodness, Melissa, you sound just like your mother.'

'I think,' Melissa told him, 'that's a good thing. Even Daddy says that Mummy is a very sensible and intelligent woman.' She paused. 'Mummy says they are going to Germany. That they are going to leave France and drive there.'

'Yes, she told me that, too.' Cynthia had not been too happy about it, but Albert had unfinished business and this seemed as good a time as any to get it tied up.

'Mummy says she quite likes Mr Stresemann who is the foreign minister.' Melissa said this as though she knew exactly what a foreign minister was. Maybe she did, Henry thought.

'And she says that she is inclined to tolerate Mr Herman Miller. He's the chancellor, you know, but she said she read an article by a Mr Hitler and she really doesn't like him,' Melissa said unexpectedly. 'I heard her say that he was a dastardly man and she wouldn't trust him as far as she could spit.' She thought about this. 'I've never seen Mummy spit, but I don't think she'd be very good at it.' She eyed her uncle thoughtfully. 'What do you think, Uncle Henry?'

'I think I'm inclined to agree with your mother,' he said. In his own letter, Cynthia had been even more forthright. She had been urging Albert to slowly but surely sever ties with his

German companies, but Henry knew she had to go carefully with this – drop hints, feed Albert with information until the idea seemed to be his own. Albert was a proud man, and Cynthia knew not to hurt that pride – not if she wanted to get her own way. He wondered if she would achieve what she set out to do on this trip.

Nanny appeared with sandwiches and a tray of tea and set them down on the little table beside Henry's chair. 'Time to get ready for bed, my sweet,' she told Melissa. 'Give your uncle a big kiss.'

Henry hugged Melissa close. 'Mickey sends his love,' he said, belatedly remembering his sergeant's message, 'and asks for one of your letters when you have the time.'

'I'll write to him tomorrow,' Melissa promised.

Nanny and Henry watched as she trundled off to the bathroom, trailing her nightdress and dressing gown like a train behind her.

'Now,' Henry was told, 'eat up and I'll pour the tea and you can tell me what's on your mind.'

'I'm not one of your charges,' Henry objected.

'Oh, yes, you are. Your sister told me to keep an especial eye on you while she was away, and tonight you look done in and bleak as winter.'

Nanny's blandishments had not really worked. Henry was comfortable talking about himself with very few people, and although he knew the woman meant well, she was not one of them. Not wanting to hurt her feelings, he told her that he was tired and had a difficult case, and managed to shift the conversation back to the children, a subject she could never resist. It turned out that his sister's nanny had worries of her own.

'Little George is growing up so fast,' she said. 'Soon he'll be going to school and won't need me.'

Henry wasn't sure what to say. 'Children do grow up quickly,' he tried.

'And then the likes of us move on elsewhere. Once a family has done with us, that's just the nature of things, I suppose.'

Henry was startled. It was a state of affairs he'd never actually considered. 'You were with other families before you came here?'

'Of course. Good families, but, oh, I will miss this one. Your sister is so kind. I feel as though this has been my home.'

Henry must have been staring at her because she reached across and patted his hand as though he might be the one needing comfort. 'It's not for you to worry about,' she said. 'It's just that as you get older, I suppose you start hoping for a place to settle. It's an itinerant sort of life.'

Henry moved the conversation elsewhere, not sure what to do and wishing he could think of something constructive to say, but the problem occupied his mind as he made his way back to his flat, and by the time he had packed his bag ready for the next day's journey, he had decided that he should mention the conversation in his reply to Cynthia's letter. That an elderly lady in his sister's employ should be afraid of being dispossessed was not something that had ever occurred to Henry. Where did old nannies go to? Did they have savings – he was certain Cynthia would have paid above-average wages – but he had not thought about the bigger problem of being without a permanent home.

He recalled vividly the day he and his sister had left their parents' house for the last time, after their father had died. He could never bring himself to refer to it as the family home; it never had been that. Their father, a doctor, had rented the house and the landlord had given them an extra week's grace before they were out on their ears. Cynthia had used the time to sell every stick of furniture, every vase, their mother's jewellery, even the fire irons, just to provide them with a little travelling money. Their father had, it turned out, been heavily in debt, and it was only the fact that a colleague had purchased his practice that saved them from worse trouble. As it was, the day they closed the front door for the last time and left the key beneath a plant pot on the porch, they possessed the clothes they stood up in, a small bag each, containing spare clothing and a few small possessions, and the money Cynthia had managed to raise.

The night before, she had counted it up and split it into four purses. Her own, their mother's and a couple of drawstring bags she had rescued from their father's pharmacy cupboard. One had contained liquorish and the other moth balls.

'I'm dividing the money into four equal parts,' she said. 'Henry, you are to put one part in your coat and another in the bottom of your bag, and for goodness' sake don't ever let that bag out of your sight. I'll do the same. We're going out into a world we hardly know, and we can't afford to fall foul of thieves.' It was a strategy that reminded Henry of Joseph, packing his emergency money in his suitcase and then leaving it behind.

Cynthia had been fifteen and at that point in their lives she had rarely travelled by train; in fact, they had rarely been more than a few miles from where they lived, their father considering money for any kind of travel an extravagance, as far as his children were concerned. They were, indeed, going out into a world they hardly knew. They would catch a train to London and then go in search of their mother's brother – a brother who hadn't even attended his sister's funeral. Cynthia had visited him once, when she was very small, before her mother had died, but she knew that he still owned a bookshop and that he had a storeroom above. She knew this because she and her mother had slept there on their visit. She had an address and that was all.

Henry reached into his jacket pocket and withdrew his journal.

> *Lord alone knows what would have happened to us had our uncle moved away and not told us. As it was, I will always remember the way Cynthia marched into the shop. She'd waited until customers had gone inside. The right kind of customers, she said, in front of whom our uncle was unlikely to make a scene. And we had stood in the cold for a full hour, watching and waiting until a well-dressed couple in their middle years went in. Only then, with what she judged to be appropriate witnesses, did Cynthia decide the time was right.*

Henry paused. He could still remember the look on their uncle's face as Cynthia and Henry had made their entrance. The tears

Cynthia had managed to produce from somewhere – certainly not at grief for the death of their father – and the performance she had put on, the upshot of which was not sympathy from their uncle but, as Cynthia had so rightly judged, such expressions of concern from his important customers that within the hour a space in the storeroom was theirs.

> *That was about all he ever offered. He might have been related to our mother but in temperament he was closer to our father.*

He stopped. No, that was not quite fair. Uncle Bart was mean and disinterested but he was never violent, and he had at least given them shelter and coal for the fire, although he'd made it clear that they would have to fend for themselves in all other respects.

Henry glanced about his little flat. It was small – a living room, tiny kitchen, functional bathroom and a bedroom – but it was his space and his sanctuary, and the view of the river made up for many of its shortcomings. He had come to depend upon this bolthole, this place of his own.

He put down his journal and picked up his sister's letter, read it once more and then took up his pen to reply. It had probably not even occurred to Cynthia that Nanny should be worried, Henry thought, so he would take it upon himself to tell her now, before the intricacies of another murder filled his brain with its mysteries and its vital trivia so that there was little room for anything else.

NINE

Bardney turned out to be a pretty and slightly sprawling village set in a flat landscape.

PC George Young had met them at the station and introduced them to the station master, and they had spoken briefly, agreeing to meet up later when the man was less busy.

It was mid-afternoon. Mickey and Henry were both tired, but also eager to see the body before it became too dark. PC Young had explained that the body was in an old dairy, now disused, on the farm close to where the body had been found. The farmer had agreed to provide oil lamps should they need them and was keen for the body to be gone as it was 'stinking the place up'.

They walked out of the village with PC Young. He told them it was about a mile to the farm and he filled that mile with chatter, pointing out the geographical features and the history of the place, clearly uncomfortable with these two officers from Scotland Yard and also uncomfortable with the fact that he had not acted sooner.

'Goes right back to the Domesday Book, so it does, and there was an abbey here until Henry VIII took against it, and now it's all agricultural land, mostly sugar beet. You see over there?' He pointed to a large and somewhat unsightly building out of keeping with the rest of the village and set a couple of miles distant. 'Sugar beet factory, that is. Got its own railway line – joins up with the line just where the river bends. See? The land is all drained by dykes and in winter it floods, so you can see it was a devil to search it.'

'It took some time for the body to be found,' Henry said, and there was no mistaking the disapproval and coldness in his voice.

The constable immediately started to make excuses: the big area to search . . . he had no manpower . . . there was absolutely no indication that the boy had really gone missing at Bardney to start with.

'I imagine local farmers could each have been persuaded to check the borders of their own land,' Mickey said, his tone milder than Henry's but no less disapproving. 'You've arranged for us to meet the man who did eventually find him?'

'Of course. I've told him I'll send word as he is needed. He's a good lad – a bit slow, but a good lad. Works hard. Trained the dog himself.'

Henry was pointedly ignoring the man and Mickey saw no reason to engage in further conversation, so PC Young was left to fill the silence. Everyone was relieved when the dairy came into view, standing some distance from the farmhouse and the barns and obviously long disused. This farm, like many others, had been turned over to the production of sugar beet.

PC Young unlocked the door and swung it open wide, but the smell had already reached them; decomposition was advanced, and Henry was glad that the weather was still cold and the buzz of flies therefore not overwhelming. The situation was also helped by the architecture of the dairy. Quarry tiles on the floor, designed to be wet to cool the place in summer. Barred and unglazed windows at either end so the prevailing wind blew through. It had been built for a specific purpose and had no doubt served that well. It had been a reasonable place to store a body, Henry thought.

Constable Young, glad now that he had something to do, lit the lamps. It was only a little after four, but dusk was closing in fast, lowering grey skies, threatening rain and ice, the wind blowing chill across the fens. Henry held the lamp high and looked down at the blackened face of Joseph Levy.

By the time they had finished their initial examination, it was too late to walk to the spot where the body had been found. Evening was closing in and so was the weather, and Henry had no wish to get a soaking at the end of what had already been a tiring day. They walked back to Bardney, and this time even the constable was quiet, each man with their own thoughts. When they reached the pub where they would be staying,

Henry said, 'I would like the young man who found the body to come to speak to me as soon as possible.'

Constable Young, glad of an excuse to make his escape, headed off with the message.

'Here we are,' Mickey said. 'And let's hope they provide decent food.'

Henry wasn't sure that his appetite had returned. The smell had got into his nostrils and into his lungs, and he knew it would be a while before he freed himself of it. He was glad that their walk had been a good way across the fields and the wind had had a chance to blow the stench from his clothes, although he knew it would still cling. Just now he was more concerned with a bath than a feed.

There were several pubs in Bardney, among them the Anchor down by the river and the Angel on the Wragby road, the Black Horse and the Nags Head, but they were being lodged at the Railway Hotel. Unlike most hostelries bearing that name, it had not been built by the railway but had previously been the Bottle and Glass, and the landlord proudly told them that the pub had been there for at least a hundred and fifty years.

'Ghastly business,' he commiserated as Mickey introduced himself and Henry. They had dropped off their bags earlier but not made proper introductions. 'The poor lad had been missing for a while, I understand?'

'Sadly, yes,' Mickey agreed.

Henry didn't pay much attention to the conversation. Mickey was better at the day-to-day than he ever was, and his head was already filled with what he had seen and with things that in Henry's mind didn't make sense but which he hadn't quite resolved into thought.

'I'd like to take a bath,' he said, his first contribution to the conversation.

The landlord looked put out, as though this was an unusual request. Then he recovered himself and nodded. 'Of course, Inspector. It is Inspector, isn't it?'

'Chief Inspector, actually,' Mickey said, quick on the uptake that such things were important to their host.

'Chief Inspector. Indeed, sir. You'll find a bathroom at

the end of the corridor,' he said. 'And when would you gentlemen like supper?'

They agreed on six o'clock, and asked that when Jed Fox made an appearance, Mickey should be notified. One look at his boss told him that interviewing Jed would be his responsibility alone. Henry's mind was already elsewhere and he would not be patient with the likes of the farm labourer.

Mickey led the way upstairs. 'So,' he said. 'This is your room, apparently, and I'm just over there, and that down there must be the bathroom.'

Henry nodded absently and said, 'Those marks on his head – he was hit with something?'

'Or he hit something when he went into the water. The body's in a hell of a state; that much is certain, if nothing else.'

'We should contact Abraham Levy,' he said. 'Tell him that we will be sending his nephew home as soon as it can be arranged.'

'I'll take care of it later,' Mickey said.

He paused in the corridor and waited until Henry had entered his room and he heard the thump of his valise drop on to the floor, and then made his way to his own quarters, taking his own suitcase and the murder bag with him.

Mickey had time only to unpack his pyjamas and toiletries before being summoned downstairs with the news that Jed Fox had arrived. He was in the company of PC Young and a rather fine-looking spaniel cross that wagged its tail at the sight of Mickey. Mickey generally got on well with children and dogs.

'Be still, Sally,' the young man said. He had taken off his cap and stood twisting it between his hands. Mickey led Jed and Constable Young to a table in the corner of the bar. The pub was not yet open, but preparations were being made. Mickey would have liked to settle close to the fire, but the landlord was busying himself with unnecessary tidying in that area, clearly eager to overhear what was about to be said.

'It must have been a shock, finding him like that,' Mickey said.

Jed nodded. 'It were Sal,' he said. 'Smelt him out, went chasing off and then started barking, so I knew summat was wrong. He were lying half in, half out the water. We 'ad floods round about and couldn't even walk in that there field up to Sunday. So we'd not been up there. But boss said I could go out rabbiting that morning. It's slack work, this time o' year, when the ground gets sodden, like; we can't work the land when it's that wet.'

'So, you'd been out shooting rabbits. I like a rabbit pie,' Mickey told him.

Jed nodded in return. 'Missus wanted a couple for the pot. Boss likes to keep to the old ways and there's always a stew on the go for anyone coming in at odd times. Bread, too,' he added.

Mickey didn't fully understand but gathered this was very important.

'And he said if I got another brace, I could take them to old Jenny. She's a widow woman, on her own, like. I was on my way there when Sal sniffed out the body. She's got a good nose on 'er, that dog.'

Sally looked expectantly, and Mickey extended a hand for her to sniff and then stroked the soft ears. 'She's a fine-looking animal,' he agreed. 'What's she crossed with?'

Jed shrugged. 'Her mum weren't all that particular,' he said. 'But she had a litter of six and boss let me pick one.'

'So, when you found the body, what did you do next?'

It seemed that Jed was well practised in his story now. He told Mickey how he had called off the dog and gone racing back to the farm to get help. How he and the farmer and the stockman had tumbled the body on to a tarpaulin and dragged it back across the sodden fields and put it in the old dairy, and the constable had locked it inside and no one had disturbed it since.

By the time he had finished, the pub had opened for the evening, and Mickey felt obliged to buy the young man and the constable a beer. He would wait until Henry was down before ordering his own. Having arranged for Jed to take them out the following morning to the place where he had found the body, he went up and knocked on Henry's door and told him that food would soon be ready.

'Come in.'

Mickey opened the door. Henry was seated in a chair by the window. He had been writing in his book and his pen was poised to continue. Mickey closed the door quietly and sat down on the bed, waiting until Henry finished his sentence. He knew this was his boss's way of thinking. He'd found it strange at first, but as their working relationship expanded into friendship, he had come to understand that Henry needed to pin things to the page in order to really see the interrelationships.

Henry set the book aside and recapped his pen, screwing the top gently back in place.

'Food is almost ready for us and I'm ready for a pint. I've delayed until you came down, just to savour the moment.'

Henry laughed. 'And what did you get out of our farm worker?'

'That he's told his story so often it's now become legend. *He* is now enjoying his pint, along with our Constable Young, and will take us out to where he found the body tomorrow morning. I've just telephoned to Scotland Yard and made arrangements for the body to be moved once we've taken another look first thing in the morning. The ambulance should be coming for it around midday. I've told them to bring rubber liners and a lead-lined coffin. I think they'll be taking it to Saint Mary's.'

'And Abraham Levy?'

'When I phoned central office I asked that our news be passed on. That his nephew would soon be on his way back to London and that we'll be in touch. It's the best we can do at the moment.'

Henry nodded again. 'No clear cause of death,' he said. 'Although I'd say the body had been in water for some time, I don't believe it was dumped there. After three weeks, skin would be sloughing and I'd be expecting more bloating. It just doesn't look as though the right foot has spent all this time in water.'

'I agree,' Mickey told him. 'According to Jed Fox, the field's been at least ankle-deep in water – not severely flooded, but enough possibly to drag a body down into the dyke as the flood receded?' He shrugged. 'No, that's not right either. If I'm to make a guess, and I'm reluctant to do so without seeing the scene, then I would pass judgement that the body was dumped close to the water, perhaps in reeds or bushes and perhaps tumbled half in and half out of the water later on, as the mud shifted or the water receded.'

'Until we inspect the scene, it's impossible to speculate,' Henry agreed. 'I'm reminded of the case last year, out on the mud flats in Kent – all that shifting ground and network of little creeks.'

'But from what we saw from the train, we won't quite find that here. This is all agricultural land – reclaimed, yes, but of a different order. There are no inlets here, only the straight dykes cut between the fields as far as I can tell. Looked like some of them might even be navigable – I saw small boats out.'

'Well, as always, we will need local knowledge. What do you make of our Constable Young?'

'Now there's a man who knows he's done a bad job and is doing his best to make up for it,' Mickey laughed. 'He was convinced that if a body did turn up, it wouldn't be on his ground; now that it has, he finds himself embarrassed.'

'And so he bloody should be.' Henry stood and put his notebook and pen back into his jacket pocket.

'Go easy on him,' Mickey told his friend. 'He's one man managing a big area, most likely alone and with very little support. Very little intelligence too, from what I've seen, but nevertheless he is going to be a respected member of the community and we need him on side if we are to learn anything useful.'

Henry grunted what might have been reluctant agreement. 'And tomorrow we speak to the station master, and anyone else who might have been present on that day. Mickey, sometimes our job seems so tedious.'

Mickey narrowed his eyes and observed Henry closely. 'You, my friend, will feel better when you get some food inside you. We've neither of us really eaten since early morning, and you're out of sorts because Cynthia's not around.'

'I'm not dependent on my sister,' Henry said sharply.

'I beg to differ. If she is not happy, you are not happy, and it cuts both ways.'

Henry harrumphed again but argued no more and followed Mickey down the stairs and back into the bar. Food had been set out for them in a corner close to the fire. The pub was filling up now, mostly with locals but also a few travellers who had broken their journey for the night or were waiting between trains, and the level of noise contrasted sharply with when Mickey had been speaking to the constable and Jed Fox. Both of those individuals were now propping up the bar and arguing loudly but companionably with a third – an older man who, from his clothing, Mickey guessed was a farmer, possibly Jed's boss.

Mickey parked Henry in the corner and went back to collect their beers, nodding to Jed and the constable as he passed, but moving quickly enough to show that he was intent on his food and not on conversation. He set the beers down on the table and eyed the plates. 'Can't beat a good pie,' he said and set to, demolishing his meal. Henry ate more slowly, but, to Mickey's satisfaction, he did actually eat and began visibly to relax.

Mickey, as always, finished first and stole a spare potato that Henry was obviously not going to eat. 'So, how's your Cynthia doing, then?'

'According to her last letter, they're heading for Germany, or at least the German border. Albert has business connections that way; I don't know when they'll be coming back to London.'

'She's still worried about him, then – about this Hatry business?'

'I think she's hoping to keep him occupied elsewhere,' Henry said. 'She's been urging him to pull out of the German businesses. She doesn't like the way the military are now dominating the landscape, and the rampant inflation is cutting the legs from manufacturing and trade. She says the mood has changed, and there's no surprise at that. You can't push ordinary people to the edge of the cliff and not expect them to push back. The reparations were far too harsh and never designed to damage those who they are now in reality targeted against. You cannot blame people for what their leaders have forced them to do, not on either side. The Dawes Plan has not helped. There is the demand for reparations that the German economy cannot pay, on the one hand, and now they are forced to take loans from the Americans to pay those reparations – and then they will owe the Americans even more. Which nation will be next to force loans on them to repay *that* debt? No, Mickey, this is unsustainable and will not end well. Disaffection will assist the rise of extreme forces, not quieten them.'

Mickey shrugged. 'I've no fondness for those who were shooting at me, killing my friends with gas, and blowing me up – you know that – but no, I think perhaps Versailles was applied in a way that was never intended. The poor are poor, whatever nationality they are. If Albert decides to pull out, then, to my mind, that's a good decision. But then I was never one for him trading with the Germans anyway – not that anybody would have asked me, of course.'

Mickey cast his eyes around the bar. A mix of agricultural workers and those who were evidently passing through; three men reading newspapers, casually conversing with one another. He caught sight of the headlines on one of the newspapers. It seemed the newsmen were still excited by the inauguration of Herbert Hoover.

He turned his attention back to Henry. 'So, what were you writing earlier?'

Henry set down his fork and took his notebook from his pocket, opened it and then handed it to Mickey. Mickey was relieved to see that he then continued to eat. And the notebook was a sketch that Henry had made from memory of the body as they had viewed it in the dairy. He had annotated the sketch.

Pockets were empty.

A wound at the back of the head? Possibly from a blow but hard to define due to insect and rodent damage.

Something has been eating at the face, probably foxes as the bite marks look larger than those of rats. There is no doubt the rats have also had their share.

Sloughing of the skin more pronounced on the right

*hand than the left. Was this hand in the water when the
other was not?*

The final comment had been underlined: *His coat was of
good quality, but they had not stolen it.*

'But he had emptied his pockets,' Mickey objected.

'We don't know that he had much in his pockets,' Henry
reminded him. 'His spare money had been in his suitcase and
he left that aboard the train. His uncle thought he might only
have had pocket change with him.'

'Watch?' Mickey asked.

Henry stared at him for a moment and then swore.
'Sometimes, Mickey, I think I am no kind of detective. Of
course he would have had a watch. His uncle is a clockmaker; he would not let the lad go anywhere without a
watch and likely a good one at that.' He struck the table with
his fist, hard enough to make the plates bounce. 'To not have
thought of that!'

Mickey, unperturbed, picked up his pint. After another
swallow he reminded Henry, 'And when you first thought
about this case, it was as a missing person, not a murdered
boy found dumped somewhere in the middle of a field. But
now things have changed, so we think differently, and a watch
is a good thought. If he owned a watch, and they took the
watch, then they will most likely try to sell it and maybe it
will be distinguishable enough for us to track it down.'

Henry was only a little mollified. 'It is still something I
should have thought about.' He frowned, took a sip of his
own beer and then said, 'What puzzles me about the coat is
twofold. First that they did not take it, and second that they
emptied the pockets completely – not so much as a pocket
handkerchief left. But then I thought about it more and it
seems to me that a man *carrying* a coat while wearing another
would attract attention. Unless he had an item of luggage to
put the coat into, the killer might have thought it prudent to
take only what he could conceal in his own pockets. Which
indicates to me that he must have been planning to be among
a crowd. So, to continue from that thought, he came back to
the station and caught the train – rather than living locally

and simply concealing what was stolen there. If someone lived in this village, then it would be expected that he would take the coat home. It's good-quality cloth and could have fetched a good price, even if he hadn't wanted to keep it for his own use.'

'Some folk are squeamish about that kind of thing, though. Mind you, if you kill someone, it's likely you would get over that.' Mickey had experience of several criminals in London who had committed murder and then proudly worn hats or coats from their victim without the slightest trace of squeamishness – or without having thought that this might be solid evidence against them. The usual excuse was that they bought the item from a second-hand dealer, which, given the lively trade in second-hand garments, was difficult to disprove.

'We assumed from the start that he had left the scene and caught the train. Or rather caught *a* train,' Mickey said. 'This reinforces the idea that from here he could have gone in any of three directions. Back towards Lincoln, off towards Louth or south to Peterborough or any station in between. If I was choosing a place to commit a crime, this route would be as good as any.'

'Choosing a place,' Henry said thoughtfully. 'Was Joseph tracked? Or is this a random act?'

'If Joseph was targeted, then the murderer would have to ensure that Joseph left the train in order for him to commit a theft and murder – whether that was intended or not is another point entirely. We have to assume, for now at least, that Joseph was lured from the train by the girl. That the girl left the carriage and he went out after her.'

'And I would like to speak directly to the Parkers.'

'That is being arranged. I have asked Sergeant Young to take care of that, as he's already been in contact with them. So, if I am correct, Joseph left the train, in pursuit of this female, then ran into trouble . . . They must have taken him from the station in some way, or perhaps threatened him so that he walked with them. The girl, whoever she was, and whoever did the deed left by the next possible train, so we presume. I doubt they'd have wanted to hang around, so discovering what the next trains would have been might give us our direction . . .'

Mickey leaned forward and speared the last potato on his boss's plate, sliced it and dipped it in his remaining gravy. 'So the girl attracted Joseph Levy's attention for some reason; he then followed her on to the platform and found himself caught up in something that he couldn't handle. We still have no way of knowing if he was targeted because of something they had on him, or if they just wished to roll a random stranger. We need to look into other assaults and thefts on this line, and for that we need the assistance of our colleagues in the railway police.'

Having finished his purloined potato, Mickey stretched and yawned. 'Not a great deal more we can do tonight,' he said.

'No,' Henry agreed.

A girl came in to clear their plates and ask if they needed anything else. Mickey went back to the bar and got another round in. Henry was unsurprised to see him in conversation or that he agreed to a game of darts with some of the locals. Henry himself was quite content to sit in the corner and watch proceedings.

He felt frustrated that they had arrived too late to get much done beyond viewing the body in the half-light and making brief enquiries, and he felt restless. Leaving Mickey to his game, Henry went back up to his room to fetch his coat and scarf, and then wandered out into the street. The air was cold and damp, and he shoved gloved hands into his pockets and wandered back in the direction of the station. A single light illuminated the platform. Henry stood in the shadows, unobserved, surprised that there were still people around but reminding himself that although this might be just a loop from the main line, it was a busy route and trains would still run through the evening.

A porter spotted him and asked if he needed assistance. 'Oh, sorry, sir, I didn't recognize you at first. You're that inspector, up from that there London.'

Henry confessed that he was. He asked the porter if he was on duty on the day that Joseph Levy had disappeared, telling him that it would have been a Sunday.

'We work a rota for Sundays, sir, and I don't think that was one of mine.'

Henry nodded; he would have to find out who had been working that day. 'Do you get much trouble reported?' he asked. 'Thefts or disturbances.'

'Lost luggage more than anything. Occasionally, someone complains that they've been pickpocketed, but nothing more than you'd expect, I suppose.'

'And records are kept of these disturbances, these complaints?'

'Well, if they're serious, they get reported to the station master and he reports to the railway police. The commonplace arguments or a lost bag, we try to deal with on our own.'

'The station master would keep a record of these events,' Henry confirmed. 'Presumably, anything really memorable would have been spoken about among the staff?'

The porter had been standing half supporting his barrow, preparing to continue his duties, but now he set it upright and settled himself to answer the question. 'Well,' he said in a confidential tone, 'you get a bit of gossip, of course, nothing improper, but we did talk to one another when Constable Young came round asking about that lad – put our heads together in case we could remember anything.' The porter frowned. 'It's a terrible business, him being found like that. And after all this time. His poor family. No doubt they grieve just as much, even if they are Jews.'

Henry took a deep breath but said nothing. He was reminded of his conversation with Abraham about the casual disregard in which foreigners and particularly Jewish foreigners were held, and Henry, of course, had witnessed this many times over. He knew it was unthinking, but even with the lack of malice, it still rankled. How much more must it have rankled someone like Abraham?

'His family are indeed grieving, and it seems to be that it doesn't matter where you are from or who you are, the loss of a child is grievous.'

The porter showed no signs of embarrassment or even of having noticed that quiet rebuke. He simply nodded. 'Far as anyone can tell, the young man got off the train and someone – I think it was Mr Paul – noticed him rushing across the platform, but people are always rushing here and there, usually when there's no need for it, so no one took any notice until

Constable Young started asking questions. He showed the photograph around, and one or two of us – not me, because I wasn't on duty that day – thought they recognized him.'

'And the reports that he had got off the train in pursuit of a young woman?'

The porter grinned. 'Well, I guess she must have been a pretty one, then.'

'But nothing has been said, among yourselves, about this young woman? Or whether he caught up with her and what might have happened after?'

'To my knowledge, sir, no.'

The porter shifted his weight and moved the barrow, suggesting that it was time he was on his way.

Henry stepped back and let him go. He stood for a time just watching the activity of the station platform. It looked to Henry like a painting: bright pools of light and great columns of darkness between, and the steam from the engine that had just pulled in.

After a time he was conscious that his feet were cold and a draught blew about his neck, finding its way beneath his scarf, and he turned and headed back towards the pub.

After the activity of the station, the streets seemed very silent and dark. Glancing up, Henry noted that the sky seemed filled with stars, far more than he ever saw in town. Frost was forming and it promised to be a cold night. He hoped that the fire had been lit in his bedroom.

Returning to the bar, he discovered that Mickey was still playing darts, completely at ease with his newfound companions. Mickey glanced in Henry's direction and nodded fractionally, and Henry took himself off to his room, knowing that his sergeant would be knocking on his door within the hour, having gathered more background information and intelligence than anyone would have been aware of having given him.

The fire in Henry's room had been lit and the curtains drawn, and Henry shed his coat and shoes and lay down on the bed, staring at the cracked whitewashed ceiling. He had almost drifted off to sleep when the knock came at the door and Mickey joined him, carrying a tray of tea.

'Thought you could do with one,' he said, indicating the teapot. 'Where did you get to?'

'I went to take another look at the station and talked to one of the porters. He wasn't on duty on the day that Joseph Levy disappeared, but he suggests that a couple of his colleagues saw the young man get off the train and hurry across the platform. I'm told they thought nothing of it because people are always hurrying here and there, and there was no mention of the girl. But we will find those who were on duty and question them. And you – what have you found out?'

Mickey had set the tray down on the chest of drawers and was now pouring tea. 'Local gossip, which may or may not be relevant, and reports that travellers on this line have been prone to pickpocketing and the odd assault. It turns out that one of the men I was playing darts with has a brother in the railway police, and the brother has told him of several incidents on the line from Lincoln, that to Louth and the one going south to Peterborough of gentlemen reporting thefts from their person. These could be unconnected, of course, but it is worth talking to the brother, and we need to bring the railway police on board in any case, as their intelligence is likely to be much more relevant than ours.'

'And the local gossip?'

'That the local shopkeeper occasionally gives short measure – but only to those he doesn't like. That our Constable Young spends more time napping or playing court to a local widow woman than he does out on the beat. The consensus is that he should have retired years ago but the local constabulary can find no one who actually wants his job. And that a young woman with red hair and a green dress was seen in this very public house on the day our boy disappeared.'

Henry sat up and took the tea Mickey was offering to him. 'And?'

'And she came in, looking somewhat flustered, according to one report. Bought a port and lemon, and sat down in the corner of the lounge and ignored everyone. About an hour after, a young man made an appearance, stood in the doorway and beckoned her out, and off she went.'

'And it's certain that was the same day?'

'Certain as can be. One Mr Richard Fellows – damned good darts player, unfortunately for me – was waiting for his wife's train and, his wife also being a redhead, he particularly remarked upon this young woman. He knows the date his wife came home from visiting her sister and the landlord corroborated that memory. It seems it was the same Sunday he was setting up the teams for the next tournament. Darts, that is. Fellows was helping him decide on the order of the round robin.'

Henry nodded, satisfied. This was the most concrete information they had yet received. 'Can they describe the young man?'

'They can describe the girl in far more detail. Above-average height and dark hair is about the best either of them could do for the man. Perhaps when we speak to Mrs Parker, she might have seen more. It's only from her evidence that we even know to look for a redhead in a green frock.'

'And women tend to notice detail when it comes to other women.'

'As do men,' Mickey retorted. 'Though it has to be said they often remember somewhat different detail. And from the male perspective, it seems that this girl was well worth paying attention to.'

'Joseph Levy seems to have paid attention.'

'Sadly for him, yes. But it still leaves more questions than we have answers for. I'd be interested to know if these other men who claim to have been robbed were also distracted by a pretty face.'

'She sounds almost *too* noticeable to be used as bait.'

'True, but if she keeps her distance, and if she and her male companion spread themselves around, they could get away with a great deal.'

'But not with murder, Mickey.'

'Odd, though, don't you think? I mean, I'm speculating with too little information right now, but from what I was told, these robberies were opportunistic. A bit of cash, a watch, a sovereign. Causing a death – now that's a whole other level.'

'It could have been an accident. Joseph follows the girl, as planned, perhaps, but then he fights back. Or maybe they suspected him of carrying more money than he actually had. The boy was clearly respectable and was wearing a good coat. Perhaps he disappointed them?'

Henry yawned. 'I confess to being tired.'

'Good. Then you'd best get to sleep while your body is still of that mind. It will be a busy day tomorrow, but maybe we can get the lad back to his family and be on the trail of whoever deprived them.'

TEN

The overnight frost looked to be set in for the entire day and the grass crunched beneath their feet as they set off to view the place where the body had been found, Jed Fox and his dog, Sally, leading the way.

'Big skies,' Mickey commented. 'I suppose that's one advantage of living in flat land.'

Henry set the pace, despite not knowing where he was going, taking long strides and hurrying everyone along. He'd slept quite well but had woken feeling impatient and angry, and he couldn't quite understand what the source of it was. He had decided that exercise would be the remedy. Jed seemed unfazed by the speed at which Henry moved them on, and Sally simply ran around in circles, sniffing everything, clearly enjoying the frosty morning. Jed pointed out anything he thought might be of interest to the two policemen.

'That cottage in the distance, that's where I was to take the rabbits. I still got there but a little bit late, so she had to wait till morning, until the stiffness went off them, before she could take the skins off and get them in the pot.'

'Rigor mortis,' Mickey observed. 'You forget it's an issue in matters of butchery. I hear that with rabbits you either have to skin them right away or wait twenty-four hours.'

'Be about right, that will. You like a rabbit, do you?'

'I'm a bit partial, yes. What's that over there, that bit of a ruin? I spotted it as we left the village.'

'That'll be the abbey. What little there is left of it. Vicar says there were monks here for centuries. And just there is where we found the body.' Jed had paused and pointed at a clump of reeds and withies at the side of a deep dyke. 'I reckon if the body had gone right in, it might have been summer before you got it back. It wouldn't be likely to float this time of year, but as soon as things warmed up, he'd have come bobbing up to the top again.'

'Do you fish many bodies out of the water?' Henry asked.

'One a year, maybe two. Not usually locals. Visitors decide it looks nice round here, go trekking across the fens and come a cropper. Especially when the fog comes down. It's dangerous land for them that don't know it.'

As is anywhere, Henry thought sombrely. He crouched down and studied the reeds where the body had been laid. Some were crushed back and he was inclined to agree with Jed's speculation. Had someone dumped the body, rolled it and hoped that it would end up in the water, but miscalculated?

'How would someone have got a body here?' He stood up and looked around. Flat fields, hedges, no clear path anywhere.

'It's a puzzle, that,' Jed agreed. 'But I suppose a strong man could hoist a fresh body – not one likely to fall apart should you move it – on a shoulder. It's not a hard walk from the village to here.'

'But it is open ground. He could be seen.'

Eloquently, Jed spread his arms. 'See anyone?' he asked. 'A whole load of nothing and no one round 'ere most o' the time.'

'How did you get the body back to the dairy? You said you and two others carried it and dragged it.'

Jed nodded and pointed to the clear marks on the ground, where they had pulled the body on to the tarpaulin and then pulled the tarpaulin up on to the bank and across the first field. 'It seemed a bit disrespectful, just to pull the poor bugger along on the tarp, and we did try to carry him between us for a bit, but it's not like *he* was in any fit state to sling across somebody's shoulder, and boss thought it might be best if we kept him flat and didn't shift about too much. So we skidded him most of the way.'

'Joseph Levy was not a big man – tall but not heavy,' Mickey speculated, 'but even so it's a fair way from the train station to here. Even if, as Jed says, he could have slung him across his shoulders, I don't see one man doing this alone.'

Henry picked up a stick and poked around in the reeds and mud, but it was not from his desire to poke something. It was from an idea that he might find anything lost there.

'Take us back by exactly the route you took on that day,'

he said. 'Just so we can be sure nothing fell off the body on the way. I can imagine all of your attention was on just getting it moved.'

Jed whistled the dog and turned for home. Henry studied the ground as closely as Sally, the dog sniffing and the other following some kind of trail in his own head. He checked his watch before they left the scene and it told twenty-five minutes had passed by the time they got back to the farm and the old dairy.

'Did you notice how long it took you to get back here?'

Jed shrugged. 'Longer than it took us today, but not much. There was three of us taking turns, two pulling and one following behind, taking it turn and turn about, like we do with most jobs.'

'And conditions on that Sunday, when Joseph Levy disappeared. Wet or dry?'

'That would be the last dry day before the flood set in. Boss was hoping we could get the plough on to the land early on the Monday, but then the rain began.'

Jed glanced over Henry's shoulder, and Henry turned to see that the farmer had come out to greet them, but his main concern seemed to be when they were going to get the body off his land, Mickey told him that the collection was due around midday. The farmer could add little to Jed's story, confirming the weather and the time they had taken.

The constable had given Henry the keys to the dairy and they went to view the body one last time before it left, now that the light was better. Joseph Levy looked in worse shape than he had done the night before, probably because they could see him more clearly. His skin was slack and grey and mottled, putrefaction held back by the cold but still well underway, the abdomen swollen and the face puffy. Henry bent to take another look at the hands, confirming his observations that one must have been in the water for longer, the skin sloughed almost from the fingertips. The other hand was blackened but not in such a bad state, apart from the two missing fingers, probably taken by a rodent or a fox.

'He will be a sorry sight for his family to see,' Mickey commented. 'I pity Abraham and his kin having to prepare this body for burial.'

'At least they have him back. I had my doubts that they would.'

Only a little later, Henry and Mickey headed back to their lodgings.

'So,' Henry said. 'I'm a stranger here. I attack and kill a young man, and I need to dispose of the body. How would I get, without being seen, from the station and its environs to where the body was dumped? How would I know where to go?'

'Maybe not so much a stranger,' Mickey countered. 'Someone who travels on that train regularly and can see how the track curves and the river bends, and that there are long, straight dykes. No doubt it is a nice walk on a summer's day, especially if you have an attractive young lady in tow.'

Henry nodded, acknowledging the point. 'So we make the assumption that they had some knowledge of the lie of the land. They must have taken Joseph somewhere private in order to rob and kill him, though I'm not yet of a mind that death was their original intent. They then had to dispose of the body, and we know that the girl waited in the lounge bar for them. And I'm saying *them*, because I still doubt one man could have got the body so far on his own.'

'Agreed, one man to carry the body in something like a fireman's lift, another to keep a lookout and, as Jed put it, take turn and turn about. The girl was left for about an hour, so that would just give them time, I think, which also suggests they knew where to go. Had the land been less flat, they might simply have dumped the body by the track for anyone to assume he'd met with an accident or had perhaps even thrown himself from the train. That way the body would have been found much sooner as there is little cover either side of the track.'

'There's little cover for anyone carrying a body, although, as our friend pointed out, there are also few people around to take note. So, we go back to the station and we trace a possible route, one that would keep them from view and allow them to reach the place where they dumped the body. Once they were away from the village, I agree that no one would have taken much notice because there would most likely be no one about to see them. A nice walk in summer would be a frigid one at this time of year, so the only people around would have been farmworkers – and there are few of those because, as Jed told us, this is a slack time for working. In that case, the lack of cover would not be such an issue, once they were away from habitation.'

They had reached the Railway Hotel and Henry pushed the door open, scraping and then stamping his feet, so as not to trail too much mud inside. Mickey paused to do the same and then went to the bar and rang the desk bell. When the landlord appeared, Mickey asked if they might have something warm to drink, perhaps a sandwich or two, as it was getting on for lunchtime.

Henry settled in a chair near the fire, his coat still wrapped around him.

'Take off your coat, let the heat get to you, or you'll not feel the benefit of it when we go out again,' Mickey told him.

Reluctantly, Henry shrugged out of his heavy coat. 'And this afternoon we board the train again and we go and see the Parkers, discover what they actually saw.'

ELEVEN

Mr and Mrs Parker lived a few stops down the line at Boston. He was a retired accountant and she taught piano to various untalented children, or so Henry and Mickey learned during the first few minutes of their visit. The Parkers lived in a bungalow and had done so for all of their married life. The half-glazed front door had panels of blue-and-green stained glass and was placed centrally at the front of their home. Mrs Parker indicated the music room off to the left and led them into the living room on their right. Their stout shoes sounded uncouth on the polished wooden floor of the hall, and Mrs Parker stared meaningfully down at their feet as though in half a mind to ask them to remove the offending articles. A bright square rug covered the centre of the floor, leaving dark boards exposed all round. The walls had been painted a drab olive and fireplace tiles were similarly brown, the tone somewhere between that of the floor and that of the walls. Apart from a clock on the mantelpiece, there was little in the nature of ornamentation, but the bookshelves either side were crammed and the bright dust covers lifted the mood of the room. It seemed to Henry that the carpets and the books had been chosen by one of the pair and the colour of the walls and lack of personal touches by another. Curious as to which was which, he asked, 'You like to read?'

'Oh, absolutely. My pleasure and my escape from the mundanity of the world. My husband only reads the newspapers and those little magazines you get with fretwork patterns in. Now that he's retired and he needs a hobby, that has become his obsession, I'm afraid. He is forever turning out these funny little picture frames and letter racks.'

Mickey glanced pointedly around the room. 'You don't display any of them in here?'

'Oh, good heavens, no. When he gets better at it, perhaps.

In the meantime, it keeps him occupied, and for that we should be grateful. I had this dread that he might take up gardening and want to undo all the work that I have done over the years we've been here. Fortunately, he knows his limitations when it comes to understanding the difference between a weed and a pansy.'

The living-room door opened and a young woman came in carrying a tea tray. She was dressed in grey and her hair was held back by a little cap. She set the tray down on the coffee table and looked to Mrs Parker for instruction.

'That will do, Betsy. We can shift for ourselves.'

Betsy departed as quietly as she had arrived.

'Maid of all work,' Mrs Parker said. 'We don't have room for a live-in, but fortunately she lives in the village and I'm getting her trained . . . gradually. Young girls don't seem to want to go into service any more – they'd rather find a job in an office or a factory.' This last word was expressed with a full measure of distaste.

She sat down and leaned forward to deal with the tea. 'And now, gentlemen, what can I do for you? I understand you found that poor unfortunate boy? He was a little fool, though, chasing after that young woman. Anyone could see she was no good, but I suppose boys today, this is what they like.'

Henry and Mickey exchanged a glance, and Mickey took over the conversation.

'So, tell us what happened on that day,' Mickey said, accepting his cup of tea and helping himself to sugar cubes. The tongs ended in claws and reminded Henry of chicken feet. He found himself oddly reluctant to use them. 'I presume you were travelling from Lincoln and Joseph Levy got on the train at the same time as you did?'

She nodded, stirring her tea distractedly. 'He was quite gentlemanly, looked decent enough, tipped his hat when he came into the carriage and then put his case on the luggage rack. In fact' – she narrowed her eyes thoughtfully – 'he left his case there but he remembered to reach up and take his hat. Isn't that strange?'

Mickey and Henry exchanged another glance. That was indeed strange, Henry thought. Of course, some people just naturally operated out of habit. It might be that Joseph always wore his hat and would have felt naked without it, so it would be a natural reaction, even when he was in a hurry. It occurred to him also that it had not been found with the body, but perhaps that was not so strange. It was most likely that a fox had taken it, or it had fallen into the water – or was left at the murder scene, in which case it might have more relevance.

'And you didn't speak to him?'

'Well, we bid each other good day, but I suppose that was it. I was reading my book and my husband was reading his newspaper, and no one really makes conversation in train compartments, do they?'

No doubt she would view that as common, Henry thought. In fairness, though, he tended to avoid conversation in train compartments, too.

'And he just sat quietly? There was nothing to attract your interest?'

Mrs Parker shook her head. 'Then the girl got on, of course. One stop out of Lincoln, I believe, so that would have been Washingborough. I must admit I thought she looked a little exotic for such a dead in the hole place. But she took a seat and read a magazine and paid no attention to anybody either. Then, when we reached Bardney, she got off the train. The young man watched her as she left the compartment and then tried not to be obvious as he looked out of the window, but I could see what he was doing.'

'She must have been worth his notice, then?'

Mrs Parker smiled frostily. 'I suppose she was attractive enough – all that gaudy hair and that coat that didn't quite cover her green frock. Young girls today! When I was a young girl, we were always taught that your coat hem should be longer than your dress hem.'

So, ankle length, then, Henry thought. Looking at Mrs Parker and making a guess as to her age, he felt it wiser not to voice this comment and commended himself on his restraint. Mickey would be proud.

Mickey had made no comment either; he simply made a note of something in his book and then looked back expectantly at Mrs Parker.

'Well, the girl sat and read her magazine. The young boy stared out of the window or stared straight ahead; it was clear that he was trying not to stare at the girl and she knew exactly what was going on. Her type always do.'

'And did it look as though she always planned to get off at Bardney station?'

Mrs Parker frowned. 'I suppose so. I didn't really give it much thought. The train pulled into the station. She got up and off she went. He, of course, was looking out of the window. I told you that already. Then, all of a sudden, he got up, picked up his hat and went chasing after her.'

'Have you any idea what made him do that?'

'I could see the girl on the platform and I suppose it was because she was having an argument with somebody. Maybe he was worried about her. Fancied himself as a gallant, I suppose.'

Mickey wrote this down in his notebook and glanced over at Henry. This was something they had not heard before. 'Did you mention this to the constable, who spoke to you before?'

'I really don't remember. He telephoned just as we were ready to go out, leaving for a friend's party, and the car was waiting for us. He promised he would only take a moment of our time and so he did. I just confirmed that I had seen the girl and the boy at the station and that he'd followed her off the train.'

Henry shifted restlessly, annoyed that they could have had this information much earlier. Mickey cast him a swift and warning glance.

'Who was she arguing with?' Henry asked.

'A young man. There was a second one with him, but he was standing a little way off and keeping his mouth shut. I fancied the two of them – the girl and the young man she was arguing with – might have been in some sort of relationship because they were going at it hammer and tongs. As though picking up on something they had disagreed about earlier, if you get my meaning.'

'And Joseph Levy saw this, got off the train and went over to them?'

'Yes, Inspector. That's exactly what he did. And then the train pulled out of the station and my husband remarked that he was a young fool and that he had forgotten his suitcase. No, actually, I think we noticed a little later that he'd forgotten his suitcase. But he's still a young fool.'

'Was,' Henry said softly.

'Yes, well, that's a shame, isn't it? So I suppose that the one she was arguing with, and his friend, I suppose they did for him.'

'Well, as yet we have no idea about that. Could you describe these two?'

Mrs Parker huffed. 'Just ordinary sorts, I'd have said. The one she was arguing with was taller than the girl and quite broad across the shoulders. He had dark hair and wore, I think, a dogtooth-checked jacket or something of that nature. It was quite loud. Young people today – everything has to be loud. The other was shorter and wore a flat cap. That's all I can tell you. The train pulled out and I would have forgotten about the whole thing if it hadn't been for the fact that the silly young fool left his suitcase behind and we had to go to the trouble of reporting it.'

She sighed and set her teacup and saucer down on the table. There was something about her face, the expression in her eyes, that told Henry that she was more upset by this than she was letting on. Mickey seemed to be of the same mind because he waited quietly, and Mrs Parker finally said, 'We lost so many young men of that age, didn't we? You must both have been there. It was a waste then and it's a waste now.'

She seemed to gather herself then, straightening her back and smoothing her skirt. 'Is there anything else?'

'Certainly not at the moment,' Mickey told her. 'Do you think your husband could add anything to your description?'

'I doubt it. From where I was sitting, I could see down the length of the platform. He was sitting opposite me so could only catch a glimpse of the young man as he went by. I had the better view.'

Telling Mrs Parker that they would telephone if they needed to speak to her again, they left shortly after. Mickey led the way down the little garden path and held the gate for Henry. Henry latched it silently, aware that Mrs Parker was watching from the window and that she would disapprove of someone who let her gate clang. Then he wished he had done it anyway, just to annoy her.

'I suppose we have a little more information,' Mickey said as they headed back towards the station. 'We can now ask about a redheaded young woman and two young men having an argument on the station platform. It's more likely people would have seen that than a young man simply chasing after a young woman. Most would have seen him and assumed he was just hurrying to catch the train or hurrying somewhere else.'

'Progress of sorts,' Henry agreed. 'And it fits with the tall young man who came to fetch the girl from the public house. He stood in the doorway, so those who spotted him had a guide to how he was built. And the other to help him get the body away.'

'I don't think murder was part of the original plan.'

'No, I agree. So what was the original plan? Was it that they would entice somebody to follow the girl from the train? That seems unlikely, chancy, especially as she didn't even engage him in conversation. She did very little to attract Joseph Levy's attention. Apart from just being there and being attractive.'

'And then looking like a damsel in distress,' Mickey agreed. 'It seems to me that poor Joseph ended up in the wrong place at the wrong time, something went very much awry and he ended up losing his life over it. We should consider those victims of crime that the railway police have recorded. See if any of those involved a young woman and two young men. My betting is they did.'

'Unless,' Henry paused, the thoughts still formulating. 'Unless the girl was arguing because she was *meant* to engage with Joseph Levy. That he *was* an intended target.'

'Possible, but a less likely scenario, I would think.'

'You'll be right, I expect,' Henry said. 'There is nothing to suggest that he had met this young woman previously, and if he had intended to follow her, surely he would have taken his suitcase as well as his hat.'

TWELVE

They arrived back in Bardney to the news that the mortuary ambulance had collected Joseph Levy's body and was now on the way back to London. The constable, left to witness the handover, told them that the body had been wrapped in oilcloth and then deposited in a lead-lined coffin.

'It was heavy, unpleasant work,' he commented, although Henry doubted he'd actually got his hands dirty with any of it.

Taking a tray of tea and sandwiches, designed to fend off hunger until supper, Mickey and Henry withdrew to Henry's room, the larger of the two. Henry removed his shoes and settled on the bed, his back against the headboard. Mickey took the easy chair and placed the tray on the bed between them.

Henry had said little on their journey back, and Mickey guessed that he'd been processing the conversation and what they knew so far.

Mickey had been doing some processing of his own. 'If that trio has been active along the railway line, targeting likely passengers wherever they find them, then they could have been working anywhere between here and the capital. Back in London, most pickpockets have a patch – except on race days, of course, or during public gatherings when it becomes a free for all – but those who work the lines are a mobile lot, and if they've ventured south, it's possible we have something on record.'

'I think that's a bit of over-speculation, Mickey,' Henry commented. 'Though, I grant you, it would be a stroke of fortune. We must speak to the railway police tomorrow and see where that takes us.'

Henry closed his eyes for a moment. He was thinking about Abraham and about how long it would take for his nephew's body to journey back to London. By evening, Joseph would be in the hospital mortuary, and Henry hoped that somebody would have been sent to Abraham to let him know, as he had instructed.

His mind turned to other matters. 'I've been thinking about the boy from the Elephant mob and about Atkins,' he said.

'And what about them in particular?'

'What if this presages greater trouble than we first thought? Atkins hinted that although he considers himself secure, there is a state of flux and others manoeuvring for power. We could do without a resurgence of the gang violence of a few years ago when the likes of Sabini and his crew dominated.'

'We all thought that Sabini had had his teeth drawn, and while it's true he is basing his operations further south, I don't like the fact that he's been back up in London and that he's a friend of Atkins any more than you do. The man to ask, of course, would be Ted Greeno. If there have been any whispers, then Ted would know.'

'Greeno's expertise is with the race gangs,' Henry objected mildly.

'And is there any gang violence that is not obliquely connected to horse racing? That's where the money is – the big betting and the razor gangs.'

Henry acknowledged that. 'Greeno has been posted to the Flying Squad, I believe. I'll send word that we could do with a meeting when we get back.'

Mickey grinned at him. 'You've no liking for the man, have you? He's rough around the edges, but he's a good copper. Gets results.'

'And as the Flying Squad themselves admit, rounding up pickpockets on race days is like picking cherries in a cherry orchard.' Henry paused, knowing that he was being ungenerous. Greeno, he remembered, had started out in the East End, in Whitechapel, although he was a country boy like around seventy per cent of those recruited into the Metropolitan Police. Before being seconded to the Flying Squad he'd been working out of Leman Street, and Greeno had a knowledge of those on his patch and a memory for faces that Henry knew was unmatched.

'I suppose I just don't understand why he is still in the job,' he confessed. 'Here is a man who, according to rumour, can make his year's salary in a week of good betting. Greeno knows his horses like he knows his criminals. If I'm honest, it baffles me that he continues to work when he could be a man of leisure. He's one of the few men I know of who *could* make a comfortable living as a professional gambler.'

'Most of his winnings go to pay informants,' Mickey chuckled. 'He has one of the biggest networks of snouts and squealers since . . . Well, anyway. I doubt anyone has done it as well as Ted. And as to why he stays, I think he just likes the chase.'

'And the capture. He's not above using his fists to get a confession.'

'And he's not the only one you can say that about, Henry. Like it or not, he'll be snapping at our heels in Central Office before you or I know it, and my betting is that he'll pass us both at a run. DS Ted Greeno has his eye on bigger prizes.'

Henry took his cigarette case and lighter from his jacket pocket, stroking the smooth brass of the case and the even smoother silver of the lighter. The cigarette case, handmade by its original owner, had belonged to a friend, lost in the mud of 1916. The lighter was a gift from his sister and, unlike the case, was engraved with Henry's name. 'Eat first, then smoke,' Mickey chided him. 'You've had nothing since breakfast.'

Reluctantly, Henry selected a sandwich and bit into it.

'Ham and English mustard,' Mickey told him. 'Not too bad at all, though I do rather fancy a pie and a pint just now. I hope supper will meet my needs on that score.'

For a while they ate in silence. 'The boy who got hurt,' Henry said, and it took Mickey a moment to realize he had returned to the subject of the kid from the Elephant mob. 'He'd been cut with a razor. Swore blind he'd just fallen through a window, but once you've seen those wounds, you always recognize them.'

'Not so unusual for the victim to be in denial, though. And, of course, he'd claim to have no idea who'd done it.'

'Oh, none at all,' Henry agreed. 'But I never reckoned on it being Clem Atkins' style.'

'Does he have a style? In my book, he's still figuring all that out. He may have taken over from Josiah Bailey and the transition might have been smoother than most such takeovers, but he's still on probation, still got to make his mark.' Mickey barked with laughter at the unconscious half-joke, then helped himself to another sandwich.

Henry nodded thoughtfully. Straight razors were the weapon of choice for some, but they killed too easily. Most of the razor boys embedded a blade in a thick piece of rubber. This not only made the blade easier to handle but limited the depth of strike, making it less likely to kill. Men wounded by the razor gangs were left with a criss-cross of scars, most often on the face – scars they were never able to hide. Marked for life, unwilling to talk but still able to earn – and therefore to pay protection or to serve as an example to others. A dead man was an unprofitable one. A dead man was more likely to lead to the hangman's noose because the full force of law was brought to bear in a murder case. The walking wounded refused to speak, often reluctant even to report the attack, often just nursed at home, so the first the police knew of it was when the half-healed man returned to the streets or to the track, denying there was anything wrong. Denying anything worse than a minor accident.

Such incidents had become less common of late, and Henry very much wished to keep it that way.

'Have you ever attended a Jewish funeral?' Mickey asked him.

'No, and I don't plan on actually attending this one. Being there, yes, but where we can observe. I've no wish to intrude further on the family's grief.'

'Not to mention your dislike of religious services.'

'I go at Christmas.'

'Because Cynthia likes the carol service.'

'You only attend when Belle is home,' Henry returned.

'True. When is Cynthia coming back?'

Henry paused, finally lighting his cigarette. 'I don't know. I think she's trying to keep Albert from gambling away what parts of the family fortune he can still get his hands on. He's not as astute as Ted Greeno.'

'Maybe Ted should try the stock market.'

'I think he likes to see the flesh he's betting on. See the way it moves,' Henry suggested. 'But I don't think he could do worse than Albert.'

Mickey helped himself to one of Henry's cigarettes and lit it with his own lighter. 'You're really worried about this?'

'I know Cynthia is. Albert is a good man and he's an astute businessman in those areas he understands – manufacturing, markets, production of commodities – but he's also easily flattered and, like most of us, I suppose, reluctant to lose face, so he tends to take risks, to believe in the get-rich-quick blags. It's too easy to end up in queer street.'

'Your sister will sort him out,' Mickey said complacently. 'What did you make of Mrs Parker?'

'I'd be interested to know how much Mr Parker *actually* noticed. I would make a bet that it was far more than his wife thinks or chooses to think, at any rate. But I doubt they can be more help to us.'

'So Joseph takes a fancy to the young woman, sees her in trouble and decides to play gallant knight. Assumes he will have time to get back on to the train – hence he leaves his bag behind – but falls foul of the young man or men she is arguing with.'

'And so was the argument staged?'

'Stage an argument just on the off chance that some young man, who might have some money, will leave the train to go to the girl's rescue? No. In my book, that's as unlikely as to be a write-off. It also seems so damnably foolish. The train halts at Bardney to drop off and pick up – a matter of minutes. Had he decided to rush to someone's aid, then any sensible person would have grabbed their suitcase and taken it with them, dealt with the incident and caught the next train.'

'Perhaps Joseph Levy was not a *sensible* young man. Perhaps – just perhaps – he had more emotional investment than we credit. We don't know that this is the first time he'd laid eyes on this young woman. He'd made the journey several times before. It's possible that so had she.'

'Mrs Parker didn't seem to think they knew one another,' Mickey objected mildly.

'No, but if I had been trying to keep a relationship secret, I would certainly have been careful around a woman like Mrs Parker. Even if she did look as though she had her nose stuck in a book.'

Mickey helped himself to the last sandwich and leaned back in his chair, gazing out of the window at the darkening sky. 'I'm not a fan of this time of year,' he said. 'It's damp and it's muddy and it can't make up its mind what it's going to do half the time.'

Henry laughed. 'Well, there is little more *we* can do tonight,' he said. 'Tomorrow we speak to the railway police and we look at the records they've identified for us of the victims of pickpockets. And we will see if any of these incidents involved a redheaded girl. Or a girl with hair of any other colour, for that matter. Wigs and hair dye are easy enough to obtain. And then it's on to speak to the fiancée's family. See if Joseph Levy and his young woman were as close and as content as his uncle would have us believe.'

THIRTEEN

There had been specialist police forces on the canals, docklands and railways for almost as long as a police force had existed, and in the early days of the railway police the duties had extended to being pointsmen or signalmen as well as their wider remit to ensure the safety of railway travel.

Sergeant Terry, however, was more concerned with the safety of individuals and he laid before them a stack of neatly type-written pages and three handwritten logbooks. 'This represents the last six months,' he said. 'I wasn't sure what you actually needed and collated everything I could that relates to robberies, both in transit and at the stations. These documents, gentlemen, cover the main line between Lincoln and Peterborough and the Witham Loop. I can allocate a constable to assist you . . .'

Mickey eyed the stack of paper dubiously. He wasn't sure if Sergeant Terry was genuinely trying to be of assistance or equally genuinely just trying to pass on his problems elsewhere.

'I would welcome an overview,' Henry said. 'You mentioned three cases in particular. Do any of the gentlemen involved remember a red-haired woman as part of the gang?'

Terry pursed his lips and separated out a number of pages from the top of the stack. 'These are the ones I mentioned to you, and these three gentlemen have agreed to be interviewed. I must tell you, Inspector, there are others, but our victims are very reluctant to come forward in the first place and extremely reluctant to make formal statements. Anyone can have their pockets picked. But when there are extenuating circumstances, embarrassment overcomes good sense.'

Henry waited while the younger officer ordered his thoughts.

'An older gentleman, approached by an attractive young woman, gets into conversation and is, shall we say, distracted and finds himself jostled as he gets off the train or as he walks across the station platform. When he turns to look, the woman in question is gone, and so is his wallet. You'll find within these records several such incidents, but the three gentlemen I have here don't mention any such distraction. Which isn't to say that it didn't exist.

'So, you understand why I have put together such a daunting-looking . . .' He faltered and gestured at the stack. 'There may well be other cases, but these seem most like the one you asked me to think about. To be truthful, the evidence in most of these is scanty and ill written, taken by constables or station masters, or in some cases by guards on the train. They took details of what was stolen and the names and addresses of the victim and a line or two of detail of what led up to the misadventure. Some complainants were angry; many were distressed, and that distress is exacerbated by embarrassment either at having been taken for a fool or at having to deal with making a report. I'm sure I don't have to tell you, Inspector, that the general public is glad we are around but they don't want to come within an arm's length of a uniformed officer. They feel it reflects badly on them.'

'You sound like a man who is not enamoured of his job,' Henry commented somewhat tartly.

'The job, I am grateful for and fond of. The general public leaves something to be desired,' Sergeant Terry said with equal asperity. He tapped the stack of paper and then leaned back in his chair and looked frankly at Mickey and Henry. 'The truth is, it is a frustrating position to be in. Crime is a daily occurrence. Most of it is petty, little more serious than small theft or the occasional blow between drunken men, but these cases still require justice to be done, and to be seen to be done, and with a population that is constantly on the move, it is nigh on impossible to keep track of everything that occurs or to have the satisfaction of seeing sufficient cases brought before the courts.'

'We all get frustrated,' Mickey said in a more conciliatory tone. 'We'll work our way through these documents, and if we need further assistance, we'll let you know. Meantime, some refreshments would not go amiss.'

Sergeant Terry left with the promise of tea and biscuits and some sandwiches later on in the morning, and a constable should they require one. Henry glared after him.

'Don't be so hard on the lad,' Mickey said. 'He has the right to feel aggrieved, and no doubt there are few people in a position to listen to him. And here we are, come up from London, brash murder detectives on the prowl, interfering on his patch.'

Henry turned his glare on Mickey and then laughed. 'No,' he agreed, 'you are probably right. As he sees it, any glory that comes out of this will not be his. You start with the logbooks, Mickey – you are better at deciphering spidery handwriting – and I'll begin on the reports.'

Dividing the task between them, they spent the next ninety minutes skim-reading and setting aside anything that required further attention. The promised tea and biscuits arrived, and by the time the sandwiches had been delivered, Henry had added two more reports to the original three and Mickey found two others that he thought warranted interview. The rest, they set aside.

'So, seven. And I feel we have not even scratched the surface.' He frowned. 'We need a map.'

Mickey disappeared and returned a few minutes later with a map of the railway lines and a copy of the timetable. 'Now,' he said, 'we have two incidents at Lincoln station, one at Five Mile Junction and another at somewhere called Dogdyke, then two at Spalding and one at St James Deeping. The incidents are not necessarily reported to the stations in question; I'm guessing that they weren't manned.'

'At least two of these took place when the train was moving,' Henry observed. 'So presumably they were reported as and when someone could reach a station master or a constable. We cannot assume that the place recorded as reporting the incident is the same as where the incident happened.'

'True,' Mickey agreed. 'But it's a place to start, and what interests me is the similarity between the incidents, which might give us an insight into our own investigation. In all of these, there are two men and one woman in some way implicated, or *possibly* implicated.'

'If we take them in sequence, starting with Lincoln. The

first I've selected was November the eighth of last year when Mr Alfred Baines reports that he was jostled on the platform; when he checked, his wallet was missing. The woman had previously asked him directions and he had "raised his arms to point" – no doubt he needed both for emphasis.

'The second, again in Lincoln, but later in the month, and again a woman with brown hair asked for the time and stood and adjusted her watch. Mr Fletcher this time reports that the station was very busy and that he was jostled by the crowd. He discovered, on leaving the station, that his wallet was missing and he had lost more than ten pounds.'

Mickey took over. 'Next in the sequence is the first incident reported at Spalding and initially this seems to have little to do with the railway. It was reported at the station that a man had lost his wallet and that previously he had encountered two hefty young men and a young woman in the market. The woman appeared to be in some distress and so the man asked if everything was all right. One of the men pushed him and the girl told him that she was fine and he should go away. He only realized when he reached the train that his wallet and his watch were gone.' Mickey put the report aside and tapped it thoughtfully with his index finger. 'The description is scanty, considering. A dark-haired young woman and two hefty young men, but they will seem larger, of course, if they are pushing you around. It's likely it's the same group, though.'

Henry nodded. 'And then we have the incident reported at Dogdyke followed by the one at Five Mile Junction. The reports aren't clear; it's most likely both happened on the train. These are both reports of loss, and one mentions a young woman, with red hair this time, who was trying to find her compartment and asked for help; the second simply states that a young man barged into the victim in the corridor, apologized and went on and disappeared into a compartment. The victim reports that he glanced in as he went by and saw an older couple and a young man and young woman. It's tenuous, but possible.'

'And this takes us back to a second incident at Spalding, again in the marketplace and very similar to the first. That was at the start of February this year, so all in all, our little group has been busy.'

'And St James Deeping?'

'Another incident on the train when a couple were robbed – she of her purse and he of his wallet. They report that they intervened in a quarrel between a young man and a young woman and took the young woman into the compartment with them, and there she remained until they got off at the next stop, St James Deeping. The girl was travelling onwards and the couple reported to the guard that she might be in trouble. Only then did they realize their possessions were missing – when the woman took a notebook and pen from her bag in order to write down their address and noticed that she had no purse.'

'And a pattern now begins to emerge,' Henry said. 'The girl is either bait or distraction in all cases, and no doubt if we go back further, we will discover other incidents. Knowing when they began would be helpful, but I think this is a job to hand over to someone who has more time than we do. We need to send messages to the local constabularies involved and ask them to follow up interviews with the victims. I have to say, though, this little group is taking considerable risks. Geographically, all of these incidents take place in close proximity. The likelihood of travellers seeing them more than once must be quite great, I would have thought. They are confident and obviously very capable.'

'And Joseph travelled this route on many occasions. So what did he do to expose himself as a target? Or was it simply random? They use their damsel-in-distress routine frequently enough, so obviously they know it is effective,' Mickey observed. 'So what happens if no one rises to the bait? Do they just move on to the next station and stage it there? You'd think, if they were hoping to attract attention on the station platform – which you'd assume to be the case, as that's where they were when the girl was showing signs of distress – then they were aiming for a target on the station platform, not on the train.'

'Presumably,' Henry agreed. He frowned. 'But you and I have both been on the station platform at Bardney. It's not a large place. The station is substantial enough, considering the village it serves – and that is only because it is on the cross-route back to Louth and up to Lincoln – but to say it was busy or overcrowded, or that an incident would be easily overlooked . . .'

'And yet we know it was,' Mickey argued. 'The Parkers noticed because the girl had been on the train and because Joseph left so peremptorily. The staff there is not large in number and the changeover between trains seems to be fast, so guards, station master and porters would be busy, distracted by the needs of passengers. And if this team is as fast as we think, there would be time for them to get off the train, rob someone and get back on again within two or three minutes. You know as well as I do that dippers work fast, and no doubt they'd already picked their targets out and noted where they kept their valuables.'

'I've no doubt they've been at it for quite some time, so they must have records. They will have been picked up somewhere for something. So we put out a call to local constabularies, see what that brings up. Something our railway colleagues ought to have considered,' Henry added, somewhat sourly.

Mickey laughed. 'They are required to report on crime that happens on the railways and to solve it where possible, but with such a mobile population, both the honest and the criminal, it's hard to follow up anything.'

Henry made no comment but his shoulders stiffened – he clearly did not approve of such professional clemency. 'We should also enquire as to whether anything that was stolen was distinctive. A watch perhaps might be engraved with the owner's name. Anything of this kind should be added to the list sent out to local pawnbrokers and jewellers. We follow the usual procedures and we will turn up results. What is needed is system, Mickey. Organization, process.'

'What is needed is lunch,' Mickey countered. 'Fortification before we meet the family of the fiancée. And tomorrow we should head back home; there is little we can do here that cannot be done by routine police enquiry, and I am eager to discover what happened at the post-mortem.'

* * *

Henry seemed in a better mood after lunch. They ate in a little restaurant close to the station in Lincoln, having been given directions to the street where the Goldmanns, Joseph Levy's prospective in-laws, were living. It was 'up hill', they were told – quite literally up Steep Hill – and by the time they reached the junction with Well Lane Mickey was wishing he'd had something lighter for lunch. The pie and mash sat heavy on his stomach, and the hill seem to go on and upwards for ever. The street would have been pretty, Mickey decided, if he had breath enough to look around properly. Henry, of course, seemed not to notice, striding ahead and pausing occasionally for Mickey to catch up. Mickey considered himself fit enough, but this steep climb was a trial.

The Goldmanns lived on Well Lane, a narrow, cobbled street that still had a public water pump on the corner. The house was a tall terrace looking across at the back wall of what Mickey thought might be part of the cathedral grounds, the towers of St Mary's visible and imposing. 'We should take a look while we're up here,' he said, knowing that Henry had a fondness for ecclesiastical architecture, even if he had no fondness for ecclesiastical personages.

Oddly, the door knocker was a Lincoln imp that stared balefully at visitors and held on to a loop of cast iron, the rapping of which echoed through the house. The Goldmanns had been told to expect them, but they were greeted with a degree of suspicion that Mickey had come to expect. No one really likes it when a policeman calls.

They were invited into the front parlour, an austere and slightly chilly room, despite the fire in the hearth. There were bookshelves on either side of the fireplace and a small, round tilt-top tea table had been set by the fire with chairs around it. Tea arrived and the family assembled and looked expectantly at Henry and Mickey. Mr Goldmann was tall and slim, and his wife was short and plump. She wore a dark-blue dress with a silver fan brooch on the shoulder and her hair was tightly curled in a fashion that was not quite a Marcel wave. The two unmarried daughters were present, and Mr Goldmann explained that their elder daughter was married and had moved abroad. The two remaining were Elizabeth and Rebecca, he said, indicating them in turn. Elizabeth was tall but also slightly plump, seeming to have inherited a little from each of her parents, but Rebecca was small and slightly built and birdlike. Light brown hair and milk and roses on her cheeks, Mickey thought. A pretty little thing.

Henry remembered her from the photograph that he had seen, the one taken when she'd been seated on a bench with Joseph; he had been looking at the camera, but she had been looking at something behind the photographer. He still wondered what it was.

'So, you found him, then,' Mr Goldmann said. 'At least he's been found.' He glanced at his younger daughter, but she sat very still and her face was utterly expressionless – almost, Mickey thought, as though she didn't know what to think about any of it.

'The body was sent back to London yesterday,' Henry said. Mickey noticed that the girl flinched. 'We are expecting the post-mortem to be done today and then we will know more about how he died,' Henry continued. The girl swallowed nervously and her mother looked at Henry as though she would like to kill him.

Mickey cleared his throat. 'We have to ask about the last time he was here.'

'We've already told the police all we know,' said Elizabeth. 'He arrived as he often did on the Friday afternoon and he left on the Sunday morning. We put him on the train and he was fine. He had spent Shabbat with us, as he often did. Sometimes he couldn't come on the Friday and so he would arrive on the Saturday. It wasn't very proper, but sometimes that's just how things are. We don't keep such strict observance that we don't understand that.'

'And did anything out of the ordinary happen while he was here? Did he seem happy? Content? Was all going well with the wedding arrangements? We understand that you quarrelled,' Henry said, addressing Rebecca directly.

The girl cast an anxious look at her father, but then nodded. 'I wanted to put it off. The wedding. I wanted to wait until my sister and her husband could be there. That was all; I just wanted to delay it for a little while. It wasn't as if I wanted to . . .'

'And Joseph objected to the delay?'

'It wasn't Joseph. I think his family were getting impatient. His mother – his mother was not happy.'

'And if she's not happy, the world knows about it.' It was the first time Mrs Goldmann had spoken, and her tone told Henry everything he needed to know about the relationship.

'If you have problems with the family, then why approve the marriage? I believe that this was an arrangement of long standing.'

'Becky wasn't marrying the mother,' Elizabeth said. 'He and Becky loved one another, and anyway he wasn't going to live there; he was going to live up here, join the family business.'

'I believe you own a boarding house,' Henry said, addressing Mrs Goldmann.

'In Grimsby, yes. We have a housekeeper in place. We also have a shop here and we run that ourselves. A jeweller's. Joseph would have been useful; he would have been happy here.'

'And his family were content with that?'

'His family had two sons and their wives already living with them; they didn't need a third. We thought to keep Joseph and Rebecca with us to help with the business because Elizabeth will no doubt marry elsewhere, when she finds a man that she can actually approve of.'

Elizabeth's eyes flashed. But she didn't speak. Henry found himself warming to this older sister. The younger was pretty but she seemed insipid. He reprimanded himself; he knew nothing of these young women.

'Is it not a strange place to settle, Lincoln? I believe there is no community here.'

'Not now; there was once. The nearest active community is in Grimsby, which is why we have a boarding house there. It is close to the docks; many of our people come through looking for a place to stay that is sympathetic to them. And there is a synagogue on Heneage Road and another on Hamilton Street. Of course, those who are more orthodox make their own arrangements and usually stay with members of the congregation.'

'Then why not live in Grimsby?' Henry asked.

For the first time Mr Goldmann smiled. 'Even the greatest of trees starts with a small seed,' he said. 'Once there was a thriving community here. I visited Lincoln when I was a boy and I liked the place. Just down the road from here, in fact – you will have passed it if you walked up Steep Hill – is the house of Aaron of Lincoln who lived here in the twelfth century. He was a rich man and even lent money to the king.'

'The congregations in Grimsby are more orthodox.' Mrs Goldmann seemed suddenly uncomfortable. 'Ashkenazi so . . . To be truthful,' Mrs Goldmann went on, 'most people who know us would barely recognize us as Jewish at all. We believe in integrating – as far as it is possible to do so without betraying our heritage and culture, of course.'

'Of course,' Mickey agreed. 'Though I understand that Joseph's family would be considered devout?'

The senior Goldmanns exchanged a glance. 'Devotion takes many forms, Sergeant Hitchens. And we had had enough of prejudice and persecution in London. We came here seeking a quieter life.'

Mickey was about to pursue this, but Henry was clearly thinking about something and Mickey didn't think that it was the murder.

'As I understand it,' Henry said, 'the way the loans worked was that a group of families would get together to underwrite a loan. When a lender died, all his outstanding loans came to be owed not to his family but to the king. Most rulers knew that if they called in those debts, it would cause financial discomfort to a great many families, and as these families were powerful, they were reluctant to upset the status quo, shall we say. It was enough for families to know that they owed their king. And the reason the loans were spread between families, I believe, was so that when money owed was acquired by the king, the impact of that was cushioned if the consequences were more widespread. A family could have been bankrupted by the death of its patriarch, had it been otherwise.'

He paused and then looked once more at Rebecca, changing direction again. 'And so, what did you quarrel about?' The question seemed to take her by surprise. She had relaxed a little during his diversion into ancient history, clearly believing that his attention was truly elsewhere.

'I told you.' She sounded a little impatient now. 'I wanted to delay the wedding so my sister could attend.'

'So it wasn't that you found a red hair on his coat or smelt a perfume that you knew was not your own?'

Her jaw dropped and she gaped at him, and Mickey cast an admiring look at his boss. Sometimes Henry took even him by surprise.

'I . . . I. You don't have to ask me things like that.'

'Your fiancé is dead,' Henry said coldly. 'He was last seen in the company of a red-haired woman who he chased after when she left the train. Did he know her?'

There were tears now, not from Rebecca, though, but from her mother. 'I told her,' Mrs Goldmann said, 'he would settle down once he had married. That he loved her – anyone seeing them together would know that he loved her. Sometimes young men are foolish. Some young girl bats her eyelashes . . .'

'He said he loved her.' Rebecca's response was so quiet, so utterly bereft, that Mickey immediately felt pity for her.

'So he had known her for a time,' he asked gently, hoping Henry would have the sense to remain silent.

'He said he loved her. He met her last autumn, on the train, and they got talking. He said he had never met anyone like her and that he could not help himself and that he was so, so sorry. He asked me to tell no one until they'd gone away. He said he knew how difficult it was for me to say yes to that kind of request. That I must want to scream at him and tell everyone just how much of a traitor he was, and how badly he had treated me, and he said he would not blame me if I hated him for ever. But he loved her and he could not deny it, and he would not lie to me by marrying me.

'I thought he might just change his mind eventually, that it was just an infatuation, so I said we should tell our families we just wanted to put the marriage off for a while. I used my sister's visit as an excuse and told everyone that I wanted her to be there. I knew I could talk everyone around, but Joseph wouldn't have it. He said they were going away and I asked him how. How could they afford it? Joseph had no real money of his own. He said that he could get money, but he wouldn't tell me how. Just that they were going away and that they would manage.'

Her family was staring at her, but Mickey held her gaze. 'That must have hurt a great deal.'

She nodded, tears streaming down her face, and Mickey searched for a handkerchief in his pocket and handed it to her, hoping it was clean.

'Did he tell you her name? Anything about her?'

'He said her name was Adelaide, but he called her Addie and he said . . . he said that she was the most beautiful thing he had ever set eyes on.'

Not the most thoughtful of responses, Mickey considered. 'And he gave no clue as to where he was going to get the money?'

Henry had not been watching Rebecca; he had been studying Mr Goldmann and the bright spots of colour that had appeared on the man's cheek, which might just be down to rage about his daughter's treatment.

But Henry had been wondering. 'Had you promised him money, Mr Goldmann? Had you some arrangement that he was party to? It occurs to me that with a boarding house so close to the docks in Grimsby, where people are coming through day after day and bringing whatever of their possessions with them, a man like yourself, owning such a place, would be in a position to, shall we say, facilitate—'

'What are you accusing me of?'

'I'm not accusing; I'm simply speculating. A little smuggling perhaps, the provision of papers that could not be obtained easily, or of cover stories. We all know how impossible it is to deport migrants from Bolshevik Russia and how easy it is to simply change accent or change a name and so have permission to settle here. To register as a legal alien from a country that you cannot be deported back to – this has advantages. Or young women coming in, brought here with promises of work, who find themselves working in ways they did not anticipate.'

The blotches of colour had spread now and Mr Goldmann's

entire face was purple with rage. 'I would like you to leave,' he said. 'This is a family in mourning, and you come here, make your accusations—'

'Will you be attending the funeral?' Henry asked, his tone calm and unmoved by his host's fury.

'I won't,' Rebecca said. 'I don't feel I can. Not now.'

'No,' Mr Goldmann said. 'We will not be there.' He strode to the front door and opened it wide.

They left and turned back towards Steep Hill and then, by tacit agreement, towards the cathedral, emerging at the top of the hill between castle and cathedral and facing towards the White Hart Hotel.

Mickey nodded in its direction and said, 'That looks like a nice place to stay, although I suppose we should be heading back this evening, as we left our bags back in Bardney.'

Henry nodded agreement. 'But something tells me we might be coming back up here,' he said, 'so bear it in mind.'

'And in the meantime?'

'We arrange to examine the Goldmanns' financial records and their business accounts. There is more going on here than anyone is admitting to. Where did the boy plan to get money from? And how much did he know about this Adelaide?'

'We have a name now, or at least part of one. That's if it *is* her name. This relationship or affair or whatever you want to call it does change the complexion of things considerably. And *their* story doesn't stand up,' Mickey said frankly. 'The idea of moving up here, from London, just because you happen to have visited and liked the place. And then to set up two quite disparate businesses, one of which you have no day-to-day control over, from the sound of it. I don't like it, I don't trust it. Although their boarding house might give service to travelling Hebrews, it seems that the family are at pains to hide or obfuscate their own identity. I would have pushed this further, but you turned the conversation.'

'Then we will revisit it the next time. Lies are certainly being told, but about what?'

They walked through the gateway into the cathedral court across cobblestones made greasy by the drizzling rain and to the entrance door. It was mid-afternoon, but the sky was densely grey and it would not be long before it was dark. Inside, the cathedral was mysterious and dim, the last of the light filtering through stained glass, but Henry guessed that even in bright daylight this was never an airy or an open place. He paused to admire the carving, foliate shapes pierced and delicate, balled up or twining in great swags around pillars, and then wandered slowly into the Angel Choir, examining the dark wood and the misericords, the space enclosed and private, almost like a church within a church.

'It's dedicated to Saint Hugh,' Mickey told him. 'His tomb is through there, apparently.'

Henry followed, and in the half-light they examined the tomb of St Hugh of Lincoln, the saint lying in state beneath a heavy carved canopy.

'He was supposed to have been able to perform miracles,' Mickey said. 'Maybe we should ask him for one.'

By the time they left, it was dark and wet, and the cobblestones shone beneath the streetlights. Their way back down Steep Hill was no less difficult than their way up, the stones slippery, worn smooth and unforgiving in their hardness.

'I feel sorry for the girl,' Mickey commented. It was the first time he had said anything for a while. 'I think she and Joseph would have made a good match. If he hadn't had his head turned.'

'Romantic nonsense.' Henry's voice was harsh.

'You don't think he had feelings for her?'

Henry shrugged. 'What difference does it make?' he said.

FOURTEEN

A s it happened, the post-mortem had already taken place by the time they returned to London the following day, and the superintendent had released the body for burial. Henry was annoyed at first, but on reading the report he realized that there was little to be gained by delaying the process.

'*Death was caused by a single blow to the back of the head,*' he read. He continued, paraphrasing. 'Small fragments of dust in the wound indicate that the weapon was probably a brick, an old brick because there were also fragments of moss and mud adhering to the bone. He had been struck once and struck hard. The brain is in a state of some decay, but it is possible to discern bleeding into the cerebral cavity, which may indicate that the victim lived for a short while after the blow. There is also a stab wound to the chest, but it's unlikely that this was the cause of death as the wound was shallow and avoided all vital organs.'

'But it wouldn't have helped,' Mickey commented. 'So they got the poor fool off the train, somehow lured him out of the station.'

'He would have followed the girl. That would have been simple enough.'

'But if he thought the girl was in danger, why not report to the guard or one of the platform men? Even a porter could have helped out.'

'That I can't answer,' Henry said. 'When do people ever think clearly?'

He dropped the post-mortem report on to the desk and stood up, wandering across to the window. 'So they left the station, and at some point shortly thereafter he was hit around the head and stabbed in the chest, which indicates that perhaps one came up behind him, one in front, and they synchronized their attack, wanting to be sure. Perhaps even wanting to share the blame . . . or the pleasure. I think the intent to kill is clear enough; we couldn't tell when we first saw the body, but now the hair and scalp have been excised and the mud cleaned away, it's hard to see how he could have survived such a wound. Whoever hit him hit him hard, and it's down to pure dumb luck that the knife missed everything important. The intent was there, I'm certain of that.'

Mickey opened the file and studied the photographs of the wound, cleaned now and the damage obvious. 'And then the two men parked the girl at the pub and went to dispose of the body.'

Henry nodded. 'Joseph was tall, but very slender; between them they could have managed him easily. Taken him along the bank of the dyke and dumped him far enough from the village that he was unlikely to be found in a hurry. I doubt they expected the body to be undiscovered for so long; maybe they even hoped for it to turn out that way. All they needed to do was come back, collect the young woman and board their next train.'

'She has to be seen as an accessory,' Mickey said. 'She must have witnessed the entire offence and she was inside the public house for at least an hour, plenty of time for her to summon help, to bear witness against her companions. And yet she said nothing. That speaks either of total disregard for Joseph's life or of great fear.'

'Fear of what? Of the men she was with? I will make a bet with you,' Henry said, 'that there was at least one more train in the intervening time. She could have returned to the station, boarded that train and been well away from both of those young men. And we know that they must have remained together – it's unlikely that just one of them could have carried a body across the fields. The girl was alone. This Adelaide had plenty of opportunity for escape, and yet she stayed where they left her, waiting to be collected when they returned.'

'The landlord said that she looked upset.'

'Upset! Upset is what happens when someone spills a drink

in your lap, not when you have witnessed the murder of someone you are meant to love.'

'You are assuming that she saw everything,' Mickey argued. 'And perhaps if she did, then she was shocked into inaction. It happens, Henry. When people are overwhelmed, they are as likely to freeze solid as they are to run or to fight. That the girl did not run is no proof either that she didn't care what was done to Joseph or that she simply didn't care for him. Love and fear often battle one another, and you know as well as I do that often the fear wins.'

'Mickey, why do you always feel the need to play devil's advocate?'

'Because that's part of my job,' Mickey told him.

Mickey looked again at the photographs of the wound. The edges were sharp and well defined, and he was inclined to agree with brick not stone, not random rock. 'If I remember right, as you come out of the back of the station, there is a part of the garden wall in a state of disrepair. It would not surprise me if the murder weapon came from there. So they went armed with the knife, but in the end used whatever was to hand. Perhaps in the beginning they had no intent to kill, but the circumstances somehow changed.'

'You'll be telling me next there was no intent to rob or maim.' Henry just sounded cross now. Petulant, as he sometimes did when a case frustrated him.

'If we are lucky, one of the local constabulary will identify this trio in the next few days. There will be a record of them somewhere. These are not beginners or amateurs.'

Henry came over and sat back down. 'You know how much I hate waiting for other people to do the work,' he said.

'Don't I just,' Mickey agreed.

Preparing Joseph's body for burial had been an arduous and unpleasant task and the men had undertaken it with great care, washing the body as best they could and redressing it. Because death had been violent, the clothes he had been wearing when he met his death would be buried with him. He had been wrapped in a white shroud, and after the preparations were made, they took turns to keep vigil beside him.

His mother had wanted to see her son, but they had not allowed it; nor had they allowed his sisters to be close by. Abraham knew he would never forget how his nephew looked: wounded and decayed and seemingly already half gone back to the earth.

He took an opportunity to speak with his brother and asked, 'Will Rebecca's family be coming?' He would have expected their presence, but they had not been mentioned.

'They will not.'

'Why?'

'It's been decided it would be inappropriate.'

'How is it inappropriate? Joseph and Rebecca were to be married. She's practically his widow.'

'But they will not be here.'

'Have you quarrelled with them?'

'Abraham, please leave it alone. I am grateful – we are all grateful – for what you've done, but now, please, leave it alone.'

Abraham stepped back from his brother and studied him carefully. They had not been close in a long time, although Abraham still cared deeply for him and had done his best to indulge his brother's children as though they'd been his own. 'I don't understand. What aren't you telling me?'

'Abraham, please, I'm begging you, keep out of this. No good will come from you asking more questions.'

'Are you involved in something? Was Joseph? Did you and the Goldmanns have him doing something? Ben, I've been hearing rumours; I'd rather hear from you that they are not true.'

'And I'd rather you simply did not listen to them. There will always be rumours. Wherever we go, there are rumours.'

'But tell me, are you still involved? Did you involve Joseph in your—'

'Enough,' His brother spoke sharply. 'Now is not the time. Let it go, Abraham. There was a time when you would have supported us in the work.'

Abraham could hear a woman crying as though her heart was truly broken. He had no particular liking for his sister-in-law – she nagged and bullied and always insisted on 'the best' and on what had to be done for show – but he pitied her now. He knew what it was like to lose a child, and she'd had hers for much longer. Did that make it a greater loss? Abraham didn't really know, but he knew the pain of it and didn't think the depth could necessarily be measured in days or hours.

He tried again. 'Has your wife quarrelled with the Gold-manns? Does she blame them in some way because—' His brother's expression caused him to break off. 'What is going on? Are you in trouble? Tell me and I will help.'

'Help by running to your policeman?'

'I went to him because I knew him to be an honest man. I went to him because we had lost our boy and our own efforts had come to nothing.'

'*My* boy,' his brother told him angrily. 'And now you wish a scandal to be attached to his name? You've done enough, Abraham. Ask no more questions. Leave things alone.'

Others entered the room and Benjamin turned to speak to them. Abraham felt himself pushed aside and excluded, and he did not understand the cause of it, only that there was deep trouble here and that somehow he had exacerbated it by asking an outsider for help.

When the others had left the room and his brother prepared to follow them, Abraham grasped his arm. 'It's almost as though you would rather he had not been found. What was he doing that might be found out? What are you afraid of? It seems to me that you fear disgrace more than you fear the loss of your son. We brought your son home. Did that disgrace come with him? And if it did, what does it matter, compared with the loss of a child?'

Benjamin pulled his arm away and turned angrily on his brother. 'You take pleasure in being so unworldly,' he said. 'You cling to the past, to a lost wife and a lost child, when you could have moved on, moved forward. The world does not stand still, and sometimes chances must be taken.'

He left Abraham standing in the centre of the dining room. The women came in to bring food and lay it out on the table, and Abraham moved to get out of their way. He heard their voices, soft and consoling, and wished for a moment those words were directed at him.

Had he done wrong? He'd acted only out of kindness and concern, but now he looked at his brother and realized that he didn't know him at all.

FIFTEEN

The funeral itself passed without incident. The police had been there, of course, as observers, but they had not interfered; as far as Abraham could see, they hadn't really spoken to anyone.

The conversation he'd had with his brother had troubled him a great deal and he'd come to question things that until this last couple of days had not bothered him at all. His brother's business was successful: a general store and a small chain of jewellery shops, two of them in the East End. But one was out in Croydon, not far from the burgeoning airport, staffed by a married daughter and her husband, and catering for a very mixed trade, whereas those in the traditional areas of Whitechapel and Limehouse largely catered to the Jewish community. These shops were not high-end, mostly serving the middling classes, but they were turning over a good deal of business. Anything to do with clocks or watches or requiring engraving was often passed Abraham's way, as was any repair work or the sourcing of something particularly unusual. Abraham was well aware that his little shop would probably not have survived without this patronage, and until now he had not really given it much thought. He was happy that his brother's business was a success; he was happy that his brother's family were growing wealthy and had twice moved house in the last five years, moving a little further out of the East End each time. The children were making good marriages and seemed content, and the grandchildren were coming along. All seemed well with the world.

Abraham saw his brother perhaps once a month, but there was nothing unusual in that. They cared about one another as family should but they were not close and had little in common, even in terms of politics. They did not even attend the same synagogue. Benjamin's wife preferred one closer to their new home, where she could mix with what she told

Abraham was 'a better crowd', and Abraham understood that for business people there was a need to see and be seen, and to look prosperous because that inspired trust in prospective customers. He understood all of that and had tried to make allowances for the fact that their plans more often than not excluded him.

Abraham's refusal to remarry had set the cat among the pigeons, too. His brother told him that it made him socially difficult to deal with, because a lone man coming to any kind of event upset the numbers.

Abraham understood what he meant: the human race was expected to appear two by two and singletons made people feel uncomfortable. From Abraham's perspective, this was never a particular issue, but that was largely because he rarely attended the social events that his brother had organized and it occurred to him only now that the impact of that was that they had drifted very far apart.

Abraham was close to Joseph because it was Joseph who undertook to deliver or collect the clocks or bring the requests for engraving of plaques or watches or for particular orders that Abraham might be able to fulfil. The two had become friends and often took time out to go to concerts, or to talk or eat together. And Abraham would be the first to admit that he had come to think of Joseph more as a son than a nephew. He realized now that he was furious at the idea that his brother might have done something to put Joseph at risk.

He was utterly taken aback by the fact that the Goldmanns had not even sent a representative. What was going on? It was a ghastly and tragic business, Abraham thought, but somehow it would have been better if he had been able to make sense of it all.

He travelled most of the way home by bus. Walking back towards his shop, he had to pass the public house that Clem Atkins had ordained as his personal domain. He glanced through the windows, noting that Atkins held court at the bar, shoulders shrugged, his hands held out as though expressing some displeasure at the world. Abraham was a little startled when, after walking on a few more steps, his name was called.

'Oi, you. Levy.'

Abraham turned. He didn't know the man but he knew what he *was*: one of the thugs always at Atkins' beck and call.

'Mr Atkins wants a word.'

Abraham sighed and turned back. He wasn't particularly afraid. Clem Atkins took his dues, as had those who had come before him, and no doubt as would those who came after, but he made little bother for Abraham. Abraham knew not to rock boats.

His boots clumped on the wooden floor and he was aware that the room had fallen silent. Clem Atkins was still standing at the bar, but this time he had a drink in his hand.

'Will you raise a glass with me?' It wasn't really a question or a request. Atkins gestured to a second glass sitting on the bar, into which the barman was emptying rather too much whisky.

Abraham picked it up. 'What are we drinking to?'

'I hear it was the funeral today. Bad business, that. From what I saw, he was a nice boy. Too often it's the *nice* boys that get hurt.'

'With that, I cannot argue,' Abraham told him. 'The innocent often suffer.'

'I never said he was an innocent.' Clem Atkins narrowed his eyes. 'Not many of them round here. Innocents.'

Abraham took a sip of his drink just to give himself something to do and to buy some thinking time, and then he said. 'Is there something you wanted, Mr Atkins?'

'Just passing on my condolences.'

'And I appreciate that.'

'I hear his girlfriend didn't come to the funeral. Nor her family.'

'No, they did not.'

Atkinson sniffed and wiped his nose on the back of his free hand. 'Strange that. Not much respect.'

Abraham wasn't sure what he should say, or whether he should say anything. What was Atkins after?

He took another drink and then set the glass down on the bar. 'Thank you for your condolences,' he said. 'I bid you goodnight, Mr Atkins.'

He almost expected to be called back or, worse still, dragged back, but as he walked towards the door, he was aware of the noise of the bar picking up again and the chatter resuming, and the game of dominoes, which had paused when he came in, continued noisily in the corner. He opened the door and stepped outside, and realized, as the cold air hit him, that he was sweating. What had that been all about?

Abraham opened his front door, stood in the hall, listening to the sounds of the house, the ticking of the clocks and the usual creaks as it settled for the night. He locked the door, turning the key and drawing the bolts, and then went around the house, ensuring that everything else was secure and that no one had been inside while he'd been gone. He would have liked to check the shop, but nothing could have persuaded him to go outside again, not tonight. He comforted himself with the fact that one of his two new lodgers, living over the shop, was usually home in the evening. He wanted some tea, but he didn't think he had the strength to make it, and so instead he took himself upstairs to bed, opening the curtains just a crack and peering down into the street, not sure what he expected to see but glad that there was no one around.

He had not been afraid when he had been called into the pub. But he was afraid now and he could not explain why. He was sure that Clem Atkins knew what his brother had been up to and, whatever it was, that it had involved Joseph, and he was sure also that Clem thought that he, too, was involved.

Nothing, Abraham thought, could be further from the truth. He might once have been in his brother's confidence but since Benjamin and his family had moved away to what his sister-in-law viewed as a safer and more civilized location and Abraham been left behind, he had withdrawn from all but the most legitimate of business. The making and selling of clocks; the engraving of messages of congratulation or love, that was Abraham's world. He had chosen to not even ask what his brother might be involved in these days. But he was far from convinced that he could persuade Clem Atkins of that.

SIXTEEN

U sually, Addie made her decisions based on looking at people's shoes. People will try to keep their clothes smart, brushed and clean, but they couldn't hide what was happening to their shoes. They might polish them and take them to the cobbler for repair, but wear on shoes meant they had very little money to spare; people with old shoes were not her targets. So the young man was not one of her usual types. His clothes were neat, his trilby had a red band, and his coat was a good cloth, well made and did not look old. But he did not wear smart shoes. His boots were polished, but they looked like those a soldier might wear, and it struck Addie that they were made for exactly that: long wear. They did not speak of a young man who was well-off, just one who took care of what he had. His suitcase reinforced her deductions. It was leather and clasped about with two buckled straps. But one corner had been repaired and the repair looked very old, so either he was very attached to this ageing case or he could not afford or did not want to spend money on a replacement.

Addie knew the type: he wouldn't have much money on him and what there was would be carefully guarded, tucked into an inside pocket. But she smiled at him anyway because there was something in his eyes that was kind and something about the long, slender fingers gripping the suitcase that spoke of sensitivity and thoughtfulness – although Addie could not have told anybody why she thought that. No doubt she was just being fanciful.

She could see Fred and Gus standing together beneath the clock and chatting about nothing in particular, and she caught Gus's eye and his look of surprise when he realized that she was going to talk to this young man, his immediate assessment of her target aligning with her own.

'Excuse me,' Addie said, 'but my watch seems to have stopped. Do you have the right time?'

He looked momentarily flustered and smiled at her, but opened his greatcoat just enough to get to his waistcoat pocket and withdrew a beautiful watch. One of such quality that it caused Addie to reassess. He told her the time and tucked the watch back into his waistcoat pocket and she made a fuss over adjusting her own little wristwatch.

'It's unusual,' she said, 'to find a young man still using a pocket watch. Family heirloom, is it?'

He smiled. 'A gift,' he said. 'My uncle is a clockmaker. He gave it to me when I came of age.'

'Oh,' she said. 'What a lovely thing to do.'

That information, Addie thought, reinforced her first impression that this was not a rich man. He just happened to have one beautiful thing. 'Well, thank you,' she said and went on her way.

She was aware that he was watching her, so rather than walk straight back to join Fred and Gus, she was about to walk straight past, just in case, when Fred caught her attention by taking her by the arm. She shook him off impatiently. 'Leave off. He's not one for us.'

She glanced back to where the young man stood, hesitating now, as though concerned about her, and for just a moment she allowed her heart to beat faster. Then, not wanting to draw more attention, she turned back to her companions and suggested they go and have a cup of tea. And when she looked back again, the young man had turned and was headed towards the train.

Addie thought back now to that first meeting, that innocent – at least on Joseph's part – encounter at Lincoln station. She almost wished they'd robbed him then and there. That way, perhaps he would still be alive. Indeed, if she'd not seen him that second time, in all likelihood he would still be alive. He would have forgotten about her and not engaged her in conversation, asking if her watch was working now, demonstrating by that simple query that she'd been on his mind and that he'd remembered her.

Addie folded her arms across her body and stared out of the window. It was raining again – not good for working because people hurried that bit more, armed themselves with umbrellas and pulled their coats more tightly across their chests. To have a really good day, you needed sunshine, and for the best, you needed warmth, people strolling unguarded and content with the world.

Addie thought she'd never be content with the world again.

SEVENTEEN

There had been a letter waiting for Henry on his return. It was from Cynthia.

By the time you get this, we will be heading for home.

Henry set the letter down on the small table beside the window and shed his coat, hanging it on the peg behind the door and taking a moment to switch on the electric fire and pour himself a drink before sitting down in his favourite chair and casting the bright, plaid rug across his knees.

Oh, Henry, I will be so glad to come home. We drove up into Belgium and then onwards to the border, following the route Albert and his men took in 1914. I've never known him hanker after doing this before. He's as close-mouthed about the war as you are, but on this occasion he seemed decided on it and so that's what we did. We made our way to Ypres, intending to stay for a few days, but Albert changed his mind as suddenly as he had first made the decision to go. We turned instead towards Liège and he left me alone at the hotel while he wandered off to God knows where. But when he returned for dinner, he seemed more content and so I asked no questions. I know he came here right at the end of the war and he spoke to me about the devastation the city had suffered. I knew then that he had come looking for someone, but I didn't ask who or why. Some questions are best left unasked.

In time we came to the border crossing near the Oostkantons and we followed the line of the Vennbahn for a time.

The Vennbahn, Henry remembered, was a railway built to transport ore from Aachen to Luxembourg, but in 1914 it had brought troops to Liège, presaging one of the first conflicts of the war, and a few weeks later Albert had led his men at the first battle of Ypres. Henry thought he understood why his brother-in-law might want to return after all this time; it was not an inclination he himself had ever had.

The next day we drove on to the factory near Aachen. You would not recognize the place. I almost did not. As you know, inflation is out of control, poverty is rife, the supply of raw materials affected by the inability of the German importers to pay in currency that their suppliers will accept. The Mark is not yet in freefall – though Albert and I have no doubt that will come – but the price of an order placed in Deutschmarks will have doubled by the time payment is made because the currency is so devalued, day on day, hour on hour. So far, Albert has bought in American dollars and British pounds and has thus kept the supply chain intact, but now suppliers are so jittery that even this means is failing and the goods, once they are ready for sale, are so undervalued as to undermine the market. Buyers know desperation when they see it. They buy so cheap as to barely cover the cost and now the factory is operating at a great loss.

Henry, it shames me so deeply, but I had to join my voice to those of Albert's business advisors, demanding that Albert close the German businesses, despite the knowledge that those who depend on the already scant wages will then have even less. But the business is haemorrhaging money. If we maintain our interest, it will bankrupt us. And so, as of three days ago, we have begun to pull all interest from the German economy, have put the buildings themselves up for sale, knowing that we may recoup only a fraction of our investment and that anything we do now will be in the nature of limiting damage only. For Albert, this has been a sobering experience and for that alone I am glad that we made this journey. He is beginning to see what I have suspected for some time now: that this is not time for expansion or for chancy investment but for rationalizing and consolidating and protecting what we can.

I feel that this lesson more than any other will help keep Albert from the clutches of the likes of Hatry and his foolish get-rich-quick schemes.

Oh, but, Henry, there are other incidents that have upset me equally. When we were waiting to cross the border, we witnessed lines and lines of people queuing up to take their money into Belgium, just to buy bread. Although few shops will now accept their currency, those that will are profiting by it by charging many times the usual cost – and yet still they tell me this is cheaper than the cost in their home town. And there is such hatred brewing, such tension.

I hope, dearest Henry, that life is treating you well. You must come and see me as soon as I return. I need to speak to my little brother almost more than I need to hug my children – and you know me, so can guess from that just how great my need must be.

Later that evening Henry called at Cynthia's house, partly in the hope of further news of his sister's return. He arrived at the same time as Malina Cooper, Cynthia's secretary and general help.

'You look cheerful,' he commented. 'You've been shopping?'

Malina smiled at him and hugged the brown paper parcel. 'I've bought the most beautiful winter coat,' she said. 'I'm going to show Nanny. Are you coming up?'

Henry said that he was, knowing that his niece would be happy to see him. 'Have you heard from Cynthia? I had a letter saying they were returning.'

'Telegrams,' Malina said. 'One to me,' which evidently pleased her a great deal, 'and one to Mrs Mullins' – the redoubtable housekeeper, Henry thought – 'saying to expect them on Friday or possibly Saturday. They will send word once they have decided on their flight.'

'Cynthia seems to have become fond of aeroplanes,' Henry commented.

'It would be so much fun to fly, don't you think?'

'Fun, perhaps, but I think the cost would be beyond me.'

'Oh my goodness, yes.' Malina opened the nursery door

and a moment later Henry was engulfed in Melissa's embrace. 'Uncle Henry, Mummy's coming home. I'm so excited.'

'So am I, my love,' Henry confessed. He allowed himself to be led to a chair, and Melissa plonked herself on his lap. Tea and bread for making toast arrived – with extra for Henry and Malina – and Malina's coat was shown off. This was such a relaxed, informal house, Henry thought. So unlike the cold, austere and uncaring place in which he and his sister had grown up. The difference still shocked him in an odd sort of way, for all that he was glad of it. He still half expected someone to come in and reprimand them, punish them for being happy.

Malina held up the coat for him to see. Deep green in some sort of soft but sturdy wool and with a heavy lining and a little fur trim at the collar.

'I like the colour,' he said.

'Thirty bob from one of those little Jewish tailor shops off Cable Street. Such a bargain.' She stroked the fabric, clearly delighted. 'I don't know how they do it at that price.'

Henry thought of the conditions the sweatshop labourers worked under, but decided not to comment. Malina was paid better wages than she had ever earned and with bed and board thrown in, but that still didn't make her well-off. It was the poor preying on the poor, he thought, but then he reminded himself that his sister's gowns were in all probability made by the same workers, in the same conditions and with no more benefit to them.

The thought suddenly left him depressed.

'Uncle Henry?' Melissa was sensitive to his moods. 'What made you sad?'

He smiled at her, stroked the red-gold hair that was so like her mother's. 'I'm just tired, sweetheart.'

She nodded, accepting if not quite believing. 'I suppose trying to find murderers must be depressing,' she said.

'Sometimes it is,' he agreed. 'Not the finding so much, but the searching.'

Melissa studied his face intently in a way that was also like her mother. 'You can only do your best,' she told him seriously.

It was something Cynthia always told her children, and Henry suddenly felt very much like a child.

Malina had departed to hang the new coat in her wardrobe, and Melissa settled by the fire to eat her toast. Henry watched as Nanny toasted a piece for him, pierced on the prongs of the long-handled fork. 'Bless the girl,' Nanny said. 'She's had to struggle for everything and now she can afford to splash out a little – well, it's a joy to behold, isn't it?'

Henry agreed that it was.

'And I want to say thank you, Mr Henry,' Nanny went on quietly.

'Oh, for what?'

'For writing to your sister. Though I never meant for you to. I didn't say what I said for that. But I'm grateful.'

For a moment Henry was nonplussed, then he recalled the conversation about the children growing up and the worry this elderly woman had about losing her position and her home. 'Oh,' he said.

'The mistress, she sent me a telegram. Oh, I was so shaken, you know – telegrams only ever bring bad news. I've only had one before this and that was . . .' She trailed off but Henry could guess what it was. It had probably said something like *'We regret to inform you . . .'*

He wondered whom she had lost. Was there anyone in the country who had not lost someone in the Great War?

'So when the telegram came, I had to ask Malina to read it to me.' She took the much-folded flimsy sheet from her pocket and handed it to Henry.

'You will always have a home with us,' Henry read. He nodded. 'I'd have expected nothing else.'

He handed it back. Melissa was waiting for another piece of toast, and Malina had returned and poured more tea. She settled with a contented sigh in a chair next to Henry's. These two women, Henry thought, had finally fetched up in a safe harbour, and Cynthia would move heaven and earth to ensure that those she had taken under her protection remained that way.

He recalled his sister's letter and the decision to close the factory on the German border. He could imagine Cynthia's guilt at the knowledge of so many now put out of work. For her to have added her voice to that proposal, Henry thought, must mean that things were very bad. Very bad indeed.

After leaving his sister's house, Henry had gone looking for Abraham at home but had been told by a neighbour that as it was Sunday evening, he had gone to the Workers' Circle in Alie Street to listen to some music. The Circle had been formed by Russian Jews back at the start of the century. Its aim was to provide a meeting place and somewhere the local people could receive an education and indulge in culture. It was a poor community, but the belief in cultural enrichment and care for the sick and the unemployed was at the heart of the first Circle.

The Circle had moved to Brick Lane and then finally to Alie Street, and Henry made his way there.

Abraham seemed pleased to see him. He had been eating a supper of herring and bread, washed down with a copious quantity of tea. Henry declined the herring but accepted the offer of tea. His cup was filled from a giant samovar in the corner of the room beside the food counter.

'I come here on a Sunday,' Abraham told Henry. 'Often there is music, or sometimes I play chess; always there is company.'

'And yet you sit alone tonight?'

Abraham shrugged. 'I should not even be here. I should still be with my family, mourning the death of my nephew. Most people here know that and don't know whether they should tell me they disapprove, sympathize because they know my brother's wife or leave me alone to grieve.'

'And which would you prefer?'

'Truthfully, I don't think I know. But what brings you here?'

'Did Joseph have a watch?'

'Of course Joseph had a watch. What kind of uncle would I be if I didn't give the boy a watch?'

'Could you describe it to me? Was there anything about it that would make it identifiable?'

Abraham dabbed at his plate with the last of his bread and chewed slowly as though needing to think about his reply. He took a sip of his tea.

'I had hoped,' he said, 'that somehow the watch would have been in his waistcoat pocket, that he could have been buried with it. They left him his coat but not his watch. A watch is so easy to dispose of, I suppose.'

'It's even possible that he was killed for it,' Henry said.

'Possible, yes. It is a fine watch, if a little old fashioned. Gold, it winds with a key that he kept always on a fob chain. A full hunter. I took it as security for a loan and the loan was never repaid, so I kept the watch. After a time I decided that the watch deserved a good home, and when Joseph had his Bar Mitzvah, the age at which a child becomes a man' – Henry nodded – 'I engraved a message on the watch and gave it to him as a gift.'

'And the message was?'

'Simple. *To Joseph with all our love.*'

'Our?'

'Inspector, my wife and child might have died but, as I told your sergeant, I never ceased to love them or to feel that my family remained with me. Had my wife lived, the watch would have been given with love from us both. Why should that change simply because she has already passed on?'

Henry thought about it but could come up with no answer. His usual resort of asking himself what Mickey would have said also failed him and so he said nothing for a while. Instead, the two men sat quietly, listening to the hum of conversation all around them, the chink of cups, the bursts of laughter.

Henry was suddenly aware of just how tired he felt, how utterly exhausted. He sorted through his mental file for something to say. 'This might seem like an odd question,' he ventured, 'but what was so important about Joseph's hat? Why would he be sure to take his hat, even when he left his suitcase behind?'

Abraham stared at him, as though this was the strangest question in the world. 'Can I get you more tea? You are sure you do not want to eat – the food is cheap here.'

'I want nothing, thank you. My question seems to have taken you by surprise.'

'It's an odd question to ask. I suppose, it is because a young man should not be seen without his hat, any more than a lady without her gloves. And' – he managed a half laugh – 'we Jews are attached to our headwear.'

'And yet he removed his hat and put it on the luggage rack alongside the suitcase. When he left the train, he made certain to pick up his hat. He could just as easily have reached for both but he did not. We know that there was nothing of value in the suitcase apart from a ten-shilling note, but he made certain to take his hat. Besides,' he added, 'you and Joseph are not Hassidic or Sephardic Jews who cover their heads at all times, and as far as I can tell, you do not even wear the *kippah* outside of religious observances.'

'A hat is just a hat. How should I know why he took his hat?'

'There is no reason,' Henry admitted. 'I'm just reminded of the people whose hats matter to them. Perhaps I am just overtired,' he admitted. 'And when I'm overtired, small things bother me.'

Abraham laughed and seemed to relax. 'I understand that all too well,' he said. 'The body wishes to relax and sleep, and the brain, the brain tugs at minor sins, at small problems, at memories you put aside years ago but that suddenly come back to haunt you in the middle of the night.'

'There was an old man who lived in the village where I grew up,' Henry said. 'He had a beautiful garden, and when he went out to visit other gardens, he would quietly take cuttings and conceal them in the band inside his hat until he had them home, and then he would put them into clay pots, and nine times out of ten they would grow for him. I came to realize that this process of stealing and concealment and smuggling was part of his process of getting something to grow. He could have asked for cuttings; nobody would have denied him, and everybody knew what he did – it was a standing joke. But nevertheless he did this. He purloined his little bit of plant material and concealed it in his hat, and he took it home and made it grow. And I know of others who hide money in their hats – blades, even.'

'Joseph just kept his head in his,' Abraham said dryly. He finished his tea and looked around. 'Do you like music?

The concert will begin in only five minutes or so. It is Mozart. I'm sure you would enjoy it.'

'I think it is a little late to buy a ticket.'

'There are always spare tickets. Anyway, if they have sold out, they still allow people to stand at the back. We believe that music is important, as important as food and tea and talk and a place to be.'

'We?'

'People who come here. The Workers' Circle welcomes all. You look around and you will see Jews like me; some of the old men here fought the Bolsheviks and still others fought against the Tsar. You will find anarchists and idealists and nihilists, and those who simply like to play chess or dominoes. You see that old man over there, reading *Freiheit*? In his mind he is no doubt plotting his next attack with Molotov cocktails and heavy sticks. If you ask, he will show you his scars.

'Or they come just to listen to the music. Joseph used to come just to listen to the music. But the problem with being here is that others see that you are here and they make an assessment of you. How can you be of use? You have come here tonight, wondering how I could be of use, and I understand that it is of use to me too, but you see what I mean.'

'I'm not sure that I do,' Henry said. 'I want to find out who killed your nephew and you want that, too. His family need to know that.'

Abraham shook his head. 'His family know that he's dead. What else is there?'

'You don't want to know who killed him? I don't believe that.'

'Of course I do. The concert is about to begin,' Abraham said. He picked his coat off the back of the chair and collected his hat from where he had laid it on the table. He turned the hat so that the inside could be seen by Henry. 'Nothing in my hat,' he said. 'But I will think about Joseph and about his hat. And if I think of anything worth telling, then I will tell you.'

The room was emptying now as people moved through into the hall. Henry could hear a string quartet tuning up, and as he rose to leave and glanced through the door, he could see that the room would probably hold about 200 people and that it was already filling up. He found he was slightly put out that Abraham had not repeated his invitation to join him, and he was also curious now. He had said something that had unsettled Abraham, but now was not the time to push that, nor was this the place. But he had no doubt that he would hear from Abraham Levy in the next few days and he wondered what it was that he was not being told.

Henry had been aware that someone was following him ever since he left Alie Street. As he turned the corner, he glanced back but could see no one in the shadows. It was a wet Sunday evening and there were few people around; most of those who had been going anywhere had already gone, and the majority were tucked up for the night, curtains closed and lights dimmed. He hunched deeper into his coat and turned up the collar against the cold. As he did so, he heard a sudden rush of footsteps and turned as a man hurtled into him, light glinting off the blade in his hand.

Instinctively, Henry dropped his weight, turned his body and blocked the man's arm with his own, pushing back with his shoulder and turning on his heel so that he threw his assailant off balance. The man staggered back, then turned tail and ran. Henry gave chase, but the knifeman had the advantage – he knew this network of streets and tiny back alleys and no doubt hoped to lead Henry away and perhaps even turn on him again. But Henry was fast, long-limbed and fit, and his would-be assailant had not made it a hundred yards before he was pushed to the ground, his knife hand bashed against a kerb stone and his arms twisted behind his back. Henry knelt on the man's back while he retrieved the knife and tucked it into his own pocket. 'Consider yourself arrested.'

The man had begun to blabber. 'I never meant it, sir, but you come out of that place and I thought you were one of them Jew boys.'

'And what if I had been? Is it not also against the law to roll a Jew?' He hauled the man to his feet. 'There's a difference under the law, is there? I think you'll find there *is* a difference under the law when you attack a policeman.'

Arms firmly twisted behind his back, Henry walked the man

to the main thoroughfare and there found a constable and handed his charge over. His crime, attacking a police officer with a knife. He handed the knife over, too.

The constable enquired as to whether the chief inspector would be coming back with them. Henry declined. 'Put him in a cell overnight. I'll deal with it in the morning. I don't see why I should spoil my evening for the likes of him.'

He watched as the constable took his assailant away and then walked thoughtfully back to his flat. Was this just something random? Despite what the man had said, Henry wasn't so sure. But it could wait till morning. What he had told Abraham was the truth: he was dog-tired and he needed a night's sleep. He hoped that Abraham would be wrong and that the stupid little details and worries that attack the mind in the early hours of the morning would stay quiet.

EIGHTEEN

Despite having been voluble the night before, the man who had attacked Henry had now decided upon silence. He'd been fed and watered, Mickey was told, but had refused to speak to anyone and now, sitting across the table from Mickey, the man was still declining to be drawn.

He was small but wiry, not frail. Bones held together with steel cables. Mickey recalled Henry's comment that when he had held the man down, he had felt strength in his back and arms that belied his leanness.

'You were sent to attack my boss?'

The man stared at the table.

'Or was it happenstance? Does Clem Atkins know that you are poaching on his territory?'

A slight flicker as the man lifted his eyes and then lowered them again told Mickey that he had landed on the truth.

'So, someone sent you to make trouble on Atkins' patch. Now, I'm wondering who that might be . . . A long list of possibilities, I would imagine, wishing to test Atkins' nerve and his security.'

A slight shift in his seat this time.

Mickey got up and paced, his steps eventually bringing him up behind the man. Mickey did not touch him but simply paused behind the chair before moving on. 'I don't imagine your master will be impressed,' he said. 'You lie in wait, hoping for a Jew, and instead you catch yourself a policeman.'

He continued to pace with slow, steady steps, as though merely taking a pleasant walk, until once more he stood behind the man. Both the man's hands were visible on the tabletop. The wrist Henry had smashed against the kerb stone was bruised and swollen. Without warning, Mickey reached for it, pressed his finger and thumb into the wrist, separating bone. The man yelped in pain, half leapt from his chair. Mickey placed his other hand on the man's shoulder and pressed him back into his seat.

'So you do have a voice,' Mickey said. 'You know it's a little late to play the mute with me. I'm told you spoke readily enough last night.'

He released the wrist and the man hugged it tightly to his chest. 'I got nothing t' say to yer.'

Mickey sighed, bored now. 'I'm guessing here,' he said, 'but my guess is that your affiliations are with the Elephant mob. One of yours was hurt and you came looking for revenge, but what the hell possessed you to come alone? Even the likes of you, someone with the most limited intelligence, must recognize the stupidity of that?'

There was a knock at the door and a constable appeared, carrying a fingerprint card.

'Ah, so we have a name,' he said. 'Tommy Price. Robbery with threats, housebreaking, even a spot of dipping. I'd never have reckoned you quick enough to pick pockets.'

He handed the card back to the constable. 'Have him charged,' he said, 'and have the word put out that we have Tommy Price in custody and that he's squealing like a little girl.'

NINETEEN

A ddie remembered the first time they had been together in the small, rundown hotel close to the railway station, on a Sunday afternoon, just a few weeks after they first met. She had a cheap dress ring that she had slipped on to her wedding finger, turning the stone to the inside of her hand. Had anyone cast a quick glance, she could indeed be Mrs Astor. She had met him there, his fiancée's family having left him at the station in the expectation that he would get the train. He had indeed boarded the train and walked the length of it, then disembarked and watched as his future relatives had left the station. He and Addie had walked to the hotel and gone in together, his suitcase lending a touch of authenticity to the story that they would be leaving Lincoln in the morning, and then they had asked about cheap places to eat. Not everywhere had a Sunday licence, but there were a few pubs close to the station that catered for travellers. He had been nervous in the little restaurant, tucked away in a side street, just in case someone he happened to know should come to the door – even though he knew that was so unlikely as to be impossible. And then they had returned nervously to the hotel, expecting to be challenged, but they had just been handed the key and wished a good evening.

Joseph was not as innocent as his family had believed, and this was not his first time with a woman, but even so he had found that his experience was distinctly lacking, and she knew that she had been a revelation to him. Afterwards they had lain together, not talking, light from the street lamp seeping in through a gap between the curtains and filtering through the thin blue fabric.

'I don't want to go home,' Joseph had said.

She had pressed closer to him. He was so skinny that she could feel the bones of his ribs. He had eaten well earlier in the evening, and she supposed he was just one of those people *who burnt energy through sheer nervousness and never seemed to put on an ounce of spare flesh.*

'Then don't go. We can go away together.'

'I have no money.'

'Money can always be got. There are always those with money that can be relieved of it.'

'I can't do that.'

'You can, if you're desperate enough.'

'I can find work.'

Addie had sighed and turned on her back. The truth was, she had thought, there was nothing either of them could do. They were imprisoned where they were, like wasps in a trap. They had flown in and now they beat their wings against the glass but could not get out.

'Do you love her?'

'Not like I love you. Do you love him?'

Addie had shaken her head. 'He's a bastard,' she had said. 'I hate him. Sometimes I think I'd like to stick a knife between his ribs.'

'What stops you?'

She had lifted her head to look at him. The question had been so unexpected. 'I don't know if I could do it. Or if I did, I don't know if I could do it right. What if I didn't kill him and he told on me. I'd hang.'

'You could leave him. He doesn't own you. You're not married to him. You don't owe him anything.'

'Oh, no? Really? And if I left him, what then? Where would I go?'

'You said money could always be got.' He had returned her words to her and it had hurt more than a knife between the ribs.

'Not on my own.' She had sat on the edge of the bed, her back to him, angry that he should understand so little.

'Addie, come lie down; you'll get cold.'

Sighing, she did lie down, but there had been a distance between them now and a cold that she knew would never thaw; it had been chilling inside her for far too long.

'And where the hell have you been?'

'What's it to you?'

He came over and twined his fingers in her hair and then pulled tight. Addie gasped. 'You're hurting me.'

'I said, where have you been?' He sniffed her as though sensing out the deceit . . . and the sex. 'And who is it this time? I hope he's paying bloody well.'

'I don't know what you mean.'

His hand tightened further in her hair and the second gripped just below her right breast, fingers digging in between her ribs, his hand vice-like. Addie gasped in pain. He never bruised her where it would show, but he knew exactly what to do to hurt her most. Abruptly, he let go and gave her a shove, and she fell backwards on to the bed. His hands moved to the buttons on his trousers and he shoved her skirt up around her hips.

Addie had long since learned not to tell him no.

TWENTY

Information trickled in, reports of interviews and enquiries put out to pawnbrokers, but there was as yet nothing useful. More than a month after Joseph Levy disappeared, the most that could be said was that his body had been found and the young man buried.

Henry had thought carefully about his conversation with Abraham Levy and the subtle change in tone he had observed. Previously, all that Abraham could think about was where his nephew might be and how he and his family could make things right for the young man by finding and bringing him home – dead or alive.

Something had happened that Henry was not privy to, but the case had stalled and other investigations now took his time, and he had not found an opportunity to return to question the clockmaker further.

He always found waiting difficult, and knowing that he must wait on other people gathering information made him restless. Henry immersed himself in other problems and a week had passed since the man had attacked him with the knife and he had spoken to Abraham Levy.

Mickey had been making his way home after a rare Sunday afternoon with friends when he found himself waylaid.

'I hear your boss had a touch of trouble the other night?' Clem Atkins blocked the pavement, two of his lieutenants behind him. 'Fancy a drink?'

'Right now I'm on my way somewhere, so I'll have to say no,' Mickey told him. 'One of yours, was he?'

Atkins laughed. 'Mine know a copper when they see one. I hear he got mistaken for one of our Hebrew brethren. Understandable, I suppose, if he decides to go where their kind congregates?'

'The Workers' Circle is open to all,' Mickey objected mildly.

'Started by Jews, though, weren't it? What did they call it – something German-sounding? Had the sense to change it when the war happened. I suppose that means they've got some nous.'

'The *Arbeiter Ring*,' Mickey confirmed, 'But it's been a Friendly Society since I don't know when. Open to all, as I understand it. The boss reckons there was a concert there last Sunday night.'

Atkins made no comment.

'You consider it fair game to attack Jews, then?' Mickey speculated.

'Me, I got nothing against the Jews. They keep out of my way and for the most part they only prey on their own kind. Especially the Russians in their black coats. Con their own, so why should *I* bother?'

'And the man who attacked Chief Inspector Johnstone? You know him?'

'Know him for a fool. And a bigger fool if he comes back this way.' Atkins leaned closer to Mickey. 'You can pass that on.'

'I'll be sure to,' Mickey said.

Atkins stepped aside, and he and his boys crossed over the road and headed back in the direction of Commercial Street. Mickey watched them thoughtfully, not quite sure what the encounter had really been about. His route home was well known, as was his tendency to walk in all but the foulest of weathers, when he might take the omnibus part of the way or scrounge a lift home with one of the official drivers. Walking home through the likes of Clem Atkins' territory was, some said, foolhardy. Continuing to live in the same streets as those who had little concern for the police's version of law and order attracted the same verdict, but Mickey had grown up in these streets, was comfortable with his neighbours and had no intention of changing his habits – and, more to the point, he was accessible this way to those who would not go near a police station but who still wanted to be able to pass on the occasional tip-off or ask for a bit of legal advice without attracting too much attention. Everyone and his dog chatted to Mickey. Chats of a more

substantial nature therefore often passed beneath the notice
of the likes of Clem Atkins.

So, Mickey thought, *what does he want me to know?* That
he wasn't in any way responsible for the attack on Henry?
Certainly. That if it had been one of his men, Henry might
not have got off so lightly? Possibly. That he doesn't hate the
Jews? Why is that little idea suddenly so pressing? Is he
anticipating trouble that way? Again, possibly.

He thought of Atkins' reference to the so-called black coats
and the cons he claimed were perpetrated within that community. He knew what Atkins was referring to when he spoke of
the black coats. The Orthodox Hassidic community, marked
out by their appearance, had been subject to some particularly
focused cons. Theirs was a community that *did* deal in
diamonds; they were currency, portable and easily hidden, and
also difficult to identify as genuine if you didn't have the
expertise.

In a community where anyone who looked like you, seemed
to hold the same beliefs or belonged to the same culture was
considered a brother, it was easy to take advantage – and for
men like Atkins to sneer at naivety.

What typically happened was that a friendly-seeming
stranger would stop a likely target in the streets. He would
plead that he was new to the area, seeking to raise some
money. He had diamonds that he wished to sell. If his new
acquaintance could recommend a dealer, then he would
gladly sell a diamond or two at a bargain price in gratitude
for the deal. He would then, likely as not, take out a little
bag and tip a handful of shiny stones, just to prove good
intent.

Often the new friends would go together to one of the
many dealers and the one genuine diamond would be shown
to the dealer. An offer would be made, but the seller suddenly
needed more time to think about it.

On leaving the store, the would-be diamond seller would
confide to his 'friend' that he had, on second thoughts, decided
he would rather sell to the man who had shown him kindness.
At a reduced price. No, at a bargain price.

He couldn't raise the money on his own? Not to worry, let

him find friends with whom to share the good fortune; after all, did the dealer not say that the diamond he had seen was of top quality?

Sometimes the bait was taken, sometimes not, but the chances, Mickey knew from the instances that made it to the courts, were even, if not better. The 'diamonds' would be bought and the delighted buyers would, often as not, go to the same dealer who had verified the one genuine stone in the collection to cash in their good fortune, only to be told that they had bought paste or even a handful of glass.

Mickey had often wondered how such an obvious con could keep on running, month on month, year on year. How could people not know, not have heard? But the answer was, of course, that many instances went unreported. Embarrassment can overpower good sense – especially in a man of otherwise good judgement. And there was suspicion of the police, of law and order that was still alien and not something the community yet owned, even for the second or even third generation.

One thing was certain: Clem Atkins had gone out of his way and almost off his patch to encounter Mickey on his way home, which meant that something was up or about to be.

Atkins was rattled. Of that much Mickey was certain. But rattled about what? Mickey thought again about the kid from the Elephant mob who'd been beaten and then so badly cut up. Was the Elephant mob a threat? A bigger threat than Atkins – or Mickey, for that matter – had reckoned. And what did they have to do with the Jewish community on Atkins' patch? The Yids had never been allied to the Elephants, and from what Mickey knew of the rival gangs, that was never likely to happen. Chalk and cheese – but with a lot more prejudice. So had Mickey got it wrong? Was *Atkins* looking for an alliance of some sort? Something that would strengthen his hand? Thinking of Atkins in alliance with either the Elephant mob or the Yids was laughable in Mickey's book, but Sabini was still on the scene, wasn't he? Or at least if he wasn't on the scene, he was hiding in the wings. So was Atkins planning some kind of alliance with him? Was Atkins looking to expand his territory?

Whichever way you looked at it, someone was going to suffer, Mickey thought. And likely there'd be police breaking heads in the midst of it and getting theirs broken in return.

TWENTY-ONE

*I*t was more than three weeks before she saw him again. *He had arrived on the Friday evening but was not due to join his fiancée's family until Saturday. He had told her that he should not be travelling, that he should be celebrating the Sabbath with his own family. He had told his father he was going to join his future in-laws and would arrive before sunset.*

'So you're lying to everyone now,' she had said.

'Everyone except you. I wouldn't lie to you.'

They had returned to the same hotel and gone out to eat, even though she could tell he was feeling guilty because this was not the way he should be doing things. Childhood, adolescence, young adulthood, from sunset on Friday, things had been special, had been family, had been faith, and now she was taking him away from all of that, and for that she felt guilty, too.

He had seen the bruises, of course. Gus had not ceased to punish her, to keep her in line, and she knew how much she was risking in defying him.

'He did this to you?'

'It doesn't matter.'

'It matters and I won't let him do it again.'

She had laughed. 'So what are you going to do? Thump him? He'd break you up and use you for kindling.'

He had looked away, embarrassed at the truth of it. 'I've got a way for us to be together,' he had said. 'A way of getting money.'

'What do you mean?'

'What I say. I've got a way of making us some money. Like you said, there is always money to be had and there are always those who have it and from whom it can be taken.'

She had looked aghast. 'You'd steal for me?'

'I already have.'

'I don't understand. What do you mean? Joseph, don't play games with me.'

'I'm not. I have a way to get money.'

'But it's not your money, is it?'

'No, but it will be. Soon.'

'I don't understand.'

'You don't need to understand. When I tell you, you just have to meet me on the train. Just go away with me.'

'I can't. He'll kill me.'

'Trust me, he won't find you.'

For an hour or so she had allowed herself to believe. But by morning she had known that this could not be true; there was no escape for either of them. She had thought again about wings beating against the glass, until eventually the wasp was dead, exhausted, bruised, broken.

She had not expected him to come back, even though she had left messages in the usual places, but he had come back, and had forgiven her for her lack of faith. Twice more they had met in the same little hotel, and finally she had agreed to go away with him.

'You don't know me,' she had argued. 'We have spent a scant few hours together. Is that enough for you to decide you want me?'

He had stroked her arm, his fingers almost too gentle. 'I've known from the very beginning,' he had said, and Addie had laughed, wanting to believe him but knowing that he was lying to himself. He didn't know her at all; the Addie he saw was an invention born of a few snatched and very precious hours. She found it hard to believe that his vision would survive the harsh light of real life. But sometimes, when she lay beside him as he slept, she had wanted to believe.

'I have money,' he had said again. 'I will have, after this weekend.'

She had tried to press him about the source of his wealth, about what he meant; she had come to the conclusion that something must be happening with his in-laws and that perhaps the money or whatever was theirs and he was carrying it back to London for some reason.

'*Meet me on the train. I will look after you. I promise I will look after you.*'

Addie had no doubt that he would have done, that he meant it. But some people are not destined to have any luck, and Addie knew she had pushed hers to breaking point. When she left the hotel with Joseph, and after they had parted and she had walked down a side street away from him, she was grabbed by the throat and pushed against a wall. '*Him!*' Gus was more furious at her choice than he was at her betrayal. '*You've been screwing him?*'

And that was it. He made her tell him everything that Joseph had said, and when Sunday came, he told her, '*You get on that train and you play your part and then you get him off that train and I will deal with the rest.*'

And Addie got on the train and she smiled and pretended to be a stranger, as she and Joseph had agreed – Joseph still afraid that someone who knew his fiancée's family might chance to see him – and then she got off the train as Gus had ordered and Joseph, puzzled and concerned, stared out of the train window, trying to understand what she was up to. And then, seeing Gus standing on the platform, arguing with her, Joseph followed, just as Gus had planned.

He rushed over to her, hand outstretched to draw her back. '*Addie, leave him. Come, get back on the train. We can tell the guard that you're in trouble.*'

But she hung back, uncertain what to do, not believing that she could really get away – not believing that she really deserved to get away.

She still did not believe that Gus had intended to kill. All Joseph had to do was hand the money over and that would have been that. He had sworn to Addie that he'd have money, enough so they could run away, and yet when it came to it . . .

All he had to do was hand it over. She would have gone with Gus. They would have gone on their way. She would never have seen Joseph again, but they would all have survived. But Joseph must have lied to her. He refused to hand over the money, and when they searched him, it turned out he had no *money. He had lied to her when he had told her that he'd make it possible for them to go away. Joseph had lied; he was just another con artist, getting what he wanted by spinning a line, and she had fallen for it.*

Now Joseph was dead and Addie's heart was broken.

TWENTY-TWO

Henry had been waylaid by Albert, which meant that the two of them had withdrawn to Albert's study and imbibed before he got the chance to go up and see Cynthia.

'How was your trip?'

'Dismal. No, that's not fair; Cynthia showed me a wonderful time. But then we had to turn to business and things went downhill with the rapidity of a bobsleigh. I think I'm done with business, Henry. I think I'll throw in the towel and become an art dealer instead.'

Henry was bemused. Albert knew nothing about art. Henry said so.

'I think that's the point, old chap. The world I know about is falling apart around my ears; I may as well embark upon an adventure. Besides, if I wanted to become an art dealer, I'd just give the whole kit and caboodle over to that sister of yours; likely she'd make more sense of it than I ever could. She at least has an eye.'

He looked more depressed than Henry had ever seen him. Albert was naturally an upbeat sort of person, not given to moods of introspection and certainly not to misery.

'Cynthia said you are withdrawing from Germany.'

'Not much choice. The way I see it, things can only get worse.' He sighed. 'I'll speak to you man to man, Henry – there are things I didn't want to worry your sister with. Cynthia has a good head on her shoulders, but she can't be expected to take on everything, not everything that's in a man's world. Women are not cut out for such unpleasantness.'

Henry raised an eyebrow, wondering how much Albert had had to drink before he had arrived. He decided, however, that if his brother-in-law was upset about something, he should let him tell his story in his own rambling way.

'I had a couple of private meetings with some chaps I

know. Consensus is that nationalism's on the rise and Germany is about to start re-arming.'

Whatever Henry had anticipated, it wasn't that. 'But they are bound by international law not to do that.'

'And what are the inspectors going to do to stop them? And what has anyone done to stop them so far? The Americans are selling steel and components, and so are we. True, we are not selling them guns, but we are doing everything but. Mark my words, Henry, this means trouble. And I don't mean just local trouble.'

Albert shook himself and got a second measure of the whisky. Henry still hadn't finished his. 'You're really worried, aren't you?' he said.

'I confess I am, old man. And I'll tell you this for nothing: I would ship those boys of mine as far away as I need to, just to keep them out of it. There will be war, Henry – maybe not in the next few years, but it will come.'

Henry said nothing. It was not a conversation he wanted to have. It was not a thought he wanted to have. Albert must have realized this, the two of them knowing each other well by now, because he sat down and raised his glass. 'To Cynthia.'

'To Cynthia,' Henry echoed.

'And now console me by telling me about these common or garden murders that you get yourself involved in,' Albert said. 'At least you secm to solve the buggers.'

An hour later Henry made his way upstairs to Cynthia's little sitting room. The bright room, with its yellow silk wallpaper, was always cheerful, and the fire burning in the grate made it warm and cosy. Malina was also there, with a work basket. She was busy darning stockings, reinforcing the heels before they had a chance to run. Henry remembered Cynthia and his mother doing the same. Cynthia was lounging in an easy chair with her feet up on a footstool, her shoes kicked off, glass in hand. A slight flush in her cheeks told Henry that this was not her first drink. She set the glass down and came over to embrace him and kissed him on the cheek. 'So glad to be home and even gladder to see you.'

'I should go,' Malina said. 'Leave the two of you to talk.'

Henry would have welcomed that, but Cynthia waved her back into the chair. 'Don't be silly. Henry, would you like a drink or have you had enough with Albert?'

She poured him one anyway and then flopped back down into her chair and lifted her feet once more on to the footstool. 'If I go nowhere else this year, I shall be very happy. Travel is all well and good, but it's so nice to be home.'

'Albert seems unusually morose.'

'Good. Not wishing him to be unhappy, but a little reality will benefit him. Anyway, let's not talk about that. How are you, my dear? What's been happening in London since I've been gone?'

For a little while they talked about nothing in particular. Malina finished darning and put the stockings away in the work basket.

'I remember you once stole a pair of stockings,' he said.

Cynthia gaped at him and then laughed. 'Oh my goodness, yes, I did.'

'You?' Malina was clearly scandalized.

'A young woman who wants to look respectable cannot go bare-legged. I had managed to find myself a better job, but the only pair of stockings I had were more darn than stocking, and I was desperate to make a good impression. I was, what, seventeen, but this was my first really good chance and I so much wanted to look right for it. I'd only got the one decent dress and one that would do at a push, but stockings – oh, for goodness' sake, stockings. I'd never stolen anything in my life before – well, almost nothing, but that's another story. But, anyway, I did – I stole a pair of stockings from the little shop next to the drapers. I felt so guilty that the first wages I got, I went and bought a pair just to try to make it up.'

Malina was torn between scandal and admiration. 'You've come a long way,' she said.

'The further to fall,' Cynthia told her. 'But no, we're not going to fall. I've already made sure of that and I will continue to do so. So, how's work? What ghastly murders are you involved in now?'

'One,' Henry said. 'And this one is as sad as it is ghastly. A young man, a Jew, travelling from Lincoln to London after seeing his fiancée. It seems he got off the train in order to help a young woman who was having an argument – perhaps a rather violent altercation with a man whom she probably knew. It's likely that our victim went to try to help – that somehow he left the station with these people and ended up dead. His body was missing for three weeks, so you can imagine the state of it when it was returned to his family. As I say, sad and ghastly.'

'Very hard on the family, if he was missing all that time,' Malina said. 'I think the Hebrews have stricter funeral rites, don't they?'

'Apparently so. His uncle came to us when the young man went missing – I'd met him briefly on a previous investigation – and he was desperately upset that the boy could not be found. And if he was dead, that he could not be given the proper rights of burial.' He glanced at his watch. 'I should be going.'

'It's Sunday. Time for relaxing. Stay a little longer.'

He hesitated and then settled back. 'Just a little longer, then.'

'Only one disadvantage in being back,' Cynthia said. 'I don't have an excuse for missing Bunty Avery's party.'

'And who on earth is Bunty Avery?'

'Old money, but married a Yank. A millionaire. Old enough money on her side that she has entrée into all the best houses, and her parties are famous for mixing those old names with the new money their daughters might just get their hands on, should they accept the right ring. I do so hate them.'

'Why?' Henry asked. Generally, his sister liked a good party.

'Because we are neither old money nor American, and you know as well as I do that most of the old families will only give me the time of day if we happen to be on the same charity board – and that's because they want a donation. Bunty is a game girl, and her husband is a nice enough fellow, but I spend the entire evening trying to navigate. Who will speak to me, and who is likely to cut me dead? After all, my dear, I'm the lowest of the low: a little girl from the typing pool who managed to snag a man who, by rights, should have been snagged by one of their more respectable daughters. They tolerate men, Henry – men who happen to have made money through trade. They do not tolerate jumped-up little secretaries.'

'I thought you were typing pool,' Henry joked. Actually, his sister had been a very efficient and well-regarded personal assistant to Albert's father, her knowledge of languages and her ability to deal with difficult customers something the old man had really valued. But he knew just what she was up against.

'You could give Malina a wig and dress her up in your fake emeralds,' Henry joked.

'Oh, no. If I'm going, I want to wear the real ones,' Malina objected.

'Not even *I* wear the real ones. No one notices the difference anyway, and I get nervous wearing that amount of money round my neck. No, good pastes are far better.'

'And you wonder why they don't take you for a lady.'

Cynthia scooped a half-melted chunk of ice from her drink and threw it at him. 'You'd be lucky to find a genuine stone on any of them,' she said. 'Crumbling estates and death duties. Rotten plumbing. That's all their airs and graces get them. I'm happy with my copious hot water and fake emeralds.'

Henry left just as the blue enamel clock on Cynthia's mantelpiece was striking nine. He had intended to go home, but some impulse had him hailing a taxi and heading for the Workers' Circle, wondering if Abraham Levy might be there. The conversation they had had the week before still preyed on Henry's mind, nagged at him in spare moments, and he wanted to make sense of it.

The taxi dropped him at the end of the street where he'd been attacked on the previous Sunday night. His assailant had appeared before the magistrate, pleaded guilty and was now locked safely away, but he had still refused to talk to anyone beyond his statement that he'd not known Henry was a policeman: *'He don't look like no copper.'*

Henry wasn't sure if he should be glad of that or not.

The Workers' Circle buzzed. There was no concert tonight, Henry was told as he collected his tea, and he wondered if that meant he should have tried Abraham at home instead.

Then he spotted his man, sitting in a corner and playing what looked to be a serious game of chess. Not wanting to interrupt, Henry took a seat close by. Abraham acknowledged him with a glance, but his focus otherwise never shifted from the game. Henry, a reasonable player, judged both opponents to be good, and it seemed others thought so, too. He realized that an interested crowd had gathered, keeping a discreet distance, as Henry himself had done, but nonetheless discussing the game in whispers. Henry listened to the mix of accents and languages. He identified Russian, Armenian, Italian and East London. And something that was not quite German. Like most coppers who'd walked their first beats in the East End, he had picked up a smattering of Yiddish and could discern, in a half-dozen other languages, whether he was being insulted or offered refreshment – each was equally likely, in Henry's experience – but he often wished he had Cynthia's faculty for languages.

She would enjoy this place, he thought. If, when this investigation was over, he was still on speaking terms with Abraham – and Henry knew, also from uncomfortable experience, that not everyone wanted the company of a policeman when their immediate need had been satisfied – he would bring Cynthia to meet Abraham Levy. They would get along, he thought.

The game of chess seemed to be drawing to a close. Henry could not see how Abraham's opponent could avoid check and mate within the next couple of moves, but the player obviously had other ideas. He moved his knight to queen's bishop four and then sat back with a satisfied look. Abraham made a counter-play, but Henry had been right. Checkmate. Abraham's opponent reached out an old and bony finger and tipped his queen on to her side. A collective sigh from the spectators and they drifted away.

The clockmaker came over to join Henry. 'It is always a pleasure, but what brings you here?'

Now the question had been asked, Henry found that his response was difficult to frame. 'Last time I was here, I felt . . . Abraham, you have not told me everything. What is it that you didn't say? If it is pertinent to the enquiry, then I can't understand why you should hold something back.'

Abraham peered into his tea cup as though he might find an answer there. 'The dead are dead; it is the living that can be harmed. Nothing can hurt my nephew now and nothing will bring him back, but I sense . . . I have come to believe . . . that others might be harmed. My brother wishes me to leave well alone – he says that you and I have done enough – and I've no reason to go against his wishes.'

'Not even to bring justice to the dead?'

'Justice?' He waved a dismissive hand. 'And what is that? The boy is dead.'

Henry stared at him. 'What's going on? We've looked into the business and financial interests of the Goldmanns, and on the face of it the family has thrived through their own efforts and some good luck. Your brother also—'

'You have investigated my brother?' Abraham looked genuinely shocked.

'Of course we have. This is a murder investigation.'

'But Joseph died away from home.'

'Even so.'

'And what have you found? About my brother?' He sounded anxious, Henry thought. Not just indignant.

'And what could I have found?'

Abraham sighed. 'I need more tea.' He took Henry's cup without asking and filled both at the samovar. It seemed in that short trek across the crowded room, weaving between tables, that Abraham had come to a decision.

'On the day my nephew was buried, I was, of course, at my brother's house. He seemed strange. Angry almost. I asked why the Goldmanns would not be coming and he refused to say. I said that Rebecca had been Joseph's betrothed, that she should be at his funeral.'

'Joseph had confessed to being in love with someone else,' Henry told him.

Abraham sat back, clearly shocked. 'Ah,' he said. 'But who?'

'A young woman by the name of Adelaide. We have no second name, not yet, but we believe they met on the train and formed a relationship. I don't know how long they had been seeing one another, but it's likely that she was involved in his death.'

'How?' Abraham had grown pale. Clearly, he knew nothing at all about this, but perhaps it explained a great deal about his brother's behaviour and about why the Goldmanns had not been at the funeral. No doubt Rebecca's family had contacted his own and let Joseph's secret out.

Henry told him what they believed had taken place at Bardney and that this young woman was implicated in other crimes.

'I thought I knew him,' Abraham said sadly. 'But he told me nothing of this.'

'He told no one until that last visit when he confessed to his fiancée,' Henry assured him. 'No doubt you would have been his next port of call. He would have felt need of your help to break this news to his family.'

'But instead she led him to his death.' There was anger now. 'Some mischance, some bungled robbery – that I could accept. But that someone fooled Joseph, and misled him, caused him to misstep, and that he should have died as a result of that misstep – that is almost more than I can bear.'

He paused and nodded to himself. 'This, I think, explains my brother's attitude on the day of the burial. He talked about disgrace, about not wanting to bring dishonour to the family. At the time I could not understand how anything could over-write his grief. What else mattered? But if he felt his son had been so unwise, had betrayed trust, had made himself a fool . . . And, of course, he blamed me. Had the body not been found, had I not drawn your attention to this, then the Goldmanns would probably have kept quiet. That pain would not have been added. So he blamed me.'

Henry watched as Abraham worked this out, gave words to the pain he was feeling. He could understand how that reasoning would make sense but felt also that something more was nagging.

'As I understand it, close family remain together after a funeral. The community looks after the bereaved—'

'And we talk about our dead and slowly, oh so slowly, we come to a place where we can recall the good times.'

'And yet your brother wanted you to go.'

'I will admit that hurt. I've not spoken to him since then.

To be truthful, Inspector, I thought he might be keeping something else from me, but what you've said makes sense of his
behaviour. I am, I admit, still hurt by it – on my own behalf
and on Joseph's – but I can understand it.'

'And before I told you, what did you think could be wrong?'

Abraham hesitated. 'So many thoughts went through my
mind,' he admitted.

'Like what?'

Abraham shrugged. 'Fleeting thoughts, Inspector, brought
on because I could not understand his attitude or his anger.
But now I feel I do understand and I have to thank you for
that. The boy acted unwisely, involved himself with a young
woman his family could not possibly have approved of. That
is the cause of my brother's grief. Nothing more.'

He sat back, looking less pale now, seeming relieved as
though a massive weight had been lifted. 'Anyone can fall
in love unwisely,' Abraham said softly. 'Most do not die from
that lack of wisdom.'

They talked for a little longer, and Henry departed when
Abraham accepted the invitation for another game of chess.
He had felt the shift in mood that often happened as an
investigation closes for a family and they feel ready to move
on and dispense with the police presence that inevitably
permeates their existence for a time. At first most welcome
it; after a while it becomes an unpleasant reminder of failure
and loss, and the welcome dies as the family tries to move
on. Henry was rarely affected by such things, but he found
he felt it keenly now, as he watched Abraham settle down
to his game, and it took him a moment or two to understand
why he did.

It was because Abraham had been all too ready to accept
Henry's story as the complete explanation for the brother's
behaviour. It was a relief to him to think, *Ah, that's all it
was. Now I understand. I can put all of those other thoughts
aside. All those ideas that have kept me awake.*

And that readiness made Henry suspicious. What else had
Abraham really feared? Henry had lied about looking into the
elder Levy's business dealings. He had wanted the Goldmanns

looked at because he had sensed lies when he had interviewed them – maybe only lies to protect their family, but lies just the same – but the Levys had not come under suspicion. After all, Abraham had approached *him*, and Henry and Mickey had believed that the family must be united in their anxiety to find their missing member.

But now he wondered.

Henry still did not turn his steps for home. Instead, late as it was, he went to the central office at Scotland Yard and set things in motion. The Levys' finances and businesses were to be examined as carefully as the Goldmanns'.

TWENTY-THREE

A ddie's life had shifted on its very foundations that day.
  They had agreed that he would leave his suitcase
  on the train. They would get off at Peterborough, change
trains there, make the decision of where to go at that point.
It had sounded so adventurous, so romantic. Joseph would
leave his past behind him in the shape of that old battered
case and they would begin again.

'There'll be nothing in it that I need,' he had told her.
'I told you, dearest, I'm leaving all of that behind.' A symbolic
act, Joseph had said, and she had almost laughed at the
impracticality. Why leave good clothes and a useful valise
behind? But she had accepted this was something he needed
to do.

She had assumed, therefore, that whatever money he had
told her about would be carried in his pockets and not in
the suitcase – and she'd liked the idea of a mystery, left
for his family. A suitcase with no owner.

Somehow it had just added to the sense of adventure.

But then Gus had forced the story from her and she had
known that the adventure was over.

And now Joseph was dead and everything had gone back to
the way it was before – for Gus and Fred, at least.

Addie stared out through the rain-streaked window. The
boarding house they were staying in was close to the tidal
river in Boston, but the tide was out just now, and all she
could see was mud with a mean little streak of water and
boats tilted at angles against their moorings. Fred had gone
into town and Gus to make his report to the police – he was
still on ticket, having to sign in every couple of days, or
sometimes more frequently, depending on the mood of the
desk sergeant.

Not that it stopped him doing much. He'd sign the book,

hop on the train an hour or so later, get up to whatever he had planned and then be back on the train to sign, good as gold, the next day. Addie knew it was a common enough scenario. Addie herself had never been arrested, and Fred had only once been charged. His prints had been taken and he'd come up before the magistrate, but when a witness withdrew – after Gus had a word – the case had been dropped.

Gus had just been unlucky – so he said. Stupid, Addie would have contradicted if she'd dared, getting himself in a fight when a would-be victim had called him out. Gus had drawn a knife, failing to realize that the victim was not alone. A friend had punched Gus in the kidney and he'd gone down. Arrested for affray, they'd found wallets in his possession that were certainly not his own.

Now they used Addie as a distraction, Gus as back-up in case anything got heavy, Fred to dip. Light-fingered and quick, Fred was born to it.

The front door slammed and Addie heard Gus's heavy tread on the stairs.

'Right, Addie girl, time to get a shift on.'

'Fred's not back yet.'

'He'll meet us at the Angel.'

Addie nodded. The Angel was close to the market and a favourite with Fred. She collected her coat from the end of the bed and her bag from the dresser.

'And put a smile on it,' Gus told her. 'What punter wants to speak to a face like that?'

TWENTY-FOUR

By Tuesday results were beginning to come in from the enquiries Henry had put out. Names had been sent to the fingerprint bureau from the various divisional head-quarters and constabularies of those picked up for crimes involving theft from persons, and had been cross-checked against fingerprint records – should they become relevant later – and prison records. These had been followed up at the local level and a handful of possible suspects forwarded to central office. It was a laborious and time-consuming process but ultimately an efficient dragnet. It was not uncommon for dippers to work in groups or for them to be mixed up with 'women of the unfortunate classes', as DI Fred Cherrill of the fingerprint bureau liked to call them – known or suspected prostitutes.

Had the crimes been committed in London, Henry and Mickey would have had a ready list of persons to be brought in for questioning, but they were well off their own patch and dependent on the knowledge and record keeping of others – and Henry chafed against the inevitable delays.

So far the investigation into the Goldmanns' affairs had turned up nothing untoward, but it was clear that they had prospered greatly in the past four or five years: from owning one small shop they now had three – and the boarding house. The similarity to the Levys' circumstances was not lost on Henry.

'In the case of the Goldmanns,' Mickey pointed out, 'there is a solution to this.' He had been reading through a set of documents released to them by the Goldmanns' bank.

'Oh, what?'

'Both Mr Goldmann and his wife suffered bereavements. Her mother was a widow; she died leaving a good-sized house, and this was sold and ploughed back into the business. See?'

He laid the paperwork on the table and indicated sales documents, bills for conveyancing and deposits into the bank.

'Mr Goldmann had an elder brother who had previously inherited the family business, that being—'

'Don't tell me. The boarding house.'

'One and the same. They seem to have refurbished and extended into the next-door property and now employ a housekeeper – as they told us. So far, all very easily accounted for. Henry, it could be that the family – *both* families – were merely embarrassed by the young man's activities and that we misread this.'

Grudgingly, Henry had to agree. 'Clem Atkins suggested—'

'And since when has he been a reliable witness?'

Henry shrugged, conceding the point. Pressure was being applied by their superintendent to put the business aside. Sooner or later, whoever had done for Joseph Levy would be picked up – probably for something else – and would be brought to justice. The family were not pressing, the newspapers showed little interest in the death of a young Jew, and evidence and leads were both in short supply.

For now, the trail was cold.

By Wednesday, Henry was willing to concede that the death of Joseph Levy was not the most pressing business. But then a note arrived from a pawnbroker. He had a watch in his possession that he believed might have belonged to the dead man. Thinking about fingerprints, Henry fired off a telegram, warning the man not to touch it, just to set it aside; he and Mickey would travel up the following day. It was not lost on either of them that the pawnbroker was in Grimsby, where the Goldmanns had their boarding house.

They would take with them the fingerprint cards belonging to the suspects that local knowledge or the railway police had provided. The chance that the watch would still bear a relevant fingerprint was remote. But it was still a possibility.

'I'm having a pint with Phil Cox tonight,' Mickey told Henry. 'Would you care to come along?'

Henry shook his head. 'Works with Ted Greeno? He'll say more to you if you're alone.'

'Likely true.' Not everyone could cope with Henry. Phil was an old friend, a detective sergeant from another division.

'Have fun.' Henry smiled at his sergeant. 'See if Ted has any tips to offer.'

TWENTY-FIVE

D S Phil Cox had already been propping up the bar for some time before Mickey arrived. Like Mickey Hitchens, he was a solid man, one who liked his food, his beer, his horses and his wife, and, like his guvnor, Greeno, possessed an encyclopaedic knowledge of the street gangs, the race gangs, the con artists and every low life in between.

When Mickey arrived, Cox was deep in conversation with two men who drained their glasses and disappeared as soon as Mickey got the next round in.

'I'd have bought them a pint,' Mickey joked.

'Best not.' Cox's eyes laughed. 'So, what can I be doing for you, Mickey lad?'

Mickey plonked the beers on the table and shrugged out of his coat. 'The Elephant mob,' Mickey said. 'You can enlighten me about them. What they're up to, goading Clem Atkins, and what all this has to do with bloody Sabini.'

'Well, you don't want much, do you? Now, where shall I begin?'

'Maybe I should make a start,' Mickey said. 'Tell you what we know so far.'

Over a couple of pints, Mickey explained the background to the problem. The attack on the Elephant boy on Clem Atkins' territory and then the seemingly random attack on Henry Johnstone a few days later. 'That second could just be coincidence, of course. Henry was in the wrong place at the wrong time.'

'Inspector Johnstone's good at that.'

Mickey let that slide. 'And there's something else. Might be connected, probably not, but we've been looking into the murder of a young man by the name of Joseph Levy.'

'Nephew to Abraham Levy.' Cox nodded. 'Bit of a trouble-maker, the uncle.'

'I've heard that before.'

'He's something of an agitator. He tried to organize the sweatshop workers into a union. Stood on a soapbox outside the labour exchange until he got moved on sharpish. Spends too much time at that place on Alie Street.'

'The Workers' Circle.'

'A favoured haunt of the East End tourists, yes.'

Mickey snorted. He had no liking for the people Cox referred to. Middle-class and even rich punters who paid for tours of the poorer streets, liked the adventure of slumming it in places like Alie Street or listening to the yarns told by some old timer in Charlie Brown's pub in the East India Docks. They put money in the hat, listened to a talk on the perils of drink and went on their way feeling virtuous. And often much lighter in the pocket than they expected.

'That didn't work out so well,' Mickey commented.

'Indeed not. Union labour is the first to get chucked when there's a downturn – and in the sweatshops that's every other week. The machinists get paid their thirty bob a week, do their sixty, seventy hours, take themselves off home. Doesn't leave much time or energy for a lot else. Mr Levy shouts a lot, but I hear he's been quiet of late. Someone threatened to break his hands and a clockmaker's not much use to anyone without use of his fingers.'

'Who threatened?'

'Josiah Bailey. Or one of his mob, anyway. I don't imagine Atkins would be any softer, but from what I hear, Levy's kept his head down and minded his own business of late. I had a little chat one time with Long Hymie – remember him? Pickpocket, added a sideline as an epileptic, close to Christmastime when the crowds could be counted on?'

'I know Hymie; don't recall him pulling that particular con. Never reckoned he'd be that good an actor.'

'What acting skill does it take to lie on the floor and shake? Bit of soap in the mouth for effect and you've got the full sideshow. And it always gets to me how many of our solid citizens get trimmed.'

'People get conned for two reasons,' Mickey said. 'Because they're greedy or because they mean too well and get taken advantage of. Know anything about the family?'

'What, Ben Levy and his lot? Nothing significant. Why?'
'Just asking.'

'He likes a flutter. Don't do too badly at it either.'

'Benjamin Levy? The brother?' Mickey was surprised.

'Owns the jeweller's shops. Yes. I don't think that wife of his approves, but I've run into him a time or two, passed on a tip a time or two, in fact. He knows his form.'

'Interesting.' Mickey finished his pint and went back to the bar to get two more in.

'So, the Elephant mob,' he said, coming back and setting the glasses on the table. 'And this conversation you had with Long Hymie.'

'I'll get to him in a minute. The Elephants have been unusually quiet and thin on the ground. Diamond Annie's been off somewhere and no one's saying where, and the boys have been playing things very close to their chests. Crime is down on their patch, if you can believe that, but what concerns me more is that the rump end of the Bessarabian mob seems keen to do business with your Mr Atkins, and, well, I don't much like it when I hear about that sort of potential dalliance between Atkins and the Tigers. I don't imagine the Odessans or the Elephants would welcome the development either.'

'I thought the Tigers were finished,' Mickey said.

'And so they were. So they *are* if we're talking about the grandfathers, but there's talk of young bloods picking up the torch.'

Mickey absorbed that. 'And Sabini? I hear he's back on the scene.'

'You think he ever left? But no, I hear he's lurking. And that brings me back to Long Hymie. We pulled him in one day, usual sweep of dippers and cons at Chepstow.'

'Chepstow? That's not on his usual patch.'

'Took a day trip by train. Whole shebang apparently decided they wanted a change of scene. Anyway, Ted Greeno took him aside and advised him that he might walk away quietly in time to use his return ticket, should he have anything useful to say. Old Hymie is of the opinion that while Bailey might have been happy just to maintain his rights to territory, Atkins has plans for a bigger presence. That our old friend Sabini might be relied upon to provide the foot soldiers for such an expansion.'

'And is Greeno taking this seriously?'

'Ted takes everything with a large pinch of salt, even bigger one of pepper, but he considers it worth keeping in mind.'

'And Diamond Annie and the Elephant boys will be wanting to keep an eye.'

'Among others, I would suppose,' Cox agreed.

'So,' Mickey pursued, 'if all is quiet on their patch and most of the Elephants seem to have gone to ground, what do we think they are concerned with? Two have been sussed on Atkins' patch. You're thinking they're more than keeping an eye?'

'Sitting in the Charlie Brown. Playing dominoes in the Workers, drinking in a local pub that gets busy enough that a stranger won't stand out, especially if he's been driving a van and looks like a delivery man.'

'And to what end? We want no more street battles, Phil. There's enough bodies poisoning the Thames as it is. And where's Diamond Annie, d'you reckon? I for one prefer to have that woman in plain sight.'

'Too true. But I reckon she'll turn up. She's not the shy and retiring type.'

Definitely true, Mickey thought. Annie was tall for a woman. At five feet eight, she was taller than most men and proportionately built, you might say. She had acquired her nickname from the wearing of diamond rings on every finger of both hands. Diamond Annie was not averse to the odd fist fight, and diamonds cut like razors.

Mickey returned to an earlier subject. 'The kid who got carved up on Atkins' patch – but, of course, has no idea who did it – his name was Sammy Butcher.'

'Sammy doesn't ring a bell, but I know Charlie Butcher. Oddly enough, he used to live over that way, when the old Josiah Bailey was in charge. The family moved about, what, five years ago. His ma was done for immoral earnings more times than I've got fingers, and the two older boys have records for petty theft, if I remember right. I wouldn't place them as members of the gang, but there's not much that happens on their ground that the Elephants don't know about. What about him in particular?'

'He had to be there for a reason,' Mickey said. 'Sammy was chased by a group of kids, so must've stood out. We've been talking about some discreet spying going on, but it doesn't seem to me that young Sammy Butcher fits the bill. So what was he doing?'

'I'll see what I can find out, let you know. Now, how's that beautiful wife of yours? It's been ages since we had you round; Mary said to ask you when I mentioned we were meeting up tonight.'

They chatted for a little longer and then Mickey took his leave with a hive's worth of thoughts buzzing around his head.

TWENTY-SIX

T he journey from London to Grimsby was a long haul, and despite an early start, it was late afternoon by the time they found the pawn shop. They had chatted sporadically on the way, Mickey recounting to Henry the conversation he'd had the night before and discussing the implications, but they were also comfortable with silence. Mickey read *Lord Peter Views the Body* by Dorothy L. Sayers and from time to time broke off to criticize the investigation. Henry had borrowed *Decline and Fall* from his brother-in-law; he'd been curious as this had been Mrs Parker's reading matter. He explained this to Mickey.

'But you didn't even like the woman. Why would you like what she reads?'

'I find I do like the book,' Henry said. 'I suppose even women like Mrs Parker might have decent taste in literature.'

Despite this, Mickey noted that Henry's attention was elsewhere. He knew better than to ask where his colleague's thoughts had drifted off to. He'd let Mickey know soon enough.

The pawnbroker was just off the Bullring. The scent of coffee hung in the air, together with the smell of cooked meats and pies as they passed a shop called Stephenson's West End Provisions.

'My stomach thinks my throat's been cut,' Mickey said. 'It's to be hoped the pawnbroker can suggest a place to stay. One that serves decent food.'

'Mr Siddons?' Henry asked as the ringing of a bell above the door brought a man through from the back room.

'I am indeed, and you must be the police from down there in London. Come through. Put the closed sign on the door; it's nearly time anyway. It's a long old journey from down there to up here.'

Mickey agreed that it was and they followed him through

to the back of the shop. There were glass-topped counters on three sides displaying goods for sale, and cabinets on the walls containing objects awaiting redemption. The back office was obviously used for paperwork and storage. The watch had been placed in a tray and set on the writing surface of an open roll-topped desk.

'It's the engraving I spotted. What you put out on the watch list.' He chuckled. 'A watch on the watch list. I must say I was surprised when I realized I had it. I wasn't here when it was taken in. My assistant did the deed. He's not in today. Should you need him, he can be summoned, I suppose. Or you can talk to him in the morning or pop along to his house tonight. Of course, all the details are in the book.' He pointed to a ledger set next to the tray.

Henry picked it up and stepped aside so that Mickey could get to the watch. Mickey set his bag down on the floor and studied the watch carefully. It looked very clean. He said so.

'Well, it will have been polished when it came in,' Mr Siddons informed them. 'Nine times out of ten, items like this don't get redeemed. We extend the best of terms, you know. We are very fair. But, of course, that means that not everyone is able to afford to redeem their items. Well, it stands to reason: if they could afford to keep them, they wouldn't be pawning them in the first place, would they? So we always clean the items when they come in and—' He broke off, raised a hand to his mouth. 'Oh dear, I suppose you want fingerprints, don't you? I expect they'll have been wiped clean away.'

Mickey glanced at Henry, rolling his eyes. Henry led the pawnbroker away and pointed to an entry in the book. 'So it came in only five days ago?'

'That's what the book says.'

So the thief had hung on to the watch for a time, Henry thought.

'And you extended credit of thirty shillings.'

'Well, yes.'

'For a gold pocket watch? You consider this a fair price?'

'The party needed ready money, I'm sure. Perhaps that was

all that was asked for. Sometimes that happens, you understand; there is more hope of a party being able to redeem
their object if the loan is not too high.'

'And this is the address given and the name. Miss Adelaide
Hay and an address in Lincoln.'

'That's right, yes. My assistant recalls her well. A red-haired
young lady with very pretty eyes, he said. Apparently, the
watch belonged to her late uncle.'

'Anything?' Henry asked Mickey, his attention snapping
from the pawnbroker. The man could not tell him anything
useful. The address was interesting, though; this Adelaide Hay
had given the address of the Goldmann family as her own.
Clearly, she knew a lot about Joseph.

'Well, the inscription is there and I think I may have a
tiny glimmer of hope. It's only a partial print and I'm guessing
from its placement that it might be a right forefinger. It might
be Joseph Levy's, of course, but we might strike lucky. Direct
that light for me, would you?'

Henry took hold of the desk lamp and directed it down
on to the watch. 'Do you have a second lamp? We need more
light.'

Siddons, fascinated now, bustled to find more light. Mickey
angled his camera, trying not to cast shadow. He took three
pictures of the partial print, picked out now in black against
the gold surface of the watch.

'It's fragmentary,' Henry commented, but he could discern
loops and whorls. 'Is that a second?' he asked, catching a
glimpse of something on the rim of the outer case.

'You could be right. Wait until I've dealt with this and
then we'll have a look.' He took another two more pictures,
changing his angle a little, and then carefully, delicately
brushed the second print.

'That looks different,' Siddons exclaimed, and Henry could
see that he was correct.

Mickey took more pictures, capturing the ephemeral print,
hardly daring to take a breath. Even with the second light, he'd
be pushing the film; the negatives would be thin and difficult
to process.

'Now, let's see what we have.'

Mickey took a glass and examined both marks closely. They were definitely different but, as Henry knew, that could just indicate different fingers on the same hand. Joseph's hand?

Mickey flicked quickly through the fingerprint cards he had brought with him. Those from known suspects that local constabularies had identified.

'Now's the time to cross fingers,' he said.

He began by comparing right forefingers, instinct and experience suggesting this might be the likeliest finger to have made that mark on the inner case.

'Nothing,' he said.

He began a comparison of the second print and a slow smile spread across his face. 'We may have a match,' he said. 'Of course, it's only a partial print, but I see enough similarities to bet money on it.'

Henry took the card from Mickey's hand. Gus Dickson, robbery with threats, violent affray and theft from persons. His description was of someone tall, well built, broad-shouldered, the sort of man Mrs Parker had observed arguing with the redhead. Or, at least, she'd been a redhead on that occasion. On others she'd been described as brunette or dark, but Henry figured that a change of hair was not so difficult to achieve.

And there was an address. Recently released, Henry noted, the man would be reporting regularly to the local police.

'We need a place to stay tonight,' Mickey said. 'Can you suggest somewhere?'

'Oh, you should try the Mucky Duck.' He grinned. 'The Black Swan. Beds are not bad and the food's not bad either.' He gave them directions and provided a box into which Mickey could slide the watch.

'So now we find the hotel, telephone our contact at the local police division and then get this boy arrested. We can be in Boston by mid-morning, I reckon.'

'We could try to get a train tonight,' Henry objected.

'I need dinner and a bed,' Mickey told the man who was technically his boss. 'As do you. The locals can pick him up and keep him warm until we get there. It won't hurt anyone for our man to spend the night in a police cell.'

Henry gave in, knowing Mickey was right. It should be the local police who collected the suspect.

TWENTY-SEVEN

G us Dickson was in bed. Addie lay beside him, pretending to be asleep. Fred was already snoring on his camp bed in the tiny kitchen, sounds that could be heard well enough through the thin walls. Fred rarely lost sleep over anything.

Gus, though, was losing a lot of sleep lately, and the reason for that was currently settled on the edge of the bed, her back to him. Although she was pretending to sleep, the stiffness of her back was ramrod and as unlike a woman at rest as it was possible to be.

Gus still got what he wanted from her, of course. She wasn't that stupid, and he didn't really care that it was given grudgingly and – increasingly, lately – passively. He didn't really care what Addie thought about anything and particularly not about sex. What right did she have to think about *that* anyway? Not when she'd given herself to some skinny Jew boy. Gus wasn't sure what offended him more: the skinniness, the lack of manliness all round or the fact that she'd given it to a Jew.

She had him; what the hell did she want or need with anything or anyone else? What right had she to expect a damn thing?

Addie moved, just slightly. She must have really dropped off, Gus thought, and then startled awake. She'd been doing a lot of that lately. And to think he'd once had genuine feelings for her. Thought she might be worth hanging on to.

Well, not any more.

Gus sat up and then leaned over to where Addie lay and took her by the shoulder. He rolled her on her back.

'Not now, Gus. Please.'

'What the fuck, Addie! What d'you mean, not now? You don't get to decide.' He took a deep breath. 'Look, I don't want to be angry with you. I don't want to hurt you, but you push me too far. You know that?'

'I'm sorry, Gus.'

But she wasn't sorry. He could hear that. She didn't give a damn; maybe she never had. 'Turned your head, didn't he? You're a bloody stupid bitch, Addie, you know that. We had it good and you . . .'

'I thought he loved me, Gus.'

'Loved you! Fuck it, Addie, you betrayed him. You can't tell me you felt a damn thing. You smiled your smile and you did everything I told you to, and the poor bugger followed you like a little lamb. All he had to do was hand it over. He said he was getting money but he lied to you, Addie. Lied. And if you try to tell me it was any different to that, you're lying to yourself.'

She turned away and he didn't stop her. She was no fun anymore. He wanted rid. She wasn't even any good as a distraction. He'd point out a mark to her and in the old days she'd be on it. There she'd have been – that smile, that little tilt of the head, that feeling she gave the poor sods that they were special and that she'd singled them out.

But now!

Gus got out of bed and wandered over to the window, drew the curtain aside and stared down into the empty street. The rain had cleared and the sky was full of stars.

'I'm off out,' he told her.

'Where are you going?' She sounded oddly panicked, as though, much as she hated him being close to her, she hated more the idea of being alone or of him being elsewhere.

The sound of splintering wood followed by shouting and booted feet on the stairs interrupted them. The constable barged through the door, truncheon in hand, another behind him.

Gus was knocked to the ground before he even had the idea of resisting. He heard Fred shout from the other room and Addie, clutching the sheets, began to scream.

'Fuck it,' Gus swore.

'Language, sonny.'

Gus yelled in pain as the constable hit him again.

TWENTY-EIGHT

'**H**as the woman said anything yet?' Henry asked. As there were no female officers in the Boston constabulary, a matron had been called in to supervise Adelaide.

'Not yet, Inspector. She was . . . in bed when the constables made the arrests. They found a neighbour to be with her while she dressed and then I came in. She slept a little and ate breakfast, but she's refused to say anything to the sergeant and said little enough to me.'

She sounded aggrieved. Henry nodded. 'We'll see,' he said. 'And the men?'

'Been interviewed, but I don't think Sergeant Todd has got much out of either of them.'

Henry opened the tiny window in the cell door and peered through at Addie. She glanced up and then looked away, disinterested.

Henry returned to the office where Sergeant Todd was waiting for them.

'I took statements,' he said. 'Such as they are. Frederick Welton is playing dumb, insisting he was just staying for a night or two and knows nothing. Mr Gregory, aka Gus Dickson, is a cocky bugger and is likewise insisting on his innocence; reckons he was manhandled and wants legal counsel.'

'What for, if he's innocent?' Henry asked.

'I'll take Dickson,' Mickey said. 'Sergeant Todd, if you can have another go at Fred Welton, and Chief Inspector Johnstone will question the young woman. Shall we reconvene at midday?'

There was a shortage of space in the borough police headquarters. Henry had been allocated a tiny room behind the kitchen that he guessed was usually just used for storage. A small table and three chairs had been moved in, but the matron would be sitting in the open doorway.

Not ideal, Henry thought, but it would do. Priority had clearly been given to the interviews with the male suspects – the woman just an afterthought. He'd seen the look of surprise on Todd's face when Henry had not chosen to interview Gus Dickson himself, and still more surprise that he had let Mickey make the allocation.

Adelaide Hay was brought in. She looked pale, wore no lipstick, and her red hair had been left to tumble about her face and shoulders. That she had dressed in haste was obvious. No stockings and an old cardigan thrown on over her green dress.

She didn't even look up at Henry as the matron seated her at the table.

'Would you like some water?'

She shook her head.

'I know you had a relationship with Joseph Levy. I know you were present when he died. I want to know what happened.'

'I don't know any Joseph Levy.' It was said without conviction.

'You went to Grimsby, pawned his watch. The pawnbroker could identify you.'

'So? I pawned a watch.'

'The address you gave – it was the address of Joseph Levy's fiancée. How did you know that?'

For the first time she lifted her gaze to look at him. Her eyes were deeply green and, Henry could see, brimming with tears.

'Tell me,' he said. 'How did you get involved with Joseph Levy? What happened on the day he died?'

Addie shook her head.

'What's that supposed to mean? Don't lie to me.'

'I'm not.'

'You know that Joseph told his fiancée he was in love with you.'

'He what?' She looked shocked. Bright colour touched her cheeks and lips and then faded again.

'Did he die because of you? He wanted you to go away with him, didn't he? I said, didn't he?' Henry raised his voice and brought his hand down on the table with a sharp slap.

Addie jumped, as did the matron. She looked about to object and Henry raised a hand to silence her.

'He asked you to leave with him. Is that so?'

This time she nodded.

'And how were you going to live? Where were you going to go? What did he offer you, Adelaide?'

'He really said he loved me?'

'Apparently so. And you repaid him how? By betraying him to Dickson? Did you tell Dickson that you were leaving with Joseph Levy? Was he jealous? Or did he think Joseph had something worth stealing – something more than his watch and chain?' He paused momentarily. 'And where did the chain go? Pawn it somewhere else, did you?'

She shook her head. 'I hid it in my coat lining,' she said. 'Gus found it.'

'And he hit you? I'm told you are badly bruised.'

She shrugged, as though it were nothing. What did anything matter now?

'And so he followed you off the train? Was that what you'd agreed with Gus Dickson? That you would lure Joseph from the train? We know from witness statements that you were involved in an altercation with a man matching the description of Gus Dickson. Did you quarrel about Joseph Levy?'

'Gus was mad with me.'

'So they had travelled ahead of you by an earlier train? You got on at another stop, hoping to avoid them? So why didn't you just stay on the train? If you saw them at the station, Gus Dickson and Fred Welton, then why didn't you just stay on the train? Why get out to confront them, if not to lure Joseph from the safety of the train? No, that wasn't how it happened, was it, Adelaide? You had it all planned with Welton and Dickson. You would get on the train as arranged with Joseph Levy and then you would leave the train at Bardney, knowing the poor sap would follow you, and you handed him over to your friends, knowing what they would do to him.'

Because that was the way we had always done it. That's what I was there for, to make a scene while they did the business.

She stood suddenly, taking Henry by surprise, and leaned

across the table, shouting in his face, 'He lied to me, didn't he? He was just like all the rest, all full of talk. I trusted him. He said he'd have money and we could go away, but he had nothing. Didn't have a pot to piss in.'

The matron grabbed Addie's shoulders and pressed her back into her chair. Henry was unmoved.

'So,' he said, continuing in the same tone as before, 'you saw your friends on the platform and you got off the train. You proceeded to argue, and Joseph, thinking you were in trouble, followed you off the train and across the platform. You and your friends persuaded or threatened him so that he left the station with you and then you robbed and killed Joseph Levy and you hid his body by the river Witham.'

Addie sat back, arms folded across her body, and looked at the wall above Henry's head.

'And you were party to all of this, Adelaide. He fell in love with you, wanted to give you a better life than you had with the likes of Gus Dickson. But no. You are as black-hearted as your friends. You betrayed him, no doubt laughed with Dickson about this poor fool you'd taken in, but that was the problem, wasn't it, Addie? He was a *poor* fool. You had expectations and poor, foolish Joseph failed to meet them, so you—'

'He lied to me.' She shouted the words and then repeated them more quietly. 'He lied to me. He said he'd have money, that he could take me away. I never wanted to tell Gus, but he forced it out of me, just like he forced every other bloody thing. But when he got off that train, all he had to do was hand it over and they'd have let him go.'

'You really believe that?' Henry asked. He had lowered his voice now, forcing Addie to pay attention, to listen closely. 'You really believe that they'd have let him go? He could name you; he could describe them. All he had to do was shout for help and the porters or the guard would have come running. But he trusted you, believed you would get back on the train with him, that the two of you could be together. Isn't that what he thought, Adelaide?'

Henry stood this time and gestured for the matron to take Addie away. It was enough for now.

Then he wandered through to the little kitchen and helped himself to a mug of tea and thought things through.

Why had Joseph and Adelaide not boarded the train together in Lincoln?

Well, the answer to that one was simple, perhaps. His ersatz in-laws had come to see him off. But did that make sense? Why had they escorted him to the station? They didn't know about Adelaide – except that Joseph had told Rebecca that he was in love. Had she revealed this to her family?

He thought back to what Rebecca had told him, checking through his notes. The girl had said that Joseph revealed his love for Adelaide and that Rebecca had tried to buy some time by asking to delay the wedding. Clearly, she'd hoped for a change of heart or at least wanted to wait until Joseph was out of the house before revealing what he'd told her.

Adelaide must have caught a train out of Lincoln, got off at the next station, ready to get back on to the next train – the train Joseph told her he would be catching. As likely as not, this earlier train had also carried her male associates to Bardney, and they'd hung around – or lain low – until the next train arrived just under an hour later.

Joseph had clearly decided that they should not acknowledge one another and had most likely been surprised when she had left the train at Bardney. Looking from the window, he must have been shocked to see Gus Dickson and Fred Welton.

'Did he know what she was?' Henry wondered aloud. 'Did she tell him about them?'

She must have done. If she and Joseph were intimate, he would undoubtedly have seen the bruises.

So where was this money supposed to be coming from? And did Henry believe Adelaide's claim that Joseph had nothing worth stealing – apart from the watch and chain – when Dickson and his associate had so brutally attacked him?

Henry enquired as to where Fred Welton was being interviewed. He slipped quietly into the room and signalled to Sergeant Todd that he should continue. A constable sat at the side of the room, taking notes, and Henry leaned against the wall beside him, watching Fred Welton.

Welton was the smaller of the two men. Skinny and

hollow-cheeked and not as tall as Adelaide Hay or Gus Dickson. So which had wielded the knife and which had struck with the brick? On balance, Henry would have Welton down as the knife man, striking slightly upwards beneath the ribs. The brick had landed with considerable force on the back of Joseph's head and spoke of a taller, more robust frame having wielded it.

Glancing at the constable's notes, Henry gathered that their suspect hadn't had much to say for himself, but Henry's presence seemed to change that. Fred kept glancing in Henry's direction and announced more than once that his being brought here was 'a bleeding liberty'. He was suddenly unsettled.

Sergeant Todd noticed this too and pressed the advantage. 'You do know that this gentleman is from London?' he said, leaning almost confidentially across the table. 'That he's a *murder* detective? That like as not he'll see you end up dancing on the end of a rope?'

Just to reinforce the point, Sergeant Todd mimed the action; sticking out his tongue and making choking noises while his hand pulled on an imaginary rope.

Fred Welton paled and shifted his chair back with a loud scrape. 'I didn't do nuffin'!' His voice rose in pitch, arms flailing to emphasize the point. 'I just helped Gus move the body. All I did! On me mother's life, that's all I did.'

'You never had a mother,' Todd growled. 'She must ha' taken one good look at you and left you for the bloody gypsies.'

Henry shifted position and Todd glanced his way, wondering if he'd gone too far, but Henry had no objection to the pantomime; it seemed to be getting the desired result. He found, though, that he did have an objection to the reference to gypsies. Not one he would have had a few months before, but that had changed after close acquaintance with Malina Cooper, now ensconced in his sister's house, and her wider family.

Sergeant Todd, understanding that the inspector was not going to interfere, carried on. 'Move the body, did you? Hide it so that poor young man's family went through agony, not knowing if he was alive or dead?'

'What did you do with the body?' Henry's voice, calm and controlled, seemed at odds with the sergeant's tone, but that appeared to upset Fred even more.

'There's a yard at the back of the station – bit of a dumping ground, it looks like. We hid him there, covered him with a tarp that was lying around and weighted it with bricks. Came back when it was dusk and took him out of town and dumped him in a field.'

Henry recalled the place. It was on the opposite side of the station to the wall that he and Mickey had speculated was the source of the improvised weapon, but it made sense. Low lying and close to the river, it was likely that it had been subject to the same flooding that had made the field inaccessible and delayed the finding of Joseph's body. He doubted there'd be much evidence worth searching for by now.

'And I suppose you were nowhere near when that poor young man was killed?' Todd picked up the questioning again. Reluctantly, Welton turned his attention from Henry.

'No, I weren't. Gus just wanted to talk to him. Get his dues, but the stupid fool wouldn't play ball. Gus and Addie took him outside the station so they could have a chat, like. I stood watch just in case anyone else took an interest. Next thing I know, Addie comes racing back, saying he's done for. I think she means Gus at first, like the kike might have had a knife or summat, but when I get there, I realize he's dead and I see Gus wiping off his blade on the grass and there's a bloody great hole in the back of the lad's skull.'

'And Joseph Levy was definitely dead.'

Fred looked surprised, as though it had never occurred to him that he could be otherwise. 'Well, if he weren't, then he were soon enough,' he said pragmatically. 'We lifted him and moved him over a bit of a wall. Then Gus took Addie off somewhere. He came back and I reckoned he dropped her at the Nag's Head or maybe the Railway Hotel – I don't remember.'

Henry nodded, knowing that to be true.

'Then we scooped up the body and hid it, just temp'ry, and then when it started to get dark, we took it across the field.

Gus reckoned we didn't know how long it would be before someone spotted it in the yard. He wanted to make sure it was a while before it were found.'

'And you didn't wonder about that? You both took a big risk, hanging round until later and then moving the body that far across open ground.'

Fred's expression told Henry that he had not. Gus had wanted this done and so Fred had done it.

'And where was the girl while you were hanging around waiting to move a corpse?' Todd asked.

It would have been Henry's next question, but he decided Todd had asked it better.

'Gus brought her from the pub and put her on a train. Told her to get off home.'

'And she did as she was told?'

Fred Welton nodded. 'She was there, asleep in bed, when we arrived. Sleeping like the dead.'

Henry, Mickey Hitchens and Sergeant Todd convened for lunch at the Angel. It was not market day, so the bar was quiet and the food was simple, but Mickey wolfed his sandwiches and then went to ask for more. Todd was a little more circumspect, given the company, but he still put on a good show and downed a pint or three.

Henry, slower as usual, was thoughtful. He wanted to hear how Mickey had dealt with Gus Dickson.

'Loud mouth, doesn't say very much with it,' Mickey told him. 'But he's shaken, I can see that. Keeps insisting he didn't do the murder but admits to moving the body. Dumped the poor bugger in a yard, covered him up and then came back with Fred Welton and moved him later.'

'And does he accuse Welton of doing the killing?'

Mickey shook his head. 'No, that's the interesting thing. Keeps insisting it wasn't him, but he's not naming names. By now they're usually wriggling like maggots and persuading us to catch the other fish.'

'Welton reckons he was keeping watch. That he helped dispose of the body but that was the limit of his involvement.'

'And you believe him?' Mickey asked.

Henry took a bite of his sandwich and nodded. He chewed slowly, thinking. 'I am inclined to,' he said.

'But there were two injuries,' Mickey began cautiously, suddenly seeing where his boss was headed.

'And Welton said he saw Dickson wiping his knife blade on the grass,' Todd put in. He stared at Henry. 'No,' he said, shocked as he realized where this was heading.

'I think Adelaide struck the killing blow,' Henry confirmed. 'She has the height, she is heavier than Welton and she was angrier than either of them. Joseph had made promises to her and she believed them broken – it doesn't matter that *she* betrayed *him*; all she can see is that he let her down.'

'So she crowns him,' Todd said. 'Never underestimate an enraged female,' he added with such feeling that Mickey had to hide a smile. 'Think you can make it stick?' Todd added.

'You want a go at Gus this afternoon?' Mickey queried.

'No, you keep with him, but face him with the idea that Adelaide Hay confessed – see where it gets us.'

TWENTY-NINE

'Y ou beat seven shades out of one of mine, cut him up real bad. I'd be entitled to do the same to you.'

Clem Atkins resisted the impulse to scream. His men were on the other side of the door, but he knew her reputation and knew that he would only get caught in the middle of the fight.

Instead, he turned and faced the woman sitting quite comfortably in the chair next to his bed. 'Annie,' he said. 'What a surprise. But your boy was on my patch – what happened to him was his own damned fault.'

'Lucky for you, I agree. But that don't make it right and I will have blood for blood – you know that. It's just a matter of when. You'd do the same in my position.'

She stood. As tall as Clem and as broad, carefully and fashionably dressed, the diamonds on her fingers gleaming.

'Just so we understand one another,' she said. 'Only we've been hearing stories about you. About you mixing with young tykes that should know better. That reckon they can revive what's been smashed. The story is you're giving them a hand.'

'The stories are wrong, Annie.'

'Damned right they are. As of now. I'm willing to let bygones be bygones.'

She opened his bedroom door and stepped out on to the landing. Her sudden appearance caused consternation. Weapons were drawn.

'Tell your boys to back off.'

'Back off,' Clem said. 'Annie was just visiting.'

He watched as she made her way downstairs and held back his men when they wanted to rush her. He could see the questions.

'She had something I wanted,' he said and grinned broadly, letting them draw any conclusion they damn well wanted. The roars and the laughter told him they'd decided exactly which one they wanted – despite the fact he'd been in the room for only minutes.

He went back inside and watched from his bedroom window as Annie got into a car and was driven away. 'You've got a bloody nerve,' he said softly. But then he'd always known that. Annie, Queen of the Forty Elephants.

One time he'd watched her walk into a big department store, Annie and her girls, dressed to the nines, looking for all the world like an exclusive group of Bright Young Things off on a spree. They'd walked out with furs, bolts of silk, jewellery . . . looking a little heavier than when they'd walked in. As time went on and the threats of violence were proved to be more than threats, it was rumoured that staff saw them coming and quietly disappeared until they'd shopped and gone.

Annie never fenced what she stole in the capital. Couriers took the small stuff to out-of-town fences; larger items were simply packed into trunks, labelled with legitimate addresses and sent off on the railway with 'for collection' labels affixed, to be collected at the station by more of Annie's out-of-town associates.

Annie was queen of organization, if nothing else – and she was definitely a hell of a lot else.

Clem smiled grimly. He opened the bedroom door again and told his men he was turning in for the night. Two would sleep in the room opposite, but he'd not be disturbed again. There was something he had not noticed until Annie had left and that was a brown envelope lying on the middle of his bed. At some point it had been posted and the address on the front crossed out and another applied. One of Atkins' men had taken it off the boy that they'd beaten up, and although they'd not got much out of him, the boy had confessed he was taking the envelope to Abraham. It had puzzled Clem at the time, but he'd held off doing anything about it while he worked out how he could use this to his best advantage.

Annie was letting him know that she'd been through his room – that she knew he had this and had laid it out on the bed for him to see just so he'd get the message.

The trouble, Clem Atkins thought, was that he wasn't quite sure what message he was supposed to be receiving. One part of it was clear: Annie reckoned she could get to him any time she liked, but that for now he wasn't important enough for her to bother with. The other was that she knew what the kid had and probably where it came from. But was she warning him off, informing him, asking for a cut? No doubt she would let him know that part soon enough.

He waited until all was quiet and then crept back down the stairs. The only problem with all the security he had surrounded himself with, Clem thought, was that it also imprisoned him, and if Annie could get in the way she had that evening, it meant there was a leak somewhere. Time for a bit of a purge, maybe. He moved rapidly through the bar, knowing his home turf well enough that he needed no light, and went out the back way. Five minutes later Abraham Levy was opening his back door to a midnight visitor.

Addie lay on the narrow bunk, staring at the ceiling. She had expected to be called back into the interview room, had heard Gus being brought back and deposited in the other police cell, but no one had come for her.

A constable brought food and she was allowed out to empty her bucket, but no one spoke to her beyond necessary instructions and no one answered even the simplest of her questions.

Addie felt herself adrift in some other world, one that had no connection to reality and that she could no longer believe she had ever been a part of.

She knew it was dark outside. The tiny ventilation grill had let in thin slivers of light but they had gradually faded completely. She supposed they would all be transferred to Lincoln at some point; they couldn't keep them in police cells indefinitely.

Addie turned on her side and tried to remember what it had been like when Joseph was asleep beside her, his breathing soft and steady, almost like a child. But even he had lied to her, and that was something she had been unable to forgive.

Henry knew the effectiveness of silence and the power of time, and after further discussion over lunch it had been decided to make use of both assets.

'Arrange for Fred Welton to be taken to Lincoln today,' he instructed. 'If we want him, we can access him there, but I see him as the least use to us, and your accommodation is already stretched. Leave the girl and Dickson in their cells and give orders that they are not to be spoken to, over and above what is necessary. We will continue with our interviews tomorrow morning, and in the meantime I'd like to visit the boarding house where they stayed.'

'And I wouldn't mind a look around,' Mickey said. 'Looks like a pleasant little town. I spotted a bloody great church tower as we came in.'

'Boston Stump,' Todd told him. 'Time was they had a light up on top of it that could be seen out in the estuary. Ships used it as a marker. It's dedicated to Saint Botolph.'

'You seem to go in for biggish churches in these parts,' Mickey observed.

'From the days when wool was king and rich men wanted to do something to save their souls.'

They could have shared it with the poor, Henry thought, aware that such thoughts might be judged Bolshevik.

So the afternoon was spent inspecting the two rooms – bedroom-cum-living room and tiny kitchen – the three had occupied in the boarding house overlooking the tidal river. It seemed that Fred Welton wasn't supposed to be there; the landlady, who lived two streets away, was outraged. The tenants in the downstairs rooms pleaded ignorance.

They also spent a pleasant hour at leisure, exploring the mix of medieval, Georgian and Victorian, wandering back and forth across the bridges that linked the two sides of the divided settlement, this town built on 'havens', little creeks in the salt marsh that had brought the early settlers to habitable land.

But the following morning it was all business again. Adelaide Hay and Gus Dickson were brought up from the cells straight after an early breakfast and seated opposite their interrogators. Welton now absent, Sergeant Todd elected to join his opposite number, and he and Mickey now faced the young man. Mickey had a wolfish smile on his face.

'You've been telling us porky pies,' he said. 'And my mother raised me not to be fond of liars.'

'I told you the truth. I never killed him; I just helped dump the body.'

'And in part I believe you,' Mickey assured him. 'You didn't strike the killing blow, although it was your knife that made the slit beneath his ribs and that you wiped on the grass after. But it was Adelaide who dealt the killing blow, was it not? Came up behind the poor unfortunate and whacked him over the head with half a brick. And a hell of a whack she dealt him, too. Laid his skull open so you could see the brains.'

Gus Dickson swallowed hard. 'I don't know what you mean.'

'So you'd rather hang for her, would you?'

On cue, Todd went through his pantomime again. Dickson wasn't quite as impressed as Fred had been.

'Adelaide whacked him over the head. You stabbed him in the ribs – and it's pure luck you didn't strike as well as you might have done. Our pathologist tells us he could have recovered from the knife wound – it bounced off a rib and went in shallow. So you might be equally lucky and the judge might not don his little black cap for you. But the girl? She's as dead as poor Joseph Levy. There's not a judge or jury in the country that won't convict her of murder. Because that's what it was. Hard and cold-blooded. She killed someone who loved her enough to give up his fiancée and his family and his security, and that's how she repaid him.'

Gus Dickson actually laughed. 'Come off it,' he said. 'The Jew boy just had his fun with her. You think someone like him would end up with someone like Addie? He just strung her along, promised her the world. But what sort of world can you buy with empty pockets?'

'You stole what he had.'

'I stole a watch and a chain. I hid them for a bit and thought to keep them. I always wanted a pretty watch. Then I took it out one day, thinking I might as well make use, and when I opened it up, there was this inscription in the back.'

He sounded so deeply put out that Mickey laughed at him. 'Sad for you,' he said.

'So I got rid – sent Addie to pawn it. She came back with sweet Fanny Adams, so it looks like I'm not the only crook.

Thirty bob for a watch like that. Then I found out she'd kept the chain. Like I say, you can't trust no one.'

Morning found Abraham on his way to his brother's house for the first time since Joseph's funeral. He was furiously angry now and more than a little frightened. Clem Atkins' midnight visit had crystalized his thinking and confirmed what he had suspected but had not been able to define.

The time it took for him to travel to his brother's home did nothing to diminish his anger; nor did the news that his brother was not home but spending the day at one of his shops.

Abraham paused outside the shop, gathering himself for the storm. This was an Orthodox street. He stood out as a stranger here, despite being of the same faith. Those who had been following him since he left home stood out even more. Abraham cast a glance in their direction, just to let them know he was aware, and then turned his back and went inside. The doorbell jangled. Benjamin looked up. He had been counting stock, checking against a list that a young woman read out. He paused, as did she, finger on the list to mark where they had got to.

'Abraham? What brings you here?'

Since the funeral Ben had continued to send watches for repair, requests for orders, engraving to be done, but the brothers had not spoken directly.

Abraham looked pointedly at the assistant. 'I would like a private word with you.'

'Then you had better come through. We will continue with this later,' he told the girl. 'Tidy this away.'

Abraham could see that his brother was on edge and he wondered if Benjamin suspected what he might be about to say.

'Sit. How are you? Can I offer you anything?'

'You care how I am? I don't think you can. You didn't care how your son died, so what hope do I have?'

'Abraham, I have no idea what you mean. I lost my son. You know what that feels like.'

'You exploited your son. He died because you wanted him to do things that were illegal and immoral.'

Ben looked confused. 'How can you say things like that?'

'You told me that your son shamed you.'

'Yes, by betraying a young woman he had promised to marry and by falling for some . . . strumpet. Some little whore. Of course I'm ashamed of that, but if Joseph had come to me and told me, I would have forgiven him. We would, between us, have found a way of putting things right.'

Abraham reached into his pocket and withdrew an envelope. He tipped the contents on to the desk. A foreign passport, identity papers, a brooch and a ring.

'What is this?'

'You tell me.'

'Where did you get this, Abraham?'

Abraham looked at his brother's face and began to wonder if his suspicions really were correct. Benjamin looked shocked, genuinely shocked.

Abraham sighed, rubbing his face with his hands. The truth was he didn't really know what to think about anything anymore. Seeing the change in his brother's demeanour, Benjamin sat down and examined the contents of the envelope closely. 'What's going on?'

'I thought you could tell me. But I think you're in the dark as much as I am. Last night Clem Atkins came to my house with this. He came alone, like a thief, knocked on my back door. He claims he took it from the Elephant boy who was beaten so badly, cut up by his thugs. You heard about that?'

'I did, yes. But why would that boy have this?'

'Look at the envelope. Benjamin. The address has been changed. Changed in a hurry, simply crossed out and the new one put there. The second address is one I do not know, but the first is one we have used before. Look at the writing, Benjamin. Look at the handwriting.'

Benjamin turned the envelope over and looked more carefully. He froze. 'I don't understand.'

'No more do I, but that handwriting is Joseph's. He changed the address; he sent this letter elsewhere – I do not know why. But there would have been money in the envelope; you know that.'

For a moment this hung in the air between them and
Benjamin stared at his brother, unable to comprehend the
implication. 'If this is not the only time, if he sent our other
letters astray . . . But how could he get hold of them? The
Goldmanns were always so careful.'

'And we were so careful to keep Joseph in the dark, but the
Goldmanns treated him like a son. He was part of their family.
It could be that they said too much, or that Rebecca told.'

'Of course Rebecca knows. She visits the boarding house,
checking on the administration of the place at least once every
week. And she was proud of what we were doing. Of course
she would tell her future husband; and would probably be
shocked that he didn't know already.'

Neither brother wanted to broach what was obvious, but
eventually Abraham did, as gently as he could. 'I can think
of no other explanation,' he said slowly, 'but that Joseph might
have taken . . . might have borrowed, perhaps – no doubt
intending to give back. He could have suggested he posts these
letters for the Goldmanns and obtained them that way. We
know he wanted to be with this young woman, this *Adelaide*.'
He almost spat the word.

'You are saying my son stole so he could run away with
this girl,' Benjamin said flatly. 'No, I cannot believe that.'

'What other explanation is there? I'm not saying he intended
to keep the money. I examined the ring and the brooch; both
are just costume jewellery, of no value, but it's likely those
who sent these things did not know that. I remember how it
was when you first became involved in these schemes.
Everyone contributes what they can; sometimes mistakes are
made.'

'And you are saying my son made a mistake?'

'I am saying that because you loved him, you did not tell
him the truth because you wanted no trouble to come to his
door. I am saying that because *she* loved him, Rebecca did
tell him what was going on, and that because *he* loved this
other woman, he took advantage where he could. An act of
desperation, Benjamin.'

His brother looked as though Abraham had slapped him in
the face hard enough to stun. Benjamin shook his head, not

wanting to believe, but not knowing how to counter Abraham's logic.

'And because of love, he's dead,' Benjamin said at last.

'It seems so,' Abraham agreed sadly.

Addie had initially been silent once more. Henry had asked her again what had happened on the day Joseph had died, but she seemed intent on ignoring him, disinterested and remote.

Henry laid Joseph's watch on the table between them. 'You took the watch to a pawnbroker,' he said. 'He gave you thirty shillings. The same wage as a sweatshop worker might earn in a week, I suppose. You might have got more if you'd offered him the chain.' He paused.

'You've not asked how we caught up with you,' he continued. 'We made enquiries about two men and a woman using distraction in order to rob. We then matched those names with fingerprints.'

'I've never been arrested,' she said.

'Maybe not, but Dickson has. Gus Dickson has a record and we have his prints. He touched Joseph's watch and left a print. We put out a call to all of the pawnbrokers in this area asking for report of a watch with a particular engraving. A message that Joseph's uncle had engraved upon his watch.'

He opened the watch and pointed at the traces of finger-print powder adhering to the inside. 'A print from Gus Dickson's index finger, as it happens. And he has to report to the local police, does he not? Which is how we got his address, and which is how we found you all.'

'And why should I care?'

'You should care because we now have you here, with enough evidence to charge you with murder. Not Gus Dickson, not Fred Welton – though both played their part – but you, Adelaide. You were the one who hit Joseph over the head with a brick. You laid open his skull and you killed him.'

Addie held his gaze and then nodded slowly. 'All right, maybe I did, but he deserved it, di'n't he?'

'Deserved it? How?'

Addie seemed to draw into herself as though gathering her

thoughts. At last, she said, 'He had no right to make promises he couldn't keep. He were just like the rest of them, all sweet talk and promises until he got what he wanted and then . . . then when it came to it, he let me down.'

She lifted her head and leaned forward across the table, almost spat the words. 'You have any idea what it's like to have nothin' and then have someone give you just a little glimmer of hope? You don't dare to believe it, but then you do and then you find out that person's just as much of a bloody liar as the last one! You know how that feels?'

'Hurt feelings don't give you the right to take a life,' Henry said coldly.

'No? Tell that to all the men what kill women just because they say no, or because supper isn't on the table when they come back from the pub, or because the babbie happens to cry in the night and wake them up. You tell them about what's right.'

'And is that what happened in your family, Adelaide? The more reason, I'd have thought, for you not to emulate such behaviour.'

She looked suddenly confused as though his words made no sense to her. 'How can the likes of you ever understand the likes of me?' she asked.

The matron glanced across at Henry and suggested softly that they should take a break. Henry ignored her. 'And so you killed him.'

Addie shrugged. The fight had gone now. She spoke tonelessly. 'Gus had a knife at his chest, just intending to scare him. Joseph kept saying that he didn't have what we wanted, that we'd have to wait until he got back to London and then there'd be enough money for all of us. He said he'd come straight back or we could go with him – but it was too far. Gus had to report and we'd not have made it back in time, not all the way to London and then back again for nine in the morning. Anyway, we didn't have the cash and neither did he – not to pay for us all. So how did he expect me to believe in him anymore? I knew he'd lied, that he was just out for what he could get and was no better than any of 'em. So I picked up the brick and I pulled back my arm and I hit him.

Hard as I could. He sort of stumbled forward and fell on to the knife. Gus never meant to stick him. It was just for show, to put the frighteners on.'

'And what happened then?'

She seemed to have detached herself from the reality of it – to be, Henry thought, not entirely in her right mind.

'Gus yelped and pulled back and stood there with the knife in his fist, and Joseph fell down on the floor. Gus sent me to get Fred, and I ran and got him and they said they'd deal with everything. They pitched him over a bit of a wall so he was out of sight in the yard, and then Gus cleaned up. There was blood on the ground but he scuffed mud over it. Everywhere was sodden wet. Then he walked me to the pub and told me to buy a drink and to stop where I was, and so I did. When he came back, he said that he and Fred had sorted it.'

'And then he put you on a train?' Henry glanced over to the young constable who was making the record, checking that he was managing to get this down. 'And you came back here?'

'I don't remember doing, but I must've done. Next morning, I woke up and Gus was there and Fred, and I didn't quite believe what had happened.'

As though a dam had suddenly broken, she burst into tears. 'I never meant to. I never meant to do it.'

'I think you did,' Henry said coldly. 'You were angry at what you saw as his deceit. Never mind that you'd arranged with your associates to ambush him. You conned him, Miss Hay, and you believed he'd be carrying money or something of value back to London, so you—'

'He saw me!' Addie yelled. 'Gus saw me with him and he beat it out of me. I wanted to go away with him, but Gus . . .'

'You were aggrieved,' Henry said. 'So you killed your lover.'

He charged her with the murder of Joseph Levy and left her, wailing and weeping, for the matron and recording constable to deal with.

THIRTY

'When did you figure it was the girl?' Mickey asked as they settled on the London train.

'When I saw Fred Welton. He seemed too poor a specimen to deliver that kind of blow. Or to feel that level of anger.' Henry sighed. 'So we know why and how the boy was killed. We are still none the wiser as to where the money Joseph promised was going to come from.'

'Which, to be fair, was not in our brief,' Mickey said comfortably. He folded his hands over his ample belly and closed his eyes. His pretence at indifference lasted five minutes, no more. He opened his eyes again and sat up.

'All right,' he said. 'I'll bite.'

'What can you carry that's of value but has no substance?' Henry said.

A slow smile spread across Mickey's face. 'Something you can keep beneath your hat. Beneath your hat and in your brain. Information.'

'My thought exactly. So what did he know? Who gave him that knowledge and what did he plan to do with it that would bring in the cash he required.'

'Blackmail?' Mickey suggested.

'It's possible, but did he have the nerve for that? Or the bravura? He seems to have been the quiet type.'

'Until he met a redhead,' Mickey suggested. 'Love can do things to a man. Cloud his judgement, but also give him as much Dutch courage as a bottle can.'

'And we can assume that he had no access to this information before reaching Lincoln; otherwise, surely he would have acted differently, have blackmailed or sold or traded. He could not cash what he knew until after he had returned to London.'

'So who did he have dealings with in Lincoln? His future in-laws and any visitors they might have had in their house. And back in London?'

'Who can say? His own family. Abraham Levy. Abraham Levy subsists in the midst of Clem Atkins' territory – is it possible the boy was drawn into something because of that?'

Mickey considered for a moment. 'I once joked with Atkins that the Goldmanns moved because of him, and Atkins replied that it was probably so.'

'So where does that take us?'

'Closer to home, I hope,' Mickey said with feeling. 'The bed at the Angel was as lumpy as hell. I'm sure it was filled with damp flock. I'm eager for my own bed tonight, so if you've a mind to be heading back up to Lincoln, you'll be doing it alone.'

Henry looked faintly shocked and then realized that Mickey was joking. 'No,' he said. 'We are heading for home, but we need to pursue this, Mickey.'

'And we will. Did you show her the watch?'

'I did and I elucidated the chain of events that led us to her and the men. I think she had no choice but to confess, but it was a relief when she did. I believe we had enough evidence without that for a jury to convict, but it is always easier when a confession is made.'

'And what thought just struck you a blow?'

'That the engraving on the watch is very fine,' Henry said. 'That our clockmaker has skills that might be put to use in ways other than mending clocks and engraving salutations.'

'That's a hell of a leap, Henry.'

'Is it? Maybe it is.'

Mickey folded his hands again and closed his eyes. 'Well,' he said. 'I will leave that with you. Wake me up when we are safely south again.'

THIRTY-ONE

She dreamed of him lying beside her in the hotel bed. His flesh soft and warm and his breathing as regular and soothing as that of a child sleeping in its crib.

She had wanted to believe him. Wanted to believe that they could run away together and start again, but she had heard him speaking of his family, of his home, of his father's shops and his sisters' children, and she knew in her heart of hearts that he'd never be able to withdraw from that life and that she could never even dream of becoming a part of it.

Addie herself had little to lose. There was Gus . . . scant loss. It had been fun at first. Exciting. And she'd been fed and clothed more reliably than at any time in her life. She had a warm bed to sleep in most nights and could put up with Gus's occasional bouts of anger.

Until they became less than occasional.

Until she had fancied that Joseph really could offer more.

Until she had fancied that maybe she could love him and he love her.

They would hang her for what she'd done; Addie had no doubt of that. She remembered the cold, grey eyes of the policeman as he'd charged her. He didn't even hate her for what she'd done. He'd pursued her not because he cared but because that was just what he did. Chase his prey and bring it down, strangle the life out of it.

His uncle would help them, Joseph had told her once. If everyone else in the world turned them away, then his uncle would still help them out. But Addie would never know now.

'Why did you say you had money?' she whispered. 'If you'd told me you were broke, I'd have believed you and none of this would have happened.'

That was the trouble, wasn't it? He'd given her hope of something better and then taken it away. At least Gus had been honest enough never to promise her anything.

'But I did want to love you,' Addie whispered. 'That's why I did it. I did want to love you and then you let me down.'

It was late when they reported back to central office, but a message was waiting from Abraham Levy asking Henry to see him at the Workers' Circle, should he return in time.

'Apparently the food is cheap there,' Mickey said.

'If you like herring.'

'I like herring well enough. Bread, tea, herring – I can be satisfied with that.'

Henry sighed. It was already past eight and he wasn't sure he had the patience.

'You've had no more thoughts about what information Joseph might have had?'

'None that make sense,' Henry confessed. 'But at least we can tell Abraham that the case has been resolved. We know who killed Joseph.'

Abraham was sitting in the same seat as before, but he wasn't playing chess this time. His tea had grown cold and he was staring into space. Henry took the chair opposite and Mickey purloined another from a nearby table. Abraham seemed slightly startled to see them, as though he'd forgotten that he'd requested their presence. His eyes were red-rimmed and he looked as though he'd been weeping.

'We know what happened, we have a confession,' Henry told him. 'It seems that the girl, Adelaide Hay, believed that your nephew was preparing to take her away with him and had the money to do so. But then she got off the train at Bardney and he followed and it seems that she betrayed him. She told her associates that he would have money on him, and they intended to rob him – possibly not to kill him – but it seems the woman became enraged when it became obvious that Joseph had empty pockets.'

Abraham was staring at him as if the words meant nothing and he could not quite take them in.

'His lover – this Adelaide Hay – she killed him.' Mickey said it as gently as he could, but the shock registered on Abraham's face and his body began to tremble as though he was suddenly very cold. Henry got up and fetched more tea; Mickey placed the cup in Abraham's hands.

'Drink,' he said. 'Sweet tea will help with the shock.'

Henry wondered if that was even true. 'I'm sorry,' he said. 'The young woman confessed and is being held in Nottingham gaol and her associates are in Lincoln.'

Abraham stared at the cup in his hands and then at Henry and Mickey. 'And so it ends badly for other young people,' he said. 'No good will come out of this, Inspector. No good at all.' He drank some of his tea and then set the cup down.

'Why did you want to see us?' Mickey asked.

'I'm not sure it matters now,' Abraham said. 'I spoke with my brother today. We just wondered if you knew anything more.'

It was such an obvious lie, and Henry was about to push things further, but Mickey gently shook his head.

Abraham pushed back his chair with a scrape on the wooden floor. 'I must be going home,' he said. He took up his coat, put it on, patted his pockets as if looking for something and then turned away. 'Thank you for telling me.'

'Now, what was that all about?' Mickey wondered.

Henry was vexed. 'No doubt we could have found out if we'd kept him here.'

'Later. Henry, we need to get some rest and so does he. Whatever is troubling him, it won't be gone by morning. He has the look of a man haunted by more than just death. We can pursue this later.'

Henry, bone-weary, decided to agree.

THIRTY-TWO

C lem Atkins had been mulling things over and decided that an example should be made of Abraham Levy. Then the man would either toe the line or be gone and no longer Atkins' concern. The truth was Clem wasn't too much bothered either way. He'd come to the conclusion that somehow the clockmaker must be treading on Diamond Annie's toes – and that, he decided, was not going to be good for the health of anyone in the vicinity. He still wasn't totally sure what to make of the envelope that the kid from the Elephant mob had been carrying. But he'd been interested to note that Abraham had taken it with him when he visited his brother. He knew this because when his men searched, it was not in Abraham's house.

He had made certain that the search left no trace. 'Just look; don't touch more than you have to,' he had told them. 'Disturb nothing.' He'd also put it out that he knew someone had given Diamond Annie access to the pub and therefore to him, and that he would find out who; whoever was responsible would be punished and, at the very least, would not be walking anywhere again. He was unsurprised to wake up in the morning and discover that two of his men had gone.

He knew damn well that Josiah Bailey would have beaten seven shades out of everybody until somebody confessed, but that seemed a waste of time when what was needed could be achieved at lesser cost. Atkins believed himself economical, wiser than his erstwhile employer. After all, look at the facts: Josiah Bailey was dead and gone, and Atkins was here, master of all he surveyed.

After a good breakfast he assembled ten of his best men and set out for the clockmaker's shop. Abraham was at work, of course; he looked shocked but not altogether surprised when Clem Atkins opened his door and turfed his customers out. He sent five of his men next door to Abraham's house and kept five to work on the shop. He searched the clockmaker himself and then pushed him into a chair in the corner of the shop so that he could watch while everything he owned was smashed and pummelled and crushed to pieces on the floor.

It was amazing, Atkins always thought, in just how short a time things could be destroyed, especially when you considered how long it took to make most of them. A life took nine months to arrive, and however many years to grow up, but it could be gone in an instant; those things made by men could cease to exist just as quickly.

One of his men appeared in the doorway with the envelope in his hands and Atkins nodded to him to hold on to it. He didn't fully understand the significance of this object, but knew it was evidence of something. He was pretty sure that it was something that he, Clem, could have profited from, but the clockmaker had not been prepared to play ball and this was the result.

Two of his men had been sent up and down the street to fetch people out of their houses to bear witness. It wouldn't be long before the police arrived, but they'd find themselves outnumbered and it was unlikely that the first on scene would hang around. It was more likely they would take themselves off to conjure up some reinforcements before they made it back. Clem Atkins figured he had plenty of time.

His men had run out of things to smash, so Clem made his way over to the clockmaker who was sitting in his chair, white-faced and shaking, staring in disbelief at the devastation. His entire life was in pieces on the floor.

Atkins leaned over him. 'You could have had it easy,' he told him. 'I came to you, nice and quiet, but you just brushed me off like I'm dirt on your shoe. But know this: this is my turf, and whatever you're doing, I want my cut.'

'It isn't like that,' Abraham told him, but Clem had stepped away and no one else was listening.

The sound of police whistles in the street told him that the game was now over, but Clem waited calmly in the clock-maker's shop, two of his men standing in the doorway. He watched through the window, the police arriving in numbers now, marching, truncheons at the ready, expecting a riot, but

Atkins' men had faded away and the only people on the street
were the neighbours who had been called out to watch.

Atkins took the envelope from the man who was still holding
it and stepped outside. He beckoned to one of the constables.
'You'll be wanting this,' he said. 'I've no doubt your Inspector
Johnstone will be wanting a look at it. And you better get that
trash out of here.' He pointed back at Abraham.

They took him into his house and surveyed the damage.
Abraham's only concern was for the photograph that had
been on his mantelpiece. Miracle of miracles, although the
vandals had broken the glass in the leather folding frame,
the photograph was relatively unscathed. He tipped the glass
on to the floor, folded the frame and tucked it into his jacket
pocket. He brushed the glass from his coat; the pocket
was torn, but that could easily be mended. The constables
waited while he found what clothing had not been shredded,
folded it into a pillow case and then left his home without
looking back.

He was grateful that he kept little of importance there,
certainly not anything that Atkins – or the police for that
matter – could use against him.

'Are you hurt?'

'No. I am uninjured. I'd like to go to my brother's house.'

But the constables were having none of that, and because
Clem Atkins had mentioned Henry Johnstone, they took him
to Scotland Yard instead of the local police station and handed
him over to a passing sergeant before going back to their own
division to make their statements.

He sat on the bench in the foyer, in the same place that
he had waited when he had first come to see Henry about
Joseph, and he thought about the circularity of things. Joseph
would still have been dead, no matter what. But if he hadn't
meddled, then all of the events that had followed on from
that would not have happened. Did that mean that he should
have left things alone?

He got up and went across to the desk and asked the
officer on duty if it would be possible to make a phone call.
'I would like to call my brother,' he said. 'Have him come
and collect me.'

The officer behind the desk was not sure what status Abraham had. He wasn't under arrest and he didn't appear to be waiting for anyone in particular, so what was he? And the telephone was for official business only.

It occurred to Abraham that he could ask for Henry Johnstone as that was why he had been deposited here, but he didn't think that he could face the inevitable questions – not yet – even though he knew those questions would come and there was no avoiding them.

Instead, Abraham left the building, walked across the yard and out through the pedestrian entrance and hailed a taxi, hoping that when they got to their destination, his brother would pay the fare.

The police constables had gone. No witness had come forward and no arrests had been made, Clem having assured the constables that no one had seen a thing. The constables, experienced enough to know that no one would speak out against Atkins, and having been given the convenience of Henry's name, had decided that Scotland Yard could call the shots on this one.

Now Clem Atkins had the street and, more significantly, the clockmaker's shop and house to himself. He had given his men orders just to have fun, not to look for anything in particular. Apart from that mysterious envelope. They had taken him at his word, and both house and shop were now wrecked. Abraham's two lodgers had been absent. One arrived back now, demanding to know what was going on. Atkins stuck his head round the door, and the man quailed and fell silent. He took a step back as Clem came towards him, but Clem merely felt in his pockets for a wad of notes, offered what he thought was enough to keep the man's mouth shut and told him to collect whatever was left of his possessions and get on his way. He watched, amused, as the young man simply took to his heels. Whatever had been left behind was now left behind.

Then he went back to Abraham's house and began his search anew. He was still uncertain what he was looking for, but the contents of the envelope gave him some idea. Travel documents and something that looked like an official letter, in a language that Clem could never recall seeing before but thought might be Russian. Coining and forging was something that Jews were known for, Clem thought. He cursed himself for not thinking of this sooner. Abraham had been too quiet for too long and that was unnatural. It was obvious that he been hiding something. Clem Atkins would happily have beaten it out of him, but some corner of his mind cautioned against drawing that much attention. Abraham Levy seemed to have become the special project of Inspector Johnstone, and what with the police and now Diamond Annie taking an interest, Clem felt that he was trapped between the devil and the deep blue sea, and it might be wiser to walk a fine, safe line for a while.

The next two hours brought him no success. There was no trace in the Jew's house of anything untoward. No trace in the shop of anything apart from tools for making clocks, stuff for mending clocks and orders for bits of engraving to be done. The customers would be disappointed about those, Clem thought.

He left, frustrated and angry. For the rest of the day his lieutenants kept a discreet distance and the barman only approached close enough to top up his glass.

Abraham arrived at Benjamin's home. His brother was not home, but thankfully one of his nieces was, and one look at Abraham's face told her there was trouble. She paid off the taxi and escorted her uncle inside, settled him in a chair and went straightaway to telephone her father at one of the shops.

Then she brought a footstool and a stiff drink, lifted Abraham's feet and handed him the glass. 'You look frozen. What on earth do you have there?'

Abraham still clutched the pillowcase that contained all he had managed to salvage from the house.

Gently, she eased the death grip his fingers had on the linen and set it down beside the chair, brought a blanket and covered her uncle gently. He was clearly in a bad way. She persuaded some of the brandy into him and then took the glass away as he closed his eyes and fell asleep. She was relieved when her father arrived a few minutes later.

'Should we leave him to sleep? I think he's in shock. Is it a good or a bad thing to let him sleep if he's in shock?'

Benjamin patted his daughter on the shoulder. 'Go and make us all some sweet coffee,' he said. 'Make it strong. I'll take care of your uncle.'

He waited until she had gone and then gently but urgently shook Abraham awake.

'What happened? Are you all right?'

'Atkins. I told you he came to see me, demanding a cut of whatever I was doing, refusing to believe me when I said that I was doing nothing. He came this morning with about a dozen of his thugs. Smashed all I own, Ben. Destroyed my shop, my house, everything.'

'What? Abraham, are you hurt?'

'He never laid a hand on me and I don't know why. I can't imagine why.'

'Well, let us be thankful for small mercies.' Ben slumped down in a chair next to his brother. His daughter arrived with coffee on a tray and set it on a table beside the window. She hovered, not sure of her welcome, made anxious by the tension, uncertain what to ask or what to say.

'Look after your uncle,' her father told her. 'Get something hot inside him, see if he will eat. I must telephone . . .'

He's going to call the Goldmanns, Abraham thought. Tell them what he revealed about Joseph as well as what happened today. Somehow that made it worse: that this other family would now know what their beloved Joseph had done and the distress, shame and guilt would spread.

Abraham could bear no more. To his niece's great distress, Abraham began to cry – deep, heart-gouging sobs he could not control and she could do nothing to assuage.

THIRTY-THREE

Henry had arrived back to find an envelope on his desk and a note that seemed to be just a constable's collar number. Enquiries took him back downstairs to reception, and he spoke to the officer on duty who told him that the envelope had been dropped in by a constable who had also brought a very distressed-looking man. The man had stayed for a while, then requested to use the telephone – a request that had been denied.

'Next time I looked, he'd gone.'

A little irritated, Henry asked for a description and realized that the man must be Abraham Levy.

'Whom did he want you to telephone?'

'His brother, so he said – wanted to be collected.'

'And you saw he was distressed and still said no?'

Not bothering to wait for a reply, Henry went back upstairs and examined the envelope again. When Mickey arrived a few moments later, he told him not to take off his coat; they were going out again to visit Benjamin Levy.

'And what's all this?' Mickey pointed to the scatter of objects on the desk.

Henry explained. 'The address appears to have been crossed out and another one written,' he said. 'And the second address is that of one Charlie Butcher and his family. Things begin to come together, Mickey.'

Mickey took another look at the objects that had come out of the envelope. A star-shaped brooch that looked impressive on first sight, but Mickey had seen enough of these to know that it was paste and not particularly good paste at that. 'It's the clasp that gives things away,' he said. 'They might look good on the front, but when you turn them over, there's no marks and there is a weak clasp.'

The ring looked better, but Mickey also stated his opinion that it was probably rolled gold rather than the genuine article.

The passport, however, was a different matter. 'Oesterreich,' he said. 'An Austrian passport?'

'Apparently so. I can make no sense of the letter. The lettering is Cyrillic so I'm guessing it's Russian. It's a strange assortment of objects, Mickey. So we will go and see if Abraham can shed any light on it. I think on this occasion we will take a car and driver and make a detour past Abraham Levy's shop. I have reason to believe that he is at his brother's house and not at home.'

As they waited for their car, Henry explained what little he knew. Phone calls to the Whitechapel and Leman Street divisions had filled in some gaps for him. Constables had been called to an emergency right in the middle of Clem Atkins' patch; it seemed the clockmaker's shop and house had been smashed and vandalized, and the constables had taken Abraham away, bringing him to Scotland Yard as Henry's name had been mentioned.

'But Abraham did not ask for you?'

'He only asked to make a telephone call to his brother, but this was denied. It seems our telephones are for official use only and not for those in distress.'

'And this envelope came from Levy?'

'I've spoken to the constable whose collar number was on the note, and apparently it came from Atkins. No doubt he's stirring up trouble, but it would be useful to know what kind of trouble he's stirring.'

Half an hour later the car stopped outside what had been Abraham's shop. A police constable stood on guard and so did one of Atkins' men, a strange juxtaposition, although both stood aside to let Henry through. He surveyed the devastation with disgust, his feet crunching broken glass. A small tool roll lay under the counter and Henry bent and picked it up, surprised to find something intact in all this mayhem. Almost without thinking, he put it in his pocket. He turned as other boots scrunched on glass and Clem Atkins stood in the doorway.

'And your excuse for this?'

Atkins grinned broadly. 'My turf, my rules.'

'And which of your rules did this poor man break?'

'You pay your dues,' Atkins said. 'I take it you got my envelope, then.'

'It wasn't addressed to you, so how can it be yours?'

'It came into my possession. You know what they say about possession – nine-tenths of the law, isn't it?' Atkins smiled suddenly. 'Anyway, you and I both know this has nothing to do with me. You'll find no one on my turf to say anything different, will you?'

Henry ignored him and went back to the car. They drove on to the home of Benjamin Levy and found the place in uproar. Benjamin's wife was not pleased that he had brought trouble to her home – again. Benjamin's daughter Ruth told them that her mother had been put to bed with brandy and sedatives and would calm down. Eventually. In the meantime, everyone was running to do her bidding. Apart from Ruth, who was looking after her uncle and glad to be out of her mother's way. She took the two police officers through to where Benjamin and Abraham both sat and then departed, muttering something about making more coffee.

'We went by your shop,' Mickey said. 'What a bloody mess. Are you hurt at all?'

Abraham shook his head.

'Take off your coats, gentlemen; I imagine you'll be here for some time.' Benjamin sounded resigned, but not happy. Henry shed his coat, dropped it on the back of the chair and then took two items from its pockets. The little tool roll he presented to Abraham. 'It's disturbing evidence,' he said, 'but as I don't imagine you'll be pressing charges, I thought it justified. They seem to have missed this; it had dropped down beneath the counter.'

Hands shaking, Abraham unrolled the dark-blue canvas. The watchmaker's tools were still inside. Only a fraction of what he had possessed, but somehow it cheered him. 'I will not be going back,' he said.

'I'll set some constables to gather anything else that can be salvaged,' Henry promised. 'But in the meantime, you can tell me what this is.' He handed the envelope to Benjamin who seemed reluctant to take it. 'Apparently, Mr Atkins made certain that this came to me. Perhaps you can tell me why? And why the address is for one Charlie Butcher, brother of Sammy Butcher, the boy that Atkins' thugs beat so badly and carved up so efficiently.'

The two brothers looked at one another. 'We know nothing about this,' Benjamin began.

'Do not lie to me.' Henry's voice was suddenly very harsh and very cold. 'And do not take me for a fool.'

Mickey glanced at his boss, but did not intervene. He could see how angry Henry was from the coldness of his eyes and the stiffness of his shoulders, but on this occasion he thought that some anger was justified and that the brothers should suffer the brunt of it.

'What did Atkins hope to find in your house and what did he hope to gain by sending this to me?'

'Inspector,' Abraham said softly. 'Believe me when I say that you could search our homes, raid my brother's businesses, examine our accounts and you would find nothing untoward. Atkins was angry with me because he believed I was doing business that he did not know about and from which he did not get his cut, but I paid my dues to him. There is nothing owing.'

'This is Joseph's handwriting, isn't it?' It suddenly occurred to Mickey what all this might be about – that in some way they were protecting the dead boy.

Even though he didn't answer, the look on Benjamin's face told them everything they needed to know.

'What was he doing? We know that he had a way of making money because that's what he told Adelaide Hay.'

'You believe anything that girl told you? That girl is a murderess.' Abraham was furious.

Benjamin looked confused, and Henry realized that the news had not filtered through to the rest of the family.

'You haven't told your brother?'

'You only informed me late last evening. I went home, I have no telephone and this morning everything was somewhat disturbed. I had intended to come over later today and explain everything in person.'

'She killed him? Dear God.'

Henry glanced his way but pushed on relentlessly. 'And so how was he going to make his money? Abraham, so far your nephew is dead and a fourteen-year-old boy, Sammy Butcher, is scarred for life. He came looking for you and someone identified him as being involved with the Elephant mob. It's reported that children recognized him and chased after him, presumably those he had known when he was younger and lived close by. Joseph knew him – or at least knew his elder brother. Did he know Joseph was dead? Had he come looking for him? Was he bringing this to Joseph, or to you? And why? Why is one address crossed out and another written? What fortune did he intend to make from this?'

The two brothers looked at one another again, but this time it was a despairing look. Benjamin seemed to have been stricken into silence.

'I have nothing to tell you,' Abraham said. 'Nothing at all. Joseph is dead and that is all I know.'

And that was all either brother would say. Henry had no doubt that Abraham spoke the truth when he said that they could search what was left of his home, or his brother's home or their places of work and business, and nothing would be found.

'And what about the Goldmanns?' he asked, his anger building now. 'Have you warned them, too? Will whatever secret you are keeping also be kept by them?'

'Inspector' – Abraham rubbed his face with his palms, as Henry had noticed he often did when he was tired or distressed – 'there is nothing more to say. We are grateful for all you have done, but I am exhausted and I cannot pursue this matter.'

'And I cannot let this matter drop,' Henry told him. 'This isn't done, Mr Levy. It is far from done.'

THIRTY-FOUR

'And so what now?' Mickey asked as they returned to the car.

'We go to St Thomas's and we talk to Sammy Butcher. And we find out what this envelope originally contained, because I am betting there was more to it. My guess is that there was money involved. A passport may be saleable – and we must have it checked against the list of registered aliens – but the jewellery has no value. Joseph was looking for cash, so either there was money in this envelope that needed changing – perhaps it was a foreign currency – or there was something in here of value that could be exchanged for cash. Or he sent the money ahead to be looked after, perhaps shared with the Butchers in payment for making use of their address or their connections. He could not risk having it sent to his own home; he had sisters and a mother who I am guessing would probably inspect his mail out of simple curiosity, and a father who does not miss a trick within his own domain.'

'And he could not have things sent to Abraham's address because Abraham would have realized what was going on. Whatever, this involves both brothers, and the Goldmanns are implicated, too.'

Mickey agreed. 'What do you think he will do now?' He meant Abraham and how he would fare, now that his livelihood was gone. But Henry wasn't thinking along those lines at all.

'When I have sufficient leverage, he will answer my questions,' Henry said.

THIRTY-FIVE

S ammy Butcher was still in hospital, but some of the dressings had been removed to reveal the long cuts on his arms where he had tried to defend himself and the criss-cross cuts on the left-hand side of his face. His empty eye socket was now covered with a lighter dressing and, unwrapped from the heavy bandages, he looked very young and very small.

His mother had been in to see him, as had most of his siblings, the ward sister told them. In fact, she'd had a hard time maintaining the rules that there should be only two visitors and that visiting hours were there for a reason.

Having arrived outside of those set hours, Mickey and Henry were aware that this criticism was aimed also at them.

'And how's the lad doing?' Mickey asked.

'Better, although he's sunk into something of a depression, and the doctor thinks he should be allowed home as soon as his wounds are in a fit state. We don't want him picking up an infection from insanitary conditions, but equally we are aware that he is just a child and he needs to be with his family.' Momentarily, the sharp tone gave way to something softer and then she recovered herself. 'Ten minutes, gentlemen. No more. There are other patients to think of and the hour is late.'

Not so late, Henry thought, although visiting had indeed ended some time before. He nodded agreement. Ten minutes should be all they needed for now.

They pulled up chairs on either side of the bed, and Sammy Butcher eyed them warily. 'I don't know nothin'.'

'Of course you do,' Mickey chided him. 'You know that Joseph Levy is dead and you know that the package you were taking to his uncle was taken from you by those men who did so much damage – but I know you know nothing about them and I'm not going to ask.' Go down that path and he was betting on a loser, Mickey knew.

Sammy looked only slightly less wary.

'When did you hear about Joseph?' Henry asked.

'Dunno. We 'eard he 'adn't come 'ome. Didn't come to pick up 'is parcel, did 'e, so we asked about and 'eard he'd not come 'ome.'

'And then you heard that his body had been found?'

The boy nodded.

'And he'd sent the package to you. The one Atkins' men took away?'

The wariness increased at the mention of the men, but he nodded again.

'Was this the first time he'd sent something to your address?' Henry asked.

'Nah, be three times now. Charlie reckoned 'e couldn't sent things to 'ome because they'd get pinched or summat. So 'e . . . redirected them our way and gave us a cut.'

'And this was the last package. He collected the other two?'

Sammy nodded.

'And was there money in the packages?'

'Money, papers, bits of jewels. He told Charlie that he would share the money with us but we had to 'ang on to the papers and give 'em to Joseph when 'e came to visit.'

'Joseph came to visit you?'

'Old friends wi' Charlie.'

'That was foolish of him,' Mickey said. 'A kid who has relatives still living in Atkins' domain visiting a member of the Elephant mob.'

'Charlie ain't no Elephant,' Sammy objected. 'That's me bruvver Mike. Anyway, Annie knew about it. She said she 'ad a use for Joseph and 'e talked to 'er one night. They drank beer together.'

Henry could guess who 'Annie' might be. 'A use for him?'

Sammy shrugged and then flinched. 'Don't know no more 'n that,' he said.

Henry let that go. 'And was there a lot of money? What did Joseph do with his share, do you know?'

'Looked like a lot to me.'

'You seem happier to talk to us this time,' Mickey observed.

Sammy looked abashed. 'Me mam said if it were to do wi'
Joseph, then I'd better spill – 'e were a good 'un.'

'I see,' Mickey said, echoing the boy's solemnity. 'So tell
me, Sammy, why were you taking those documents and those
bits of jewellery to Abraham?'

'Jewels were fake, no use for pawning or owt else. Like I
said, Joseph said the papers 'ad to be kept safe and given
back. He said folk depended on them to prove who they were.'

Mickey cast a quick glance at Henry. He was aware that
the ward sister was hovering now.

'But it was a dangerous thing, to be taking this package to
Abraham in the territory of a rival gang. Did Charlie want you
to take such a risk?'

Sammy looked embarrassed for the first time. 'Charlie di'n't
know. Mam di'n't know eiver. But Joseph said people depended
on 'em to be safe, and now Joe was dead, and I thought I'd
be just fine and dandy, quick in and quick out, but it di'n't
work out that way.' He paused. 'Me ma's so mad wi' me. Says
she won't ever let me out of 'er sight again.'

'Did you not think of just posting it?' Henry asked.

He was rewarded with a withering look. Sammy clearly
regarded the question as imbecilic. 'Don't be daft. Atkins 'ad
all Mr Levy's post taken to 'im first. That's why Mr Levy's
brother always got Joe to take things to 'im hisself.'

The sister made it clear their time was up and the policemen
left.

'So Atkins may be intercepting Abraham Levy's post,' Mickey
said thoughtfully. 'Fact, do you suppose, or just paranoia?'

'Where Atkins is concerned, I think a healthy dose of
paranoia would be advised. The boy's a mess,' he added. 'He'll
carry those scars for the rest of his life.'

'Most of us do,' Mickey observed. *It's just that not all of
them show.*

THIRTY-SIX

I t had, Mickey thought, been a tricky day, but it was not about to let them go quite yet. It was already past nine when they returned to the central office, hoping to report in and then head for home. A phone call was put through to Henry's desk.

Addie's suicide was not noticed until late that evening, by which time her body was already growing cold. The method she had used, the police surgeon thought, showed a rare commitment and determination.

'They had, of course, taken her outdoor clothes and given her a prison uniform of calico and canvas, so very hard to tear. Prisoners have been known to use whatever is to hand to hang themselves, of course, and this is why they are given only blankets and not sheets that can be torn into strips.'

'So how did she contrive to arrange her suicide?' Henry was already angry with the world after his visit first to the Levys and then to see young Sammy Butcher. His impatience must have been evident because the surgeon was eager to say, 'All that could have been foreseen had been dealt with. This was a very, very determined young woman.'

'Of course.' Henry tried to modify his tone.

Mickey was leaning in to listen to the call and he laid a placating hand on Henry's arm. 'Just listen to the man,' he said softly.

'So the young woman was checked at four in the afternoon and nothing seemed untoward. She had been allowed her hour of exercise, in the yard, with the other inmates. No one noticed that she had picked up anything from the ground, but she had. As I say, she was very determined.'

Henry's irritation was growing more inflamed by the second.

Mickey took the phone and spoke to the doctor, introducing himself. 'I'm terribly sorry but the inspector has just been called away.'

Henry sat back in his chair and fumed, but he knew his sergeant was right. He was likely to say something that would upset a man who did not deserve it and, more to the point, with whom he might have to meet later when this case was placed before the coroner.

'The yard is used also for hanging out the washing from the prison laundry. A broken dolly peg had been left on the ground from last time the washing had been pegged out. She must have picked it up. Back in her cell, she unravelled the blanket-stitched thread – a heavy woollen thread, you understand – that hemmed the blanket. An end must have come loose and she was very patient, I can tell you that.'

'I'm sure,' Mickey said. 'So what did she do?'

'Well, I have to say, it was very clever. The thread could not possibly have taken her weight, of course, but that was not her intent. She wound the yarn round and round her neck and she used the peg like a tourniquet to wind it tighter and tighter, and just before she lost consciousness, she must have wedged the peg beneath her chin and somehow wedged her head in the little gap between the end of the bed and the wall so that it wouldn't fall back when she became unconscious. She had placed the peg so that this had the effect of maintaining the pressure on the carotid artery, and eventually she lost consciousness and then died.'

'Like a mechanical sleeper,' Mickey suggested.

'A very good analogy,' the doctor approved. 'Wrap your arm about a man's neck and keep tight hold and he'll pass out. Keep the pressure on for too long and he'll expire. I have to say, though, it's a strange method for a woman to employ. Women are rarely so technically inclined.'

'I suppose desperation leads anyone to be inventive,' Mickey suggested.

'Well, quite so, but all in all hanging would have been swifter. We rarely leave the accused to strangle these days. It's all very scientifically done, you know.'

Mickey rolled his eyes, thanked the doctor for his help and told him, yes, he supposed they would be coming for the inquest.

He settled the receiver back on the cradle and gave Henry the short-form version of events.

'Damn the woman,' Henry exploded.

'Why? She's dead either way. It saves the expense of a trial. You and I both know there would have been no mercy for her.'

'I know and I know I'm being unreasonable,' he apologized.

'I'll walk you home and bunk on your settee,' Mickey said.

'And why would you do that?'

'Because we're walking home via any and all public houses we might find. I'm not going to sleep sober tonight, Inspector Johnstone, and neither are you. And tomorrow we visit the Levy brothers again and we tell them what we already know. See if they come up with the rest of the tale.'

THIRTY-SEVEN

R uth Levy greeted them like old friends when they arrived at Benjamin's house the following morning, both slightly hungover and a little bleary, and grateful for the coffee she offered.

She showed them into the same room as before and said she'd tell her father they had arrived. It seemed they had been expected.

Henry took the opportunity to look around the room today. He'd been too agitated to take much notice the afternoon before. The house was Edwardian but the room was dressed in contemporary style, with Art Deco chairs and a marble clock garniture on the tiled mantlepiece. The old-fashioned cabbage roses on the carpet looked to be from an earlier time.

Benjamin Levy came in, shook hands and suggested they all sit down.

'Where is Abraham?'

'Not here, I'm afraid. We thought it best that he go away for a while, but he left a letter for you and asked me to explain the contents.'

'A letter or a confession?' Henry asked.

'What is there to confess to? Search my house, raid my shops – you'll find nothing untoward. My conscience is clear, Inspector, as is Abraham's, and the Goldmanns'. The letter is an attempt to piece together a hypothetical situation, you might say. An attempt to suggest what *might* have happened. Of course, none of us know. None of us claim any part and none of us will deviate from that.'

Henry could feel his irritation rising again. He clamped down on it, knowing it would get him nowhere. Ruth arrived with the coffee and took a seat beside her father. She looked Henry in the eye, as though challenging him to be ill-mannered enough to upset her father in his own home. Her direct gaze reminded him of Cynthia. It was Ruth who handed him the letter she had brought in on the tray. It was thick and clearly held many sheets of paper.

Henry opened it and started to read.

> *In 1904, the British Government enacted the first of its acts of alien registration. Then came the war and the government tightened its control, interning many, including members of my family. Then in 1919 and 1920, they followed these actions with the Aliens Restriction Act and the Aliens Order, designed to keep out undesirables who came to this country without jobs or means of financial support, and with the requirement that all must report to the police, must register, must prove that they had work – and women prove that they were married according to the law of the land. A religious marriage or an informal but witnessed promise no longer counted under the law; a woman not wed according to British law could be deported, parted from her husband and infants, and sent away.*

Henry frowned. 'Is this a history lesson?'

'In part, I suppose, it is. If you wish, I will summarize it for you, and you can read the rest at your leisure.' Ruth leaned forward to put her cup and saucer back on the tray. 'Hypothetically, what if someone came to this country fleeing for their lives. Hypothetically, they came without money or papers or any offer of work, bringing their family from Russia – no, that is a bad example; Russian Jews have a better chance under the law. But from other places where your birthright brings with it certain persecution, where you are treated little better than slaves, where you see your children dying of violence and poverty.'

'Hypothetically,' Henry returned harshly, 'your people do not have a monopoly on suffering.'

'That point aside,' Benjamin continued, 'they land, they find lodging and in that lodging house they find help – with food, with clothing, with offers of work – but to get further, they must have papers and papers that prove they have enough money and enough support so that they don't threaten to become burdens on the state.'

'The Goldmanns,' Henry said.

'This is a hypothetical exercise,' Mickey reminded him.

'Like hell it is,' Henry growled.

'Now, those who have money perhaps contribute to funds for those who do not. They give what they can – be that money or jewellery or gold or whatever can be cashed or exchanged or passed on to those who need it. Those who make the travel documents or who create the offers of work or who ensure that bank accounts not only exist but actually hold money take nothing for the work they do. It is duty, it is brotherhood, but nevertheless money is required for expenses – paperwork must be copied, created.'

'Plates engraved for printing,' Henry said.

'An interesting skill,' Benjamin said. 'With a multitude of uses. Now, consider. What old men choose to do should not be the burden of the young. Hypothetically, if the elders are accused of doing wrong, then the young should be able to say, with honesty, "We knew nothing." Not all believe that, of course; some families are more comfortable with involving their children than others and it might be that children speak to children, not knowing of the prohibition.'

'And the Goldmann girls told your son what was going on. And enough with the hypothetical,' Henry snapped. 'Speak plainly or not at all.'

Benjamin held up his hands in defence. 'As you wish, but remember, this is all speculation.'

'So,' Mickey said more gently, 'a scheme is set up to help unfortunates. Only the deserving, it is hoped, and not those who might do the country harm.'

'I also fought in the Great War, Sergeant Hitchens. This is my home, too.'

Mickey nodded acknowledgement. 'And so the Goldmann girls spoke about this and were taken by surprise when he did not know. At that point, of course, he no doubt coaxed the rest from them. So this money and these documents – how were they collected and where were they sent? I assume someone went to the boarding house, explained the situation, and whatever was collected was sent somewhere else so that it could be used for the cause. You realize this is not only illegal, Mr Levy, but it could also infringe the Defence of the Realm Act. The war might be over, but for the most part DORA still stands.'

'And none of this happened, Sergeant. It is merely a possibility. What could have taken place?'

'I don't like these games,' Mickey said bluntly. 'But get on with it, so we can get it over.'

Benjamin gathered his thoughts. 'If my son had discovered something like this, and if he had found that he had access to the packages that were sent with contributions inside, and if, by the simple ploy of offering to go to the post and then readdressing these envelopes, he could divert these funds—' He broke off. Clearly, this part of the confession that was not a confession was difficult for him.

Ruth took her father's hand. 'If a young man like my brother was led into temptation because he fancied himself in love and saw no other way of protecting the person he loved—'

'Than by stealing from others who might need it more,' Henry said acerbically.

She swallowed nervously but ploughed on. 'That young man might have done wrong, Inspector, but he paid for it with his life because he acted unwisely and dishonestly. He—'

'So God smote him down – is that it?'

'Inspector!' Benjamin could not hide his shock.

'You might be interested to know that the young woman he fancied himself in love with is also dead. She killed herself in her prison cell.'

Father and daughter exchanged a look.

'You can't expect us to feel pity for her,' Ruth said. 'She led him into temptation.'

'Don't parrot such rot. You don't believe that any more than I do. Your brother wanted to be led.'

'You didn't know my brother!'

'Does it matter now?' Mickey said gently. 'Both are dead; that's all we know for certain.'

'And God will judge,' Benjamin said.

'I wouldn't know about that,' Mickey told him. 'Strikes me that God would have a hell of a time trying to work it all out.' He sighed. 'You know, no one has come out of this with any glory. You and the Goldmanns might believe that you are doing the right thing. For all I know, maybe you are, but if it turns out we can prove any of this, you'll be arrested, same as any criminal.'

Benjamin Levy began to object, but Mickey held up a hand. 'No, hear me out. Your son is dead. That girl is dead and saved the hangman a job, but we'll never get to hear her story now. A young boy is lying in a hospital bed with scars he'll never hide and the loss of an eye. He is fourteen years old, and the reason for his injuries is that he tried to get some of your precious papers back to Abraham. Your Joseph had told him that he'd share the cash and the gold and the jewellery, but that people were depending on the passports and the papers, and young Sammy, hearing he was dead, decided he was honour-bound to make sure they ended up in the right place. Whether your brother, Abraham, was still involved or not, he was the only link to Joseph that young Sammy had, so he took the risk and he paid for it.' Maybe that was stretching the truth a little, but Mickey didn't really care. 'So you can comfort yourselves with your hypotheticals and your belief that you're doing the right thing, and maybe you are, but all actions have consequences, Mr Levy, and none of us can escape from them.'

He stood and picked up the envelope. 'We done here?' he asked Henry.

'I think we are.'

'So, you reckon we can get them on anything?' Mickey asked as they got into the car and told the driver to take them back to Scotland Yard.

'Hand what we have over to the Fraud Squad,' Henry said. 'I doubt it will come to anything, but it might give the sanctimonious bastard a few sleepless nights.'

'A little harsh, Henry.'

'Rich, coming from you, considering your last little speech.'

'True,' Mickey agreed. 'And to give them their due, I believe they had the best of intentions. And I liked Abraham,' he added. 'Despite everything, I find I wish him well.'

Henry nodded. He too had liked Abraham and, as Mickey had pointed out, no one had come out of this well. Everyone had suffered.

EPILOGUE

Clem Atkins sat by himself in what was left of Abraham's shop, wondering what he should put in the clock-maker's place and considering his options. He could let the place out. A family in the house and lodgers in the flats above and a tenant in the shop. There would be profit in all of that, considering he was now de facto owner of the place.

At Paddington station, Abraham collected his bag from the left luggage office and watched as the porter labelled a small trunk: *To be collected.* His bag had been packed months before, left in the locker against such a day as this. His brother had arranged the trunk. Nothing that mattered had been kept at the house or at the shop. Nothing that could prove anything against him or Ben or anyone else. For all that, though, it had been decided he was better away, and not even Ben knew where he might go.

'Inspector Johnstone will make trouble for us,' Abraham told his brother.

'Of course he will, and we will survive it. Be at peace; you have done nothing wrong.'

Abraham picked up his bag and went to catch his train. He had his precious photograph in his pocket, his tools in his valise and sufficient money. He could begin again. Not like poor Joseph. For Joseph there would be no new beginning.

Mickey walked back home past the clockmaker's shop and saw Clem Atkins sitting inside.

'Proud of yourself, are you?'

'Not so you'd notice. But to stay in charge, a man has to look strong.'

'Don't let it go to your head,' Mickey told him. 'There's

always someone snapping at your heels, no matter how far you think you've come.'

Mickey walked on slowly, unconcerned. He'd received a telegram an hour ago, one that made him feel as if nothing in the world could touch him. Belle was coming home – in fact, by the time Mickey got there, she might already have arrived.

As he turned into his street, he noted with great satisfaction that the light was on. Mickey turned the key and called out that he was home. Moments later, Belle was wrapped in his embrace.

'God, it's good to have you back.'

'It's good to be back. Oh, but I've missed you so.'

Henry wended his slow way to Cynthia's home and was told that his sister was out. He was welcome to wait, of course, although the children would be asleep by now. He wandered through to the library and settled with a brandy and a book, content just to be in a friendly place.

He thought of Joseph Levy and the mistakes the young man had made. He thought of the girl Joseph had loved, who had killed herself and whose inquest he must attend in a few days' time. And he thought of Mickey and the pleasure on his sergeant's face when he received the telegram.

And then he stopped thinking at all. By the time Cynthia had returned home, Henry was soundly asleep.

DBC.

Bly